P9-CMK-873

My Soul to Keep

The Moon Chasers Series

Sharie Kohler

POCKET BOOKS

NEW YORK   LONDON   TORONTO   SYDNEY

Pocket Books
A Division of Simon & Schuster, Inc.
1230 Avenue of the Americas
New York, NY 10020

This book is a work of fiction. Names, characters, places, and incidents either are products of the author's imagination or are used fictitiously. Any resemblance to actual events or locales or persons, living or dead, is entirely coincidental.

First Pocket Books paperback edition September 2010

POCKET and colophon are registered trademarks of Simon & Schuster, Inc.

For information about special discounts for bulk purchases, please contact Simon & Schuster Special Sales at 1-866-506-1949 or business@simonandschuster.com.

The Simon & Schuster Speakers Bureau can bring authors to your live event. For more information or to book an event contact the Simon & Schuster Speakers Bureau at 1-866-248-3049 or visit our website at www.simonspeakers.com.

Interior design by Jacquelynne Hudson
Cover design by Min Choi; art by Craig White.

Manufactured in the United States of America

10 9 8 7 6 5 4 3 2 1

ISBN 978-1-4391-0159-9
ISBN 978-1-4391-2703-2 (ebook)

For my editors, Lauren McKenna and
Megan McKeever, on our fifth project together.
You never stop making me work for it.

"Thank you" doesn't say it enough.

My Soul to Keep

Sorcha's heart slammed against her chest.

It couldn't be him. She stared at the man before her. No. Not a man. Never that. As long as she'd known Jonah, he'd never been just a man. She trained her face into an impassive expression.

Her gaze scanned the well-carved features of his face. His dark blond hair was cut shorter than the last time she'd seen him. He was just as tall, though, just as lean muscled as she remembered. And despite herself, her stomach knotted and clenched with hot desire.

Here? What was Jonah doing here?

PROLOGUE

Rough hands pulled Sorcha awake, abruptly ending the dream that shouldn't have colored her sleep and made a smile slip over her lips. But it always came. It was always there when she closed her eyes and dropped her guard and let hope creep in. *He was there.*

Tonight, her mother put a stop to it, tearing her from glimpses of what *wasn't*—glimpses of what could never be.

There was no world without her father, tormenting her every breath. There was no world with just Sorcha and Jonah in it. Such a world was a girlish fantasy.

Danae's hard hand released her shoulder. "Get up. Your father wants to see you."

Sorcha blinked herself alert. Swiping the tangle of dark hair from her face, she quickly rose, swinging her legs over the egde of the bed. Her father did not like to wait. He didn't like a lot of things. All of which she sought to avoid.

She smelled the wine on her mother's breath as she fell into step beside her and was reminded of tonight's celebration. Her father, Ivo, had claimed yet another pack. Sorcha slept in another strange bed. Ivo had gained more soldiers for his army— almost a hundred lycans swore service to him this day. He would be in a good mood. That was something at least.

Still, she could not stop the cold shiver from scratching down her spine as her mother led her to the room where her father reclined like a great, sated lion on a sofa. Why should he want to see her now? At this hour? Why, when he usually ignored her existence?

A fire crackled in the hearth, casting the room in shades of red and yellow, making the handsome lines of her father's face appear even more ominous than usual.

Sorcha pulled up hard, hanging back on the threshold at the sight and sound of the beast at the room's far wall, fighting his chains, his hunger glittering madly in his pewter eyes. His huge tawny-haired frame pulled at the restraints.

She hated this time of the month when the full moon rode the night. When the air was charged and dangerous, thick with death. When her father seemed the scariest, taking pleasure in tormenting the depraved, soulless lycans subject to him . . .

and any other hapless soul to fall into his web.

The silver manacles burned into the creature's heavily corded wrists, weaving tendrils of smoky ribbons in the air. Ivo was excellent at capitalizing on his prey's weaknesses. And silver was poison to a lycan.

She moved slowly into the room, her bare feet sliding over the cold rock floor until she reached the edge of the rug. A quick glance around confirmed her worst fear. Jonah was missing. A sick feeling coiled through her. He was probably patrolling, rounding up rebel lycans who resisted Ivo.

She bit her lip. She always felt safer when her father's second-in-command was around. Even if he served her father, he always treated her with kindness. No surprise he invaded her dreams. He gave her what her own family never did. There was humanity in him. Even if he was of the same species as her parents.

Errand completed, Danae glided past her, dropping down and curling around Sorcha's father like an elegant cat. Ivo pressed a kiss to her mother's arm, stroking her like a fine pet. Looking up, he fixed his steely gaze on Sorcha.

"Your mother tells me today is your birthday."

Sorcha blinked. They'd never cared about her birthday before. A birthday, she'd learned over the years, ceased to matter to hybrid lycans who could live a very long time—if not forever. Even if this was only her thirteenth birthday, the passing of a year had never mattered to them. They never cared about anything except amassing their army of lycans.

Sorcha nodded, distracted. Her gaze drifted to the snarling lycan battling his restraints. She watched him in rapt horror. His muscles and sinews bunched and twisted beneath the hairy dark flesh. The pewter eyes drilled into her through the steam of his smoldering flesh, his hunger reaching out for her. She swallowed tightly, almost imagining those wet teeth sinking into her flesh, tearing her apart . . .

Her eyes ached from staring at the lycan, but she couldn't blink, couldn't look away. As though that split second might be all it took for him to break free to devour her.

"Sorcha," her father snapped. "Look at me."

She swung her gaze obediently to her father.

Ivo waved a hand impatiently. "Come closer."

She inched deeper into the room, watching in disgust as her father fished a piece of raw meat from a bowl and tossed it to the lycan. The creature lunged for it like a mad dog, shoving the scrap of flesh into his mouth and devouring it without chewing.

Ivo chuckled, watching her more than the pathetic creature chained to the wall, prisoner to his sick amusements. In that moment, she felt little different from the beast. They were both captives to her father's will, prisoners to his whim.

"Your mother tells me you are now thirteen."

"Yes."

"Yet you have not transitioned." He cocked his head, the firelight gilding his dark hair. "Why is that?"

"I don't know," she whispered, the pulse at her neck growing twitchy, an anxious staccato, jumping against her skin. She glanced over her shoulder to the door, longing to escape.

"A little old, aren't you?"

Sorcha shrugged helplessly.

"I have no use for a daughter who is, in effect, human. If you're not one of us, you are useless and weak."

She bit back the retort that she would never be like him even if she did transition. She would make certain of that.

Ivo stared hard at her, his eyes cruel and penetrating, deepening her impulse to flee. The only problem was that she would never make it two feet before he pounced on her.

"Maybe you have not been given the proper impetus, hmm?"

"W-what do you mean?" She swallowed, despising the tremor in her voice. She wanted to be brave, wanted to act as though she wasn't frightened of her own father, even if it was a lie.

Ivo stood, his hand wandering across the table littered with the remnants of their dinner. His fingers hooked around a slim knife. The blade flashed in the firelight.

"You understand the nature of our race. We are not like our unfortunate brethren." He gestured to the lycan at the wall. The creature's ugly snarls dulled to background noise, blending with the howling winds outside. "Our race possesses control, free will. We determine when we will and will not turn." As if to drive home his point, his face flashed, blurred into sharper lines. His eyes blasted ice, a pale glow twisting where his pupils should be for a mere moment before fading to black again. "That said, intense emotions can push us over the edge. At times . . ."

She sucked in a sharp breath as he stopped before her and raised his knife, examining it as if he found some truth etched there in the gleaming blade. Something no one but he could see.

"Pain, for example. Pain can prompt a dovenatu to turn."

Before she could react, before she could think, her father lashed out and brought the knife down in a hissing swipe.

She cried out, jumping away, but too late. She slapped a hand over her bicep. Blood seeped between her fingers, warm and sticky as syrup. The lycan went wild, spitting and snarling, scenting the coppery flow, straining against his chains with no thought to his sizzling flesh.

Sorcha bent at the waist, a pained breath escaping through her clenched teeth at the burning agony of her arm.

Her father circled her with slow steps. "No?" he murmured. "Nothing? Do you feel it? The turning? The heat building inside? The strain in your bones . . ."

She shook her head fiercely, dark hair tossing wildly, tears warm on her cheeks. "What do you want from me?"

His voice cracked liked thunder in the air. "I want you to be strong. To be a dovenatu." Hard, punishing fingers circled her arm.

She cried out, dragging her heels as he hauled her toward the ravenous lycan. "Perhaps you need further incentive."

She shrieked as he thrust her toward the deadly creature.

The lycan strained his thick neck, jaws wide and dripping saliva as he stretched for a taste of her flesh.

Tears blurred her eyes. Pathetic little whimpers

choked from her throat. A sound she loathed, but could not stop.

Her father wrapped an arm around her waist, positioning his larger frame behind her. Struggle was useless. Her feet dangled, toes grazing the floor.

"Come, Sorcha, show me your fangs, show me that there's a reason I should keep you around. Prove to me you are my daughter."

She moaned, tossing her head from side to side as he forced her hand up, *out*—closer and closer to the hungering jaws. Her curled fingers shook, spasmed. The lycan's hot breath fanned her knuckles.

"Father, please," she begged, her terror thick and terrible.

"I've no use for a defunct dovenatu, Sorcha. Turn!" He tugged her hand closer and that was when she knew he was going to do it. This was no test, no game to him. She'd either become what he wanted of her, or he'd see her dead.

Sorcha turned her head, jammed her eyes tightly shut, unwilling to watch as her hand was ripped from her body.

"Let her go!"

Sorcha's eyes snapped open at the sound of the voice that whispered to her in her dreams. *Jonah*.

JONAH STORMED ACROSS THE room with no thought to his actions, no thought to the consequences. In that moment, he did not even care that interfering in Ivo's games could mean his death. He wrenched Sorcha from Ivo's grasp, a hairsbreadth from the slavering jaws stretching for her.

She stumbled against him, crying out sharply. He pulled away and looked down. Bile swelled in his throat. He choked it back, gulping in a breath at the sight of the blood coating his palm and fingers—her blood, thick and dark as tar. A dangerous heat stirred at his core, a killing fury aimed at Ivo.

Danae rose, hissing at him, her face instantly flashing into hard animal lines, the centers of her eyes glowing torches. "You forget your place, Jonah!"

A growl erupted from his lips, vibrating from deep in his chest. He was ready to fight, to defend. Unwise perhaps, but he could not stop the impulse . . . or the urge to tear both Ivo and Danae apart. They were her parents! If they didn't protect her, who would?

Ivo held up his hand, stalling his mate from pouncing on Jonah.

Jonah's gaze shot back to Sorcha. Blood pumped freely from the deep gash in her arm. The sweet copper scent flooded him. Her frightened eyes locked on him, and he felt her pull, her need. She always looked at him that way. Her dark eyes devouring him, her heart laid bare in her youthful expressive face—as if he were her only hope in a roiling sea. He hated and relished it, hating the burden but relishing the fact that there was something as sweet and pure as this girl in the cesspit of his life.

"Jonah," she said, breathing his name, sighing it like a benediction. He grasped her uninjured arm and pulled her behind him.

Ivo chuckled, the sound brittle as dry leaves. "So possessive, so loverlike. How heartening."

"Are you trying to kill her?" Jonah jerked his head toward the salivating beast at the wall. The lycan's pewter gaze fixed on Sorcha, the sounds grinding from his teeth desperate and inhuman.

Jonah was well aware of Ivo's penchant for tormenting the lycans they captured, pitting them against each other—sometimes with live human bait—and then watching the ensuing bloodbath. But he'd never thought he'd play one of his gory games with his own daughter.

Ivo's chuckle faded. "As good as it is to see you so protective of your future mate, tread carefully when you speak to me."

Jonah inhaled, chest lifting deeply, nostrils flaring at the aroma of Sorcha's blood. Ivo had long planned to mate Sorcha with him. It was all part of his agenda to build a master race of dovenatus—a race that could dominate both humans and lycans. With Ivo at the helm, of course.

Ivo settled his gaze back on Sorcha. "You're spared for now." Jonah felt her shrink behind him and he hated that her father had that power over her. "But you'd better concentrate on transitioning."

"It will happen when it happens," Jonah growled, taking her with him as he moved to the door. "You can't force it by cutting her with a knife, or scaring her."

"It had better happen soon," Ivo spat. "She'll serve her purpose for me, or I have no use for her."

Jonah's flesh crawled at the statement. He glanced down at Sorcha, so young, so very . . . *human*. She looked like any other teenage girl with a splotchy face and a body given to chubbiness. She barely reached his shoulder. If she didn't shed her humanity soon and become one of them, she would perish in the world her father was intent on carving.

"Come on," he murmured. He had almost cleared the door when Ivo's ice-cold hand on his neck stopped him. "Go," Jonah quickly said, pushing her down the corridor. Sorcha obeyed, fleeing, her nightgown swishing at her ankles. Immediately, the tightness in his chest eased. He was relieved to see her gone. Even if he was left to face Ivo's wrath.

Ivo had moved without a sound, without the

faintest stirring of air. A cold reminder of his power, of the years and experience he had on Jonah. Those fingers tightened around Jonah's neck, crushing, digging into the flesh until he broke Jonah's skin.

Inhaling deeply, Jonah smelled his blood mingling with the coppery sweetness of Sorcha's that still clung to the air. But he didn't flinch. Didn't show the faintest sign of weakness. Like the animal he was, Ivo would sense that, exploit it. Jonah had already revealed Sorcha to be a weakness. He would give Ivo no more power over him.

Ivo's fingers pressed harder, digging into bone, testing Jonah's long-sustained loyalty. Ivo had saved him from the gutters when he was just a boy, newly turned, wild and crazed with the confusion of what he had become.

He clenched his jaw against the clawing pain, resisting the impulse that burned darkly inside him, hungering for Ivo's blood, begging Jonah to turn around and unleash all his animal fury on the bastard who would dare lay a hand on Sorcha and drive the innocence from her.

"Know this," Ivo rasped, his voice close, ruffling tendrils of hair at Jonah's neck. "You live because you amuse me, and I find you useful. Your possessive feelings toward Sorcha please me. Fitting, as she will be your mate. But heed me well.

Her life is mine. If I ever want to end it, I will. And you." Saliva flew from his lips in a hiss of air, landing on Jonah's neck. "You work for me. You do what I say, and don't ever forget it."

Ivo released his neck and shoved him through the door, apparently finished with him.

Jonah, however, wasn't finished with Ivo. In the corridor, he turned and faced the dovenatu he had served for too many years to count, knowing it could all end over Sorcha. That maybe one day it would. "And heed me, if you ever harm your daughter, all your grand plans will never happen." He paused with a heavy breath. "Because I will kill you."

Ivo's lips peeled back from his teeth in an unnatural grin. "You can try."

With a curt nod, Jonah strode down the corridor. He scented Sorcha before he spotted her in a shadowed alcove, a mullioned window at her back, her face a pale smudge in the darkness. His chest clenched at the innocent vision.

She stepped out into the moonlit corridor in a swirl of coppery-sweet blood. The small hand she pressed to the flesh wound did little to mask the aroma. Beneath that scent lurked *her* smell, a whiff of chocolate and mint, testament to her sweet tooth.

Stepping forward, he moved her fingers aside

and examined her arm, gingerly probing the angry slash. "We should take care of this."

"What if I don't transition, Jonah?" she whispered, her voice a desperate rush, as though she feared expressing the possibility aloud. He mulled that over for a moment—Sorcha, human. Forever. A part of him wished for that. Wished she'd never be like him. Never know the dark animal that stirred beneath the surface.

"He'll kill me," she stated. Her dark eyes glanced nervously down the corridor, as though she expected her father to appear and finish her off.

"He won't. I won't let that happen." Jonah held her gaze, staring intensely at her, hoping to convey his determination to keep her safe. "Do you believe me?"

"Okay." She nodded slowly, the fear ebbing from her eyes, giving way to the hero worship he was accustomed to seeing. Before he could stop her, she wrapped her arms around him in a hug, pressing her cheek to his chest. "I wish we could run away, Jonah. Just the two of us." She breathed the words against him in a small sigh.

"Ivo would find us," he said gently, patting her on the back, knowing he shouldn't encourage her infatuation with him. She was just a girl, a child he would keep safe, above his own life, if need be.

Yet he loathed her fear and would do anything to chase it from her eyes. Even let her pretend he was the hero he wasn't.

"But you'll protect me."

"Always. Now let's go tend to your arm." Taking her smaller hand in his own, he led her back down the corridor, shivering at what he imagined to be a draft, and wondering if he had just made a promise he had any power to keep. If there was any way to keep either one of them safe.

Any way to escape the dark world burying them both.

ONE

Sorcha stared at the street below and felt a lonely chill watching the people flow past like so many fish in a stream. At this hour, they were couples mostly, and groups, out for the evening, heedless of the lightly falling rain. They existed simply, taking their pleasures, living their uncomplicated lives.

A couple passed directly below, hand in hand, crossing her building's front door. The woman's laughter drifted up, curling like sultry smoke on the air. Sorcha followed her brightly bouncing scarf as she faded down the cracked, uneven sidewalk into the water-soaked night.

Humans had no clue that creatures like Sorcha existed, walked among mankind, observing from the shadows,

They could never know.

Strange how life worked. As a girl she'd desperately craved the moment when she would grow up and transition and become like Jonah. So he could finally love her. So her father would approve of her and no longer frighten her.

Now here she stood, a dovenatu, powerful and strong.

Alone.

Rain shivered down the glass surrounding her top-floor loft. She'd bought the building a year ago, shortly after Gervaise's death. It was a world away from the Central Park penthouse she'd shared with her husband. As far as anyone knew, the rundown building was just one of many sandwiched together in the crowded Soho neighborhood.

No one would ever expect that the wife of the late tycoon Gervaise Laurent lived within its molded brick walls. Precisely why she'd bought it. That and the windows. They gave her a view of the world she could only ever observe from the fringes. Flattening a palm on the cold glass, she exerted the slightest pressure . . . as though she would break through and leave everything behind. Fly away from the memories of her pack— from *Jonah*—and now Gervaise. All dead.

She shuddered, chafing her arms. Nothing was left. Nothing except an appetite for revenge that fed her heart.

Alone since Gervaise's death, the dark beast inside her prowled, clawing to come out. She could deny it no longer, not with this constant hunger for vengeance.

She had become as dangerous as her father, her mother—consumed by a thirst for the blood of whatever thing had killed her husband.

Her pulse beat faster as she recognized a shiny town car slowing and pulling up at the curb below. Finally, she was here. Sorcha watched as the woman stepped onto the sidewalk littered with bags of late-night trash. Hopefully, she held the answers to Gervaise's death.

Turning, Sorcha moved to the elevator and waited. A small shiver chased down her arms as the motor revved, carrying her much-anticipated guest up toward her.

When the door slid open, she spared not a glance for Cage, her late husband's trusted man and a former NFL linebacker. Eventually, she'd have to let him go. Once it became too obvious that she wasn't aging as she should be.

Sorcha's gaze settled on the woman. The female was nervous, but tried to hide it, holding her chin awkwardly high. Her unnaturally dark hair was all the more striking for its contrast with her crystal blue eyes.

"Maree?" Sorcha inquired, her nostrils flaring, scenting her. *Mothballs*.

The woman nodded briskly, her gaze darting

around, as if she expected something deadly to emerge from the shadows. Little did she know that the deadly thing already stood before her.

"Thank you for seeing me."

"Like I had a choice?" Maree shot a glare over her shoulder at the hulking Cage the moment before the elevator doors slid shut on his impassive face. "He wouldn't take no for an answer."

"You'll be generously paid for your time." Turning toward the area she'd designated as the kitchen, Sorcha pushed the sleeves of her loose sweater to her elbows and motioned Maree to follow.

She did, the heavy thud of her boots echoing across the wood floor. "This is pretty nice. Wouldn't have thought this was tucked up here. Looked like a real dump from the outside . . . thought I was being dragged into some crack house."

Sorcha smiled. Exactly what she wanted. It kept people from sniffing about where they shouldn't. "Can I get you anything before we begin?" She sank down in a chair at her table as if she dragged unwilling clairvoyants into her home every day.

The woman hesitantly lowered herself across from Sorcha. "No. Thank you." She buried her hands beneath the line of the table, somewhere into the folds of her skirt. "Most people come to me for readings."

"I'm not most people." That was putting it mildly. Since Gervaise's death, she'd avoided going out in public. Her anger, her sadness . . . It was just too dangerous.

Sorcha cocked her head. "I hope you won't disappoint me. Everyone else I've spoken with has been less than helpful. You've come highly recommended, however, so let's just cut to it and save us both time and see if you're legit."

Maree's pupils seemed to darken and overfill her bright eyes. An alertness that hadn't been there before swept over her. She glanced toward the elevator as if prepared to bolt. "What do you mean?" she asked, her voice as tremulous as a feather drifting on the air.

"Are you a *real* witch?"

"A witch?" Maree's gaze shot back to Sorcha. She laughed, the sound cracking on the air. "I have a gift. Nothing more. Witches don't exist."

Sorcha leaned across the table, her nostrils flaring, scenting something besides the odor of mothballs rising on the air . . . an earthy aroma that reminded her of freshly tilled soil. She'd never smelled such a thing on a human before. Maree's body temperature changed, dropped several chilling degrees. Sorcha smiled, slow and deep, satisfaction rippling through her. "You're a witch," she announced.

Sorcha had not known until this moment if this woman was a con like all the rest she had questioned. She had faced too many brick walls to count in her hunt for a real witch. She knew they existed, knew one had started the lycan curse over two thousand years ago. Which was why, deep at her core, in her bones, she knew that a witch could lead her to Gervaise's killers.

"Listen, lady," Maree began, "you're wrong. I don't—"

"When I asked you if you were a witch, your pulse quickened, your body temperature dropped. Not the reaction I would expect if I was off base."

Maree shook her head, tossing her black hair. "What are you, some kind of—" The witch stopped abruptly, her voice dying as a look of dread passed over her face, bleeding it of all color.

Sorcha nodded. "It's safe to say we're both extraordinary females."

"What are you?" Marre asked quietly, her gaze darting again to the closed elevator as if she might rush it. She moved in her chair, turning her body slightly, and Sorcha knew she was about to try.

"You'll never make it," she warned, her blood heating up and pumping faster. The darkness inside her frothed, eager for release.

Maree fell back in her chair and seemed to shrink where she sat.

Sorcha stood up and moved a safe distance from her, breathing thinly through her nostrils until she felt in control again. She loathed it that her beast could rouse so quickly. It never used to. She stared at her reflection in the dark glass. The face that stared back at her was beautiful, an elegant, sculpted beauty. She couldn't help but wonder if Jonah would have liked her this way. Would he still have pushed her away?

"Do you really want to know what I am?" Sorcha's voice scraped through the air, the words thick in her mouth. She angled her head, waiting.

"It's safe to say we both know the world is composed of many unnatural things. Can you not guess whose den you've entered?" Sorcha swung an arm, turning from the window. "Why don't you just do what it is you do, and then you can leave." She fluttered a hand. "Forget you ever met me."

Maree nodded jerkily, her blue eyes overly large in her pale face.

"Good." With a brisk efficiency she didn't feel, Sorcha reclaimed her seat. Crossing her arms over her chest, she lifted an eyebrow. "Read for me. Do whatever it is you do." The words felt strangely thick on her tongue. Oddly, after all her efforts to locate a true witch, she felt unsettled sitting across from one. She could only think that it was one of Maree's kind who had started the lycan curse . . . which created so much misery for the world. For Sorcha.

The witch exhaled. "This isn't television. I do not *read*. I can't see the future. That's not my particular skill. Every witch has a different gift."

"And what is your gift?" And how could Sorcha manipulate it to find her late husband's killers?

The scene of Gervaise's death had been terrible. Bloody. Violent. There hadn't been much of his feeble body left. Their marriage might not have been real in the sense of couples who came together physically, but she had loved him. Gervaise had been the father to her that Ivo never was. Her elderly husband had known what she truly was and accepted her anyway.

He should not have died the way he did. He should not have suffered such a horrific end. She'd known instantly that the perpetrator couldn't be human. It was a massacre—the kind that a lycan would commit in a feeding frenzy. Tonight she would learn everything about the creature who'd taken Gervaise from her. She would find him and his pack and destroy them all.

"I can see only the past," the witch explained. "That's all I do."

Sorcha sat up straighter. "Perfect. That's all I want to know."

"I cannot guarantee that I will see the past event you wish to see . . . it could be something else from your past."

"I will see my husband's death," Sorcha vowed, her jaw tight and aching where it clenched.

"I can try. But first, the fee you promised me."

Sorcha removed a neatly folded wad of cash from the large front pocket of her sweater and dropped it on the table's gleaming surface. Maree stuffed the money into the handbag she wore strapped across her chest. "Let's do this then." Sliding to the edge of her chair, she motioned for Sorcha's hand.

Sorcha obliged, stretching out her arm, showing no reaction as Maree's moist fingers took hold of her hand.

"Can you remember the event?" Maree asked.

Sorcha swallowed tightly and nodded. She would never forget the bloody sight.

"Good. Visualize that and I will try to channel the moment."

Silence stretched. Sorcha studied the witch's face as she pictured the night she'd found her husband torn to pieces. Sweat soon beaded Maree's creased brow. Her breath grew raspy and Sorcha was convinced she was somewhere else, removed from this setting.

"Maree?" she whispered, and then felt silly because of her hushed tones. "Maree? What do you see?" she asked, her voice louder.

"A great fire," she said, so softly that Sorcha leaned in. "It fills the night sky, lights up the entire city. I see you. Running down a street, the heat of the flames warm on your back . . ."

Sorcha sucked in a deep breath, knowing instantly where Maree had gone. And it wasn't to the scene of Gervaise's death. She was seeing Istanbul . . . the night Sorcha escaped from her pack and left Jonah behind forever.

She swallowed, fought the sudden thickness in her throat. Almost as if she were choking on the smoke from that night all over again.

She had never wanted to leave Jonah, but she couldn't remain with the growing danger of her father. She still recalled Jonah's eyes, heard his voice . . . felt his rejection in her heart. He would never take her to mate, never love her as she loved him. So she had fled. Raced headlong into the night, escaping her father and pack shortly before a group of hunters blew up the building.

Sorcha shook her head, returning to the sound of Maree's voice recounting that event. "Tears run down your face, but you keep running . . ."

A breath shuddered through Sorcha, seeing

herself through the witch's words. As if she were there again, she tasted the salty fall of tears on her lips, smelled the smoke and ash.

She had wept for Jonah that night—and long after. Losing him had killed her young heart, stolen the last scrap of her youth. And this witch forced her to relive that.

"Move on," she hissed, squeezing the witch's hand that held hers. Maree made a small noise of pain and Sorcha relaxed her grip. "Look for Gervaise." She lowered her voice to a coaxing pitch. "It was a spring night. I left to pick up dinner from his favorite delicatessen. He was listening to *Der Freischütz*."

She gently hummed some notes, imagining their elegant penthouse as she left it. Gervaise reclined in his leather armchair, a book in his lap, the soft lamplight casting his craggy features into relief.

Maree nodded. "Yes, I am there. I see him. The old man has a blanket over his lap. . . and a book . . ."

"Yes." Sorcha's blood raced. "Yes. Do you see his killer?"

No one had seen anything, not the building's surveillance, not the doorman or the countless people who passed through the lobby. For a time, Sorcha had been a suspect. The police finally gave up on her, unable to explain away the lack of blood anywhere on her body or the several witnesses who had seen her walking to the delicatessen.

She shook her head. So much blood. More black than red. It covered the elegant pinstriped wallpaper, the windows, the furniture. Everything. She could still hear the staccato drip of it from the ceiling . . . could still smell the coppery tang.

A lycan was the only explanation. The only thing that made sense. The creatures moved faster than the human eye could detect. Hell, they could scale the side of her building. A lycan had killed Gervaise. Or a hybrid like herself, but their numbers were small when compared to the lycans who roamed the world.

Maree grew oddly quiet, her lids drifting shut over her bright blue eyes.

"Do you see the killer?" Sorcha pressed, shaking the woman's hands, determined to have the truth. She was close now. She could feel it just as she felt a telling heat building at her core. At that moment, Maree started to shake with great full-body shudders. The hair at the nape of Sorcha's neck tingled.

Maree's eyes flew open then, and Sorcha gasped at the dark orbs—deep, black space, void of any white. Her eyes gleamed like twin marbles, polished to the point that Sorcha could see her reflection.

She dropped the witch's hands as if stung and leaned back. "Maree?" she questioned in a low voice.

Maree cocked her head, the motion quick and birdlike. "You shouldn't stick your nose into affairs out of your realm . . . *dog*. Or should I call you mongrel? You're only a hybrid, after all. Not even a real lycan."

Sorcha dug her hands into the edge of her chair. The voice was Maree's, but not. It was different, dead and hollow sounding. "My husband *is* my concern." Her voice sounded far calmer than she felt, considering the sudden rush of searing blood in her veins. It was as though her body knew what her mind struggled to grasp.

"Your husband is dead because of you."

Sorcha dragged a hissing breath between her teeth. She tossed her head, the dark strands of her hair slapping her cheeks at these words. Denial surged hot and heavy in her chest. Gervaise had *not* been targeted because of her. No way. He was all she had, all that was left after she'd lost her pack—lost herself. He was the one thing that had come close to filling the hole in her heart Jonah had once occupied. She sucked in another deep breath. It couldn't be her fault.

Maree continued, "I hoped you would be blamed for the murder . . ."

Two things became instantly clear as that comment sank in. First, Maree was no longer speaking to her. But Gervaise's killer was.

The blood rushed to her head. She swallowed the dizziness and blinked past the sudden haze clouding her eyes. "What are you?"

"Safe to say, I'm not some useless witch who only harnesses a fraction of her power by resisting possession."

"Possession?"

"You really are a stupid cow, aren't you? Hard to imagine you could be any real threat."

"*What* are you?" she demanded again, leaning forward. "Where's Maree?"

"Cowering inside herself at the moment . . . like most white witches. Always running, hiding from my kind. If she knew what was good for her, she would give herself over to me."

"What are you talking about?"

"Haven't you figured it out? I'm a demon. I possess witches . . . at least the ones who let me. You might have heard of one witch I own." A heavy pause followed this. "Tresa."

Tresa. The name struck a chill in Sorcha's heart. "The witch who started the lycan curse?" Her lips moved numbly around the question. Tresa was the reason Sorcha existed . . . the reason any lycan or dovenatu existed.

Maree smiled. At least her face did. But Sorcha now knew it was really a demon smiling at her—Maree's mouth stretching over teeth the color of bone. "Well, well, you do know something then. Maybe you *are* the clever mongrel the Dark Prince warned me of, after all. The Master predicted you would bring me down if I didn't stop you. Looking at you, listening to you . . . it's almost laughable to consider."

"Tresa," she whispered. "She still lives."

The demon nodded. "As long as I exist, she lives. When she cursed Etienne Marshan long ago, she signed away her soul. To me."

Sorcha pressed her fingers to her temples, struggling to take it all in. "You killed Gervaise . . ."

"Well, Tresa did it, but at my behest." The demon leaned in, his lips moving slowly around the words. "Take it as a warning to stay out of my way."

Sorcha stared in bleak fury. "I was living my life. I didn't give a damn about you . . ." *Until now.* "You've made a serious mistake." Heat erupted at her core, zipping along every nerve ending, pushing at her tightening flesh.

"What are you going to do about it, mongrel?" The demon sneered. "I've lived over two thousand years. Think you can stop me?"

In a flash, Sorcha turned. Could not stop herself.

Her bones pulled, snapped into place in a burning instant. Her voice spat past her lips, thick and gurgling. "Why don't you stop hiding inside Maree and come out so we can fight this properly?"

"Oh, I would love that. Tell you what, find Tresa. Destroy her. Then you and I can finish this. And I'll show the Master that no pathetic mongrel has the power to kill me."

Sorcha lurched from her chair, sending it clattering to the floor, forgetting at that moment that the demon wasn't really there. She grabbed the witch by the shoulder, her fingers digging, eager to hurt, hungry for vengeance . . . until Maree cried out sharply. Sorcha pulled her hand back as if stung and stared hard at the witch's face.

The black liquid pools of her eyes blurred, shrank and faded away. The startling blue flashed back into place. The witch sagged in her chair, blinking in confusion.

And Sorcha knew. The demon was gone.

Glancing wildly around the room, convinced the demon could still hear her even if he no longer possessed Maree, Sorcha shouted, "I'll find Tresa! I'll destroy her and then we'll finish this!"

For Gervaise. For the misery Tresa's curse had caused across ages. *I'll finish it.*

Nothing would stop her.

TWO

Jonah woke to a heavy pounding on his door, wrenched from his usual nightmares. He sat up in bed, sheets tangled around his legs, his heart sinking back down into his throat.

The nightmares were always the same. Even all these years later. Always fire. Fire clawing up his body, eating at him, melting his flesh until it fell away in liquid sheets, until his bones burst into char and ash. Always he fought the flames, plunging into the mawing heat, screaming for Sorcha, desperate to save the only thing innocent and good in his life.

Useless.

With a curse and a shake of his head, he slid from the bed, the nightmare slipping away like smoke until its later return. As the scalding burn faded from his nose, he fought off the thought that always followed his dreams, plaguing him still, all these years later. *I should have been there. If I had only been there, Sorcha would be alive.*

The pounding at his door grew more savage and he snatched his sword from where it rested beside the bed. Before he even reached the door, he heard Darby's shouts from the other side.

"Jonah! Jonah, let me in!"

As soon as he flung the door open, the witch barreled past him into his condo. She slammed the door shut behind her and drove the bolt home. Her body shuddered with angry breaths, her red hair a flaming halo around her head.

Both her hands pressed against the door as if she expected something to burst through, as if her slight frame might prevent that from happening. He almost smiled. For all that she was a witch, she was small. A brisk wind could knock her over . . . which might have been what had drawn him toward her that first night so many years ago.

Her vulnerability had reminded him of Sorcha. Still did. Darby possessed a wide-eyed innocence that prompted him to protect her, to step forward and rescue her time and time again. He'd only ever acted the role of hero before with Sorcha.

"A demon—following me," she panted.

"Ah, hell, Darby." He lurched forward to stare through the peephole, his every nerve swinging into alert. "You led him here?" Seeing nothing, he stalked toward where several weapons hung above his couch.

Darby glared over her shoulder at him as he tossed aside his sword and removed a scimitar from its hooks.

"Sorry," she bit out. "I was on my way to your place anyway when it—"

"You should have called me. I would have come to you." He didn't need a demon knowing where he lived. Now he had no choice but to destroy the bastard—or leave his condo behind and relocate.

Almost on cue, his nape started burning, heat rising up from beneath his skin. He didn't have to look in a mirror to know that the mysterious markings on the back of his neck would be glowing. He rubbed a hand on the irritated flesh. The markings had appeared years ago, the same night he'd met his first demon. The night he'd first saved Darby.

The white witch's eyes followed the motion of his hand. "You feel him? He's coming?"

"Yeah," he ground out, jerking his head toward the bedroom. "Get in there, and—"

The rest of his words were lost. A great gust of air rushed through the room. The dark shadow passed through the door, swirled into a cyclone that touched down and materialized before him.

Darby ran for cover with a sharp oath. Jonah didn't blame her. The demon was after her, and a white witch had little defense against a demon bent on possessing her. The only thing she could do was avoid using her powers and stay under the radar. An impossibility for Darby with her particular gift. Her visions came to her unsolicited, and demons constantly tormented her because of it. If not for Jonah, she would probably have given up the fight years ago, relented and signed away her soul.

With the back of his neck scorching, he squared off in front of the demon. His lips curled at the gruesome sight of it. Great knotted horns jutted out from its head and a long, barbed tail whipped about its purple-black body, hissing on the air.

Fortunately for humans, they never saw this. Humans saw only shadows, blurry winds. Only witches and slayers could see demons as they truly were. For some reason that Jonah had ceased to understand, he was a slayer. Darby insisted he was chosen by God—like all slayers. With his past, his many sins and failures, he thought that unlikely.

The demon filled the doorway, feverishly muttering in its strange tongue. The words rolled over Jonah, weaving throughout him, almost spell-like, transforming inside him, unfolding, whispering in his head . . . becoming a language he could understand.

"Stand aside, slayer. I want the witch."

"You can't have her." Swinging his sword, Jonah whirled and swiped the scimitar across the demon's gut.

The demon roared, more annoyed than harmed. The long, slashing wound sealed itself almost the instant the purple dark flesh parted.

Crouched low in striking pose, Jonah searched for the mark of the fall that signified the demon's descent from grace—God's abandonment. It was a demon's Achilles' heel, the only spot he could strike to kill the creature.

Darby cried out as the demon swung a great clawed fist at Jonah's head. He ducked and spun around, air hissing in his ears at his speed. And that's when he saw it. The mark of the fall glowed brightly, beckoning.

With a roar of his own, he drove his sword into the demon's back. With a screech that could have broken glass, the demon crumpled, blurring into a twisting plume of smoky air as it dropped to the floor. Gradually the air cleared, leaving nothing. No sign of the demon that had once stood before him.

His breath fell hard, fast with the rush of adrenaline. Turning, he faced Darby. She stepped from his bedroom, her eyes bright with relief. "That wasn't so bad," she murmured with a shaky smile.

Jonah tossed his weapons to the floor and wiped an arm across his brow. "Have you thought of relocating, Darby? Someplace isolated where the temperature doesn't get higher than twenty degrees?" Demons were accustomed to the fires of hell and could not tolerate cold climates. Even demon witches were known to reside in cold locations where they could at least wrest some control from their possessors.

"I thought it smarter to stick close to you. It's not every witch who has a dovenatu slayer at her back."

"And what if I'm not there to cover your back? What if you didn't get here in time?" Shaking his head, he moved into his kitchen. It had happened before. When he'd failed Sorcha. When he lost her.

Sucking in a shuddering breath, he turned on the faucet and scooped up a handful of icy water, splashing it on the nape of his neck, where the flesh still throbbed and burned from his proximity to a demon. Would he never be free of the memory? Never take a breath when he didn't think of Sorcha? When she wasn't there to torment him?

"What were you doing out this late anyway?" he growled.

"I had to see you. I had another vision and it involved—"

"Damnit, Darby," he snapped. "Why not wear a sign around your neck? The last thing you should have done is traipse around town in the aftermath of a vision. They can smell the magic on you."

"I thought you needed to be warned."

"You could have called—"

"You hardly ever pick up."

Turning off the faucet with a jerk, he inhaled deeply, reminding himself that Darby hadn't asked to be what she was. Just as he hadn't asked to become a demon slayer. It wasn't her fault she was a demon target. She hadn't asked him to save her that long-ago night in the park where he'd first spotted her, cornered by a demon.

At first he thought he had snapped and finally gone mad. Or walked onto a movie set. What else could explain the grotesque creature? He had helped Darby then, and countless times since. He was kidding himself to think he would stop now—that he even could.

With a suffering sigh, he asked, "What did you see, Darby?"

"Tresa . . . someone's going to kill her." She winced. "Or try at least."

Running a wet hand down his face, he stared hard at her. "Tresa . . . the witch who started the lycan curse. Shit. That *can't* happen."

She nodded. "Her demon can't be set free, Jonah."

He exhaled. Darby's visions were rarely wrong.

"You have to stop her, Jonah."

"Her?"

"The woman who's after Tresa."

"Is she after Tresa or Tresa's demon?"

"There's a difference? If she kills Tresa, then her demon gains corporeal form. It will materialize on earth, hidden no longer. It will destroy all in its path. It could be the apocalypse."

Jonah lifted an eyebrow.

Her cheeks colored. "Don't look at me that way. I'm not being dramatic. I've seen the demon witch with a sword at her throat . . . we have to stop whoever it is from killing her."

Gazing at Darby's flushed, earnest face, he saw her as he had all those years ago, a teenager being brutally attacked by a demon. She'd reminded him so much of Sorcha. If he were honest, it was *this*—her needing him, admiring him—that mimicked, albeit poorly, the way he'd felt when Sorcha gazed up at him with her doe eyes.

"Why not?" He stalked from the sink into his bedroom, craving space, distance. "I don't have anything else to do," he called. There'd been nothing since Istanbul. Since he'd failed Sorcha. Lost her. Darby was the closest thing he had to a friend. Family, he guessed. She never left him alone, constantly inviting him to dinner with her aunts, even after his many refusals.

He'd had a family before. A pack. As fucked up as Ivo was, Jonah knew what it felt like to belong to a group, to something larger than himself. And there had been Sorcha. She had been everything good. She had looked to him, and he let her down. Failed her. Losing her had killed his soul, wrecked what little heart he possessed. He'd never let himself care that much again. Not even for Darby or the witches in her coven.

He jerked a shirt over his head and stalked back into the living room of his condo. He hadn't bothered to close the blinds, and the lights of the bay winked at him like multicolored stars.

Darby turned from the window, her arms folded in front of her, a serious look on her face. "There's more. It affects you directly."

He motioned for her to elaborate.

Darby uncrossed her arms and then crossed them again, clearly agitated.

Sinking onto his sofa, he murmured, "I'm listening."

"This woman has found out Tresa's location and she's determined to take her head." She said this last with heavy emphasis. Decapitation was the only way to kill a demon witch. Not that he ever had. A witch under the influence of a demon was bad enough . . . why would he want to free her demon?

Darby's eyes glassed over, appeared faraway as she recounted her vision. "I've seen her. She's strong. She won't quit until she sees Tresa dead.

I've discussed it with my aunts. As ugly as it sounds, we can't let her live."

He nodded grimly. If there was one thing Jonah knew how to do, it was kill. He'd ended lives for years at the behest of Ivo. Killing for a good reason would not give him a moment's pause. "Fine. Tell me where she is."

"There's more you have to know." Darby swallowed. He watched the cords of her neck visibly work. "I almost debated coming to you because of it, but if you don't stop her, the risk is too great for all of us. This woman . . . I saw her kill you." She blurted out the words as if they were too much, unbearable to keep bottled inside. "She was standing over you with a knife. I saw her pull it from your body . . ."

He stilled, imagining the scene. He'd lived for so long that death had become something elusive to him. There had been moments when he wished he had died with Sorcha and the others, that in living he had somehow cheated what was meant to be.

"Did you hear what I said?" she asked.

He nodded once, slowly. "What of Tresa? Does she live? Did you see her alive?"

"Yes. You help her escape."

And thereby keep her demon leashed. It was enough. All that mattered.

"I had to tell you," Darby said, eyeing him anxiously. "I couldn't just send you into this without knowing—"

"That I'm going to die?" He almost smiled at the stricken look on Darby's face.

She shook her head. "Of course it doesn't have to be. This is your fate as of now, but you have the power to change your fate's course. If you do the unexpected, something contrary to your nature, then maybe it can be averted."

Maybe. She was banking on a maybe.

"Jonah." Darby grabbed his hand. "I'll understand if you decide not to go."

His lips pulled tight in a semblance of a smile. "I'll go, Darby. What do I have to lose?" He'd lost everything already. There wasn't anything left for him to fear.

She grimaced, and he knew she was thinking his life was something worthwhile. Only he knew it wasn't. His life did not amount to much except a stretch of empty years. "Where is she?"

She nodded, stoic and soldierlike. Moistening her lips, she said, "You'll need a heavy coat."

Of course.

THREE

THE ALASKAN TUNDRA

With a glance at her GPS, Sorcha pulled to the side of the rough-hewn road and turned off the engine. She gave the steering wheel an encouraging knock of her knuckles, hoping the Land Rover would start later when it was time to leave. In these temperatures, one never knew. Not that fear of ending up stranded out here would stop her. Nothing would stop her.

With a steadying breath, she took a slow, measuring glance around the barren landscape. A misty gray hung on the air, like a hazy twilight even though her watch read 11:15 in the morning. According to the GPS, she was still several miles from her target, a lodge just beyond the deep snow-dotted ravine where she was parked.

Her gaze crawled over the desolate, white horizon, broken here and there by dead brown earth. If she didn't know better, she'd say there was nothing out here. No life at all. The wind howled across the stretch of frozen tundra, shaking her vehicle.

But Tresa was close. Just beyond the ravine. Sorcha's heart pumped blood, hard and fast, through her body. This was it. Saliva pooled in her mouth. She had worked closely with Maree until they were able to pinpoint the demon witch's location. Despite the cold, her palms started to sweat, the heat churning at her core. She had been ready for this moment since Gervaise's death. If possible, her pulse thrummed even faster, a rapid staccato at her throat.

Stepping from the vehicle, she zipped up her heavy white-and-tan camo parka—perfect cover against the wasteland that swallowed her. She removed a long leather scabbard from the backseat. The saber inside was honed to deadly sharpness, able to cut through flesh and bone like softened butter. Sliding the strap over her shoulder, she faced the lonely landscape. Perfect isolation. A slow smile curled her lips. Tresa wouldn't expect her.

She pulled her fur-lined hood over her head, and the subzero winds had little effect on her as she set out with sure strides. The beast simmered inside her, just beneath the surface, protecting her from the cold, keeping the freeze at bay.

Instinct hummed through her, propelling her forward. Her boots crunched over loose snow and dead rock as she moved in quickly, her body taut and quivering as her legs worked fast, at a near run. Tundra air buffeted her. She welcomed the bite of cold on her face, never felt more alive and awake.

Before cresting the top of the rise, she dropped and belly-crawled over burning-cold ground. Unzipping her backpack, she pulled out her infrared heat goggles and put them on, tugging her long ponytail free of the strap. Shaking her dark, choppy bangs back from her eyes, she looked through the goggles to the sprawling lodge below. A steady stream of smoke rose from the chimney, assuring her that it was occupied.

"There's my girl," she murmured. Aside from the glow of the burning fireplace, she easily identified a lone figure through the walls, marking the blurry red silhouette. *Tresa.*

The pulse at her throat raced. Her skin snapped and shivered, the beast in her prowling with excitement, stirring up heat like sparking embers, eager to break free and unleash itself on the demon witch responsible for the lycan curse. For so much death and mayhem over the last two thousand years. For Gervaise.

"Let's do this," she announced to herself,

her voice thick already behind her teeth. She re-adjusted her infrared goggles.

Her target was in the back of the house, lounging on something. Maybe asleep on a bed or couch. Sliding the sword from its scabbard, Sorcha flexed her fingers around the leather grip with an easy familiarity. She'd trained and practiced long hours with the blade ever since Gervaise's death.

Dropping the scabbard in the snow, she left it behind and advanced on the house, her boots cracking over icy earth as she moved with the stealth of a stalking predator. The witch hadn't moved. Her pulsing red figure still reclined in the back of the house.

Sorcha's palms grew damp inside her leather gloves. She stopped at the front door and listened for a moment to the howling winds. Holding her breath, she tried the doorknob. It turned. Of course. Who would bother locking doors all the way out here?

Soft music wafted on the air as she stepped inside the lodge, sword brandished, at the ready in front of her. She eased her foot down, wincing as it creaked on the wood floor.

Swallowing against her tightening throat, she assessed the comfortably appointed room. A fire crackled in a hearth large enough for a body to stand inside. The furniture was oversized, brimming with bulky pillows. It looked like someone's vacation retreat. A pot bubbled on the stove in the open kitchen overlooking the living area. She sniffed the savory aroma of meat and vegetables. Stew?

She clenched her teeth until her jaw ached, refusing to let herself be lulled by the domestic scene. Tresa lurked in the next room, a demon witch who needed to be put down like a rabid dog. And then Sorcha would have what she really craved, what she was really after—a confrontation with the demon who'd orchestrated Gervaise's death.

She moved toward the bedroom. Through the wall, she eyed the shape of a female glowing several shades of red as her heat levels varied.

Sorcha's pulse thumped wildly in her neck as she took careful steps over the wood floor. She paused at the sudden creak beneath her, the old wood betraying her yet again. Her heart a loud pounding in her ears, she shot a glance down at her boots, holding her breath. When she looked back up, her heart seized altogether.

The hazy red figure had vanished.

Shit! Where did she go?

She dragged a deep breath inside her smoldering lungs and reminded herself that she was dealing with a powerful witch who had all manner of magic at her disposal . . . and an especially brutal demon guiding her. Of course this wouldn't be easy.

Sorcha moved forward another step. At the threshold, she peered inside the room. Nothing. Empty space stared back at her. Her gaze narrowed on a chaise longue where a book sat faceup, forgotten. A page fluttered, undecided about which direction to fall.

She held still and listened. *Felt.* Scented the air. Let her beast find its way from deep within her.

Something was different. The air felt charged. Crackled around her like an electrical storm.

An odor clung to the room, definitely not human, but not beast, not like her. Not even like the witches she had interrogated in her quest to find Gervaise's killer.

This scent was different from the woodsy aroma of a witch—at least any witch she had met. It was acrid, like a recently snuffed-out match.

Then she felt it. Breath on her neck.

Her skin snapped, burst like wildfire. Her bones pulled, scorched down to the marrow. Primal and animal, her beast emerged to answer the threat.

Flexing her hand around the leather grip of her sword, she turned.

JONAH GUIDED THE CHOPPER over the desolate landscape. He held the controls with both hands as a sudden moaning wind shook the aircraft, hoping he wasn't too late, that he hadn't flown all this way simply to fail. Failure wasn't a possibility.

He checked his coordinates and then assessed the frozen wasteland beneath him. He didn't dare set down too close to the dwelling. Not unless he wanted to alert Tresa and the woman hunting her of his arrival.

He acted with cold calculation, refusing to let his thoughts stray too long to the woman he was sent to kill. To be fair, he would try to make her see reason first. Give her that chance at least. If she failed to listen, he would do what needed to be done. Even as tasteless as he found taking an innocent life—the life of someone who believed she was doing something good, something right, by killing a demon witch—her death could mean the future of the world.

Serving Ivo, he'd killed plenty. All lycans, though. He shook his head, shoving off the distasteful memory. Killing was killing. It blackened his soul, dragged him down. Now, years later, he could admit he'd stayed with Ivo for one reason. Sorcha.

The hero worship in her young eyes had held him prisoner. Innocent eyes for all the evil and corruption that surrounded her, hungry to pull her in. True, he had been the intended vehicle for that corruption. Her father fully expected him to ruin her, to drag her into the darkness and shatter her youth.

Of course he'd refused. Maybe he would have surrendered to the temptation someday, but he never had the chance. Her father's madness had killed her first.

He winced, hating the thought of that night in Istanbul. The explosion that lit up the air, turned the ink sky red.

Why should he think of that now? Here? On the brink of a mission that bore such importance for all. Humans, witches, lycans, dovenatus. No one would be immune if this demon was unleashed.

A dark voice shivered through him, insidious as the cold wind seeping into the chopper's cockpit and penetrating his layers of clothing, into his very bones.

Because you might kill a woman. A human . . . vulnerable, as Sorcha had been. A woman who probably thought she was doing a good thing taking down a demon witch.

Banishing the thought before it softened him, stealing him from his purpose, he lowered the aircraft onto the barren landscape. The skids bounced as he set the chopper down. The blades slowed their frenzy to a dull beat.

Killing the engine, he gathered his gear and set

out, forgetting the past and wrapping his head around what lay ahead of him.

He covered ground in good time, his long legs pumping hard. The white-and-brown landscape, both soft and hard, whipped past in a blur. Wind floated over the land like something alive, crawling, frozen curls of white seeking something, just as he was.

Soon the house came into view. A sprawling lodge with smoke streaming from the chimney. He reached inside his bulky jacket and pulled his gun free.

SORCHA STARED AT THE witch who had killed her husband. Even if it was at the behest of a demon, it had been her hands that tore Gervaise apart. Sorcha pulse stuttered, slowed to a choking halt as her gaze drifted to the female's pale, slim fingers . . . as though she expected to see Gervaise's blood still there, a stain never to be washed clean.

"Tresa." Her lips moved numbly around the name. A sweeping cold filled her, shriveling her veins. Every wound, every pain she'd ever known, suddenly ripped open, tender and raw again.

Standing before the two-thousand-year-old witch responsible for her every sorrow, she felt dizzy, almost as if she stood outside her own body. Her father's face flashed before her eyes. As did all the lycans she'd ever crossed paths with. She relived the memory of their cruelty, their brutal power. Tresa was responsible for all of them.

The demon witch was beautiful in a strange, otherworldly way. Even in a cream-colored fisherman's sweater and dark jeans, she looked extraordinary, out of place and time. Her hair gleamed, blue-black as a raven's wing, the ends cut bluntly, stopping just past her shoulders. Buff, fur-lined boots encased her long legs up to the knees. Her eyes gleamed whiskey-gold, catlike in a face that was sharply cut, exotic. Pure and ancient.

Those finely arched brows winged high. "You know my name."

"Yes," Sorcha hissed, thinking again of her demented father and the lycan army he had amassed before his death. The destruction he had wrought. Countless deaths and misery. This witch had brought all that on the world. Death and misery and destruction. And not to be forgotten—Gervaise. Vengeance would taste sweet. She would make this bitch and her demon suffer for all they had done.

Somehow, intricately woven in her head, was the not entirely reasonable belief that this witch and her demon were responsible for Jonah's death, too. The agents that had blown up their building only existed because of Tresa, after all.

Tresa's expression turned bemused. "It's been

a long time since anyone has spoken my name."

No denial then. It was the only validation Sorcha needed. She'd found her target. With a triumphant shout, she let her blade fly, brought the razor tip inches from the creamy throat peeping over the high-necked sweater, stopping a fraction of a second before making contact.

Tresa didn't even flinch with the blade's tip at her throat. She simply stared at Sorcha with her whiskey-warm eyes. As if a sword placed at her throat was an everyday occurrence. "You don't want to do that."

"Oh, but I do." Sorcha flexed her fingers around her leather grip and wondered why her palms were sweating inside her gloves. She inched her face closer. "I've dreamed of meeting you, of watching you die. You killed my husband."

Finally, she would end it. She licked her lips and tried to still her suddenly shaking hands. Tried not to think about how very human the witch appeared. Not a monster at all.

"Did I?" Tresa asked in a voice laced with an indefinable accent. "I'm sorry for that."

The words enraged Sorcha, increased her loathing. "You're *sorry*? He's dead. You viciously murdered him . . . and you're sorry?"

"I have little memory of the things I've done under possession."

"You mean you're not possessed right now? Your demon isn't . . . here right now? He's gone?"

Tresa's lips pulled tight in a frown. "He's never truly gone. I'm bound to him, but yes, presently he's not here."

"But once you're dead, I imagine he'll surface."

The witch smiled without mirth. "Even as much as demons abhor the cold, yes, if I were killed, he would instantly materialize. But you don't wish to do that."

"Oh, I think I should like that very much," Sorcha growled, her words distorted through her thickening teeth.

"You're not human," the witch announced, looking at her intently with her fiery gaze, her nostrils flaring slightly, as if she scented Sorcha's unnatural origins.

Sorcha resisted the temptation to touch her face, to feel whether she had fully transformed. Her emotions ran high, and she'd never been very good at wielding control over her inner beast.

"That's right, I'm not. I'm a creation of *your* making."

"Ah." Tresa nodded, her sleek, dark hair moving fluidly over her shoulders. "Not full lycan, though. Some relief, I suppose."

Considering her loneliness since Gervaise's death, it was hard to imagine anything good about being a species that walked on the fringes of two worlds, never belonging in either. Relief? What a joke. There was little relief in her solitude, her isolation from mankind, from . . . anyone. Trapped in her cursed existence. No real friends. Only strangers for lovers because that was all she could ever allow a man to be. On the rare occasion she had let a man into her bed, it was always temporary. A fleeting satisfaction of the flesh to fill the emptiness. She never permitted more. She couldn't allow that. All she ever had was Gervaise.

Thoughts of her husband tightened her throat. "Why?" she whispered hoarsely. "Why did you have to kill him?"

"I didn't have a choice—"

"But you did once. Long ago, when you decided to sell your soul to a demon bastard."

Tresa gave a single hard nod, her features tightening. "Yes. I did do that."

Sorcha sank her blade a fraction closer, readying it to slay her.

"Heed me," Tresa continued. "I'm many things, but never a liar. Even when it might be good for me." Her eyes flashed and Sorcha suspected she was remembering something else, thinking of a time when a lie had hurt her. Those whiskey-gold eyes narrowed. "Kill me, and you'll know true regret. The kind I've lived with for two thousand years. I wouldn't wish it on anyone. You don't wish to free my demon."

Sorcha's brow creased, certain it wasn't human decency she heard in the witch's voice. It couldn't be that. Tresa couldn't possess a scrap of humanity. "Rest easy. I'll dispatch your demon to hell fast on your heels."

Just then, the witch's head cocked sharply to the side. She closed her eyes as if she were listening to something. Or someone.

Not about to let her establish a connection with her demon—that would make her harder to kill—Sorcha dug the blade deeper. Blood swelled around the point. "Stop that. Open your eyes."

The blood continued to pool, more black than red, but Tresa didn't wince, didn't even seem to feel the pain at all. Finally, the witch opened her eyes. "You must go. He's coming." As stoically as she stood, her voice betrayed her, trembling to a vibrating chord on the air. "God help us, he's coming."

Sorcha didn't miss the irony that a witch in service to a demon asked for God's help.

Anxiety surged through her despite herself, despite the fact that *he* was the reason she had come here. "Let him come," she hissed.

"Quickly, flee, go. Once he's here, I can't stop—"

"Your demon," Sorcha finished. "I get it. Bring him on. Let him see his precious witch destroyed—"

"No." Tresa shook her head fiercely, her voice angry now. "You don't understand. He *wants* you to kill me and free him. You can't kill me!"

"Wanna bet?" Sorcha leaned forward, adding pressure. Black-red blood ran, a steady river down her throat, staining her sweater.

A shutter fell over Tresa's face, banking the glow in her eyes, making them appear dull, lifeless.

With blood running thickly down the column of her neck, she looked to a point over Sorcha's shoulder. Lips barely moving, she croaked, "It's too late. He's here."

Sorcha followed her gaze and looked. Nothing was there.

Well, almost nothing.

The wind outside grew louder, howling like a beast. The air in the house seemed to darken, thicken with swelling shadows. She shivered with a foreboding sense of awareness. The temperature inside the lodge rose several degrees, as if someone had tossed more logs onto the fire.

"Go," Tresa hissed, her face pale and drawn. Her lips trembled, as if it took her very will to speak, to spit out the words. "Run."

Sorcha's beast stirred, awake and alert on a primal level.

Suddenly the shadows converged into one great cyclone of air. Tresa screamed as she was enveloped in the dark gust. Her body and arms were flung backward, as if struck with the force of a truck.

Her scream faded, dwindled to a prolonged hiss, like a drop of water on a hot stove.

Sorcha watched, grasping the fact that the shadow was no trick of light. No shadow at all.

The demon she hunted was back and bent on reclaiming his witch.

Tresa twisted and writhed, devoured within the dark, whirling shadow.

Finally, she stilled. Faced Sorcha.

Now she resembled the dark, evil entity that Sorcha had expected to find here. She stood taller. Those lovely whiskey eyes were gone, swallowed up in a sea of black that sent a chill straight to Sorcha's heart.

Eyes wide and aching in her face, Sorcha focused on Tresa's bloodied throat, peeking above the collar's edge. It had to be the throat. Decapitation was the only way.

Before she lost her chance, before the demon intensified his hold on Tresa and proved harder to kill, Sorcha pulled back her arm and brought her saber down in a flashing arc of steel.

Air hissed as her sword fell, descending toward Tresa's neck.

Sorcha's arm jerked, caught hard on something. A cry ripped loose from her throat. Her shoulder constricted, her muscles pulling and straining to bring down her sword.

Her heart froze in her too-tight chest. She glanced up at her blade, suspended above Tresa's head, locked, motionless. Her gaze flitted up, resting on the strong, masculine hand clamped over her own hand, squeezing her fingers until the blood ceased to flow. The rough-looking knuckles whitened, not loosening despite her effort to pull free.

He was strong. Stronger than she was.

Her senses flared, filled with *him,* and she knew she was in the presence of something inhuman. Something like herself? A lycan or dovenatu. It had been a while since she'd been around one, but she knew.

She remembered.

Relaxing the tension from her shoulders, she eased her arm down. Still, he clung to the sword, to her hand that gripped it. She turned halfway to face this new threat.

Her nostrils flared anew, overcome by the male, heady scent of him.

Before she lifted her gaze, before she locked eyes with the interloper, she marked him—knew he was one of her kind. A dovenatu. As a species recognizes one of its own, she knew, and every pore snapped wide, her skin stinging and alert.

FOUR

Nothing could have readied her for the sight of him.

As she locked eyes on his face, a blistering cold swept through her, killing the feverish beast inside. Her bones shrank back down, the animal vibrations at her core falling silent.

She blinked several times, doubting herself, wondering if coming face-to-face with a dovenatu might not have confused her, made her see what wasn't there. What couldn't be there. *Who* couldn't be there.

Her heart slammed within her chest. It couldn't be *him*.

Ripping off her goggles with one hand, she tossed them to the floor with a thud and shook the dark fringe of bangs from her eyes, staring hard at the man before her. No. Not a man. Never that. As long as she had known him, Jonah had never been just a man.

Her stomach heaved and she thought she might

be sick. *Jonah*. Swallowing bile, she lifted her chin a notch and schooled her face to reveal nothing, not happiness, not the betraying thrill in her heart.

She couldn't look away from him. Her gaze scanned the well-carved features of his face, drinking up the sight. His dark blond hair was cut shorter than the last time she'd seen him, almost spiky. He was as tall as she remembered, as lean-muscled. And despite herself, her stomach knotted and clenched with the pull of longing.

Some things never changed.

He hadn't changed, hadn't aged. Not that she'd expected he would had he lived.

Had he lived.

He did live. A bitter taste filled her mouth as she processed that. He stood before her, alive. He had survived the explosion. He stood before her now. *Here*. She felt the insane urge to strike him, slap his face again and again for daring to be alive after what she'd gone through when that building blew into a million particles.

She had grieved for him, even blaming herself for living when he had not. Her fingers curled inward, nails digging into her palms.

Light glowed at the centers of his eyes, tiny torches within the orbs of blue. "Sorcha," he rasped, killing any hope that he might not recognize her.

He tugged the sword free of her hand. Numbly, she watched him take it as if he were taking it from someone else and not her. Plucking a toy from a child's hand.

He took a step toward her. She quickly side-stepped him.

Standing a wary distance away, Tresa forgotten, she breathed his name. "Jonah."

From the ruthless cut of his mouth, the sight of her didn't affect him. Twelve years had passed. He knew her only as a chubby prepubescent. She need only glance in a mirror today to know she looked different since her Initiation. Taller. Lean-limbed as any jungle cat. Even her face had changed. Her cheeks less full, her face narrower, her eyes larger, luminous.

She wasn't the same girl he'd pitied all those years ago. She'd changed. Inside and out. No longer to be confused with the helpless, doting puppy she once was.

She never wanted to be that girl again. Helpless and needy, in love with a man who would never love her back. Whose supposed death had nearly destroyed her. Even more than his rejection had.

"Give me back my sword." Pulling herself together, she stretched out her hand, proud that her voice did not shake.

"I think I'll keep it." His voice rippled across her skin, the same as in her dreams. Oh, she had loved him. Wanted him with a foolishness that bordered on obsession. *Idiot.*

But not again.

"Good to see you, Sorcha."

"Yeah," she retorted, her gaze tearing from him to her sword and back again. Her chest felt tight, a twisting mass at its center. "Good to see you, too. *Alive.*" She could not stop the sting of accusation from entering her voice.

He didn't miss it either. He cocked one eyebrow, several shades darker than his sun-kissed hair. "You sound angry." He dragged out the words with a mildness that only infuriated her further.

"Angry? Why should I care whether you're alive or dead? Should I care that you're here, trying to stop me from finishing off this murdering bitch?"

"Not trying," he stated, his voice as flat and cold as his eyes. "Stopping. You can't kill her."

"You've really made something of yourself in the years since I've last seen you—protecting demon witches." She shook her head with disgust. "I would rather you were dead than find you alive and like this."

He sneered at her with his well-carved lips. "You didn't miss me even a little?"

In answer, she brought her leg up and kicked him solidly in the chest, launching him back through the air, taking immense satisfaction in propelling him fifteen feet, into the wall.

Somewhere behind her Tresa released a brittle, horrible laugh. Or rather her demon did. Sorcha couldn't spare a glance for the creature. Not now. Not as Jonah watched her, his glowing eyes narrowing to slits. The eyes of a predator.

He jumped back to his feet like a springing cat. She knew a moment's alarm, forgetting that she possessed equal ability, remembering only that he had been her father's perfect machine. A born killer.

He crouched low, an animal ready to pounce. His fingers brushed the floor with a dangerous idleness that belied the tension humming through him . . . reaching across the distance to where she stood. "Don't do this, Sorcha. I don't want to fight you."

The demon spoke, the cadence of speech recognizable from their conversation before, even when speaking in Tresa's accented tones. "My, my. What a fascinating turn of events."

Still, all Sorcha's attention remained on Jonah. She didn't dare look away.

"You don't want to fight me? Sure. You just want to protect her." Sorcha braced her legs apart, grounding herself, holding her head up with forced bravado. Her sleek ponytail brushed her back. "You think I can't handle you? That you're still so much better than I am?"

"I never thought that," he shot back.

"Right," she snapped, thinking of herself at fifteen, the night she had offered herself to him. His rejection had demoralized her. He was the one person she had thought cared for her.

She'd been wrong.

His glowing eyes seemed to home in on her, intent and probing. She fought to swallow, hating the sensation that he could read her mind, that he was thinking of that night, too, remembering her humiliation.

"Why are you after her?" he asked.

"None of your business. We're past the days where I tell you anything," Sorcha snarled, moving in a slow circle around him. From the corner of her eye, she marked the black-eyed witch. She seemed to be having trouble of some sort, bending at the waist, holding on to her middle as if in great pain.

"Oh, but it is my business. And let's face it, you always have been."

"Not anymore." She spat out the words. Did he dare behave as though he held some authority over her? She was not a child anymore.

Beyond him Tresa suddenly hunkered over, keening shrilly, her hands pulling at her dark hair before flinging back her head. Her whiskey-warm eyes were back, darting and wild. Desperate. Instantly, Sorcha understood. She was fighting her demon, trying to expel him from her body.

The witch bolted toward the open door, like a crazed creature seeking its last chance at survival.

In a flash, Sorcha sprang, launching herself over her. She landed on the balls of her feet before the witch, the stinging cold wind at her back.

Unarmed, she could at least keep her penned. Until she reclaimed her sword from Jonah, anyway.

"Going somewhere?" Sorcha hissed, her voice altered, thick in her mouth. With a growl, she grabbed a lamp near the door and knocked the shade free. She tossed the cold, solid metal pole in her hands, figuring it could work to slice off a head.

Just as she hauled back the pole, she was yanked by her hair and flung through the air. She hit a wall and landed on her side. Scalp stinging, she swallowed a cry.

Shaking with fury, she lifted herself up and watched through slitted eyes as Jonah stood between her and her prey, a great wall of muscle shielding the murdering bitch. Betrayal stung her, flayed her like a whip. He was so quick she had not even seen him move.

Jonah, her mind seethed, any lingering tenderness for him dying instantly.

"Go," he barked over his shoulder at Tresa, motioning with an angry wave. "Flee this place."

Tresa turned for the door. Jonah protecting her—it was more than Sorcha could stand!

"No!" Sorcha shouted, surging forward as the demon witch escaped out into the ice-burned wasteland. She quickly became obscured in the white swirls of freezing wind.

With a wild glance around, Sorcha spotted her sword where Jonah had abandoned it. Sprinting across the room, she snatched it off the ground, ready to give chase, but Jonah blocked her.

"Get out of my way," she hissed, flexing her grip.

He shook his head warningly. "You're in too deep here, Sorcha."

"Yeah?" She glanced beyond his shoulder, spotting the dark smudge of Tresa shrinking on the snow-craggy landscape.

She was getting away. *Gervaise's killer was getting away.*

All her probing, waiting . . . for nothing. Desperation hammered against her pulse. She had to go after her.

"I've faced worse than you." It was a miracle that she'd survived that year before she met Gervaise, alone, a scavenger on the streets, fleeing man and lycan predator alike. In those days she still hadn't transitioned, but that hadn't stopped every lycan within miles from sniffing her out.

Jonah smiled a humorless grin. Pity lurked in the curving lips. *Pity*. Again. It had always been pity with him. He'd never looked at her as an equal, as a potential mate. That's why she'd left that night.

To see that same smile on his face now drove her over the edge. With an enraged cry, she lunged forward, arm raised, knowing the saber wouldn't kill him, not a dovenatu, but it sure as hell would hurt. And hurting him sounded pretty good right about now.

All these years she'd thought him dead. Instead, he was running around protecting the likes of Tresa. It was beyond imagining. She almost wished him dead . . . or at least she wished she'd never found out he was alive. She would rather have kept the bittersweet memory of him. Better than this reality.

He sidestepped the sword, so that she only grazed his shoulder. He glanced at the blood well-ing through his coat. The wound would have been deeper if not for his thick winter gear. "You're out for blood?" he murmured, his voice lethally soft, deep and intense, silently questioning: *Is this the way it has become between us?*

"I didn't come here to play. Let me pass and you may still live." She shrugged aside the whispering voice that asked if she could really kill Jonah. For all that had happened, all the bitter feelings he roused, he was a part of her past . . . her beginning. Could she snuff out that life?

She swallowed the tightness in her throat and allowed herself to be honest with herself. Okay, she couldn't kill him. But he didn't need to know that.

"You packing silver?" He cocked his head to the side, a muscle feathering the flesh of his jaw. "Explosives?"

She looked over his shoulder again, craning her neck desperately for a glimpse of Tresa. Nothing.

He continued, "Because I'm not."

Her gaze inched back to him.

He held his hands palms out. "You want a go-round, Sorcha? 'Cause we can beat each other to death all day and never die."

"You're right." Sighing—and hoping she didn't exaggerate the effort—she turned with feigned defeat. "All right. I guess this is pointless . . ."

She waited, let a moment pass for her words to sink in . . .

"I'm glad you feel that—"

She whirled.

His eyes flickered with the barest surprise as she barreled past him, striking his shoulder with her fist to push him out of her way.

He stumbled, caught off guard. Righting himself, he caught her around the waist with one arm.

Air crashed through her lips as he lifted her off her feet. That steel band of his arm shot a hot ripple through her. Shock and awareness. She couldn't recall a time when he'd ever held her so intimately, their bodies locked flush together. Never when she was a woman. She could feel the wild pounding of his heart against her, and her body reacted, came to aching life.

A sound, almost like a growl, burned in her ears. It was with some shock she realized it was *her*.

It was unique and not a little terrifying to have met her match—to be so vulnerable again. She almost felt like that helpless fifteen-year-old once more. Almost.

Clutched close to him, her body tingled. Her stomach clenched. This was Jonah. She had never thought him cruel or sadistic. Not like her father. Jonah had never been heavy-handed, forcing her into extreme situations just to see if he could urge her through Initiation.

Even though Jonah had acted as her father's henchman, he stood apart from all the brutality, especially anything that might have caused her harm. He'd tried to help her, spare her . . . and comfort her when he couldn't. Those memories were dangerous. They made her body soften against him, the backs of her knees quiver. The growl at the back of her throat turned into a purr. In that moment, it was as if they were the only two people on earth.

His arm muscles bunched. His hand on her hip spread wide, fingers fanning out, each one a separate brand, searing her through her layers of clothing.

He said her name, the sound soft and dragging, ruffling the loose strands of silky hair near her ear.

It sucked the fight from her, urged her to melt into him. The muscles in her neck loosened, sagging her head back into his shoulder.

His fingers brushed her cheek, the barest touch. "Sorcha," he said again, sighed really. "I . . . I missed you."

A shudder racked her. *He* missed *her*? Right.

She jerked her head away from him. No. *Hell, no!*

Remembering her purpose—and that he intended to keep her from it—she kicked his knee out with the heel of her boot, satisfied at the crunch of bone. He released her, cursing in pain.

She dropped to her feet. Panting, warm and flushed despite the arctic temperature, she jerked her gaze back to the open door. *Tresa*. She dove for the opening, screaming when a rough hand clamped around her ankle and brought her down hard.

Her body crashed flat, stretched out on the wood floor. She twisted around and kicked.

He dodged the attack of her boots, his expression furious, eyes like ice, the flame at the center twisting blue-cold.

"Stop that," he hissed, crawling up the length of her and flattening his chest over her, trapping her arms at her sides.

"Go to hell!"

His body pressed, hard and heavy, like a rock weighing her down. His face loomed above hers, so close she could see the tiny white scar above his right eyebrow. She'd always wondered about that. It had to have happened when he was a boy. Before his Initiation, before she knew him.

She released a ragged breath. The hot air fanned against his face in a frothy white cloud. They'd never touched like this, body to body. Adult male to adult female. As a girl, she had fantasized about it, but it never came close to happening.

Her heart hammered with alarming speed against her too-tight chest and she worried that he heard it. Felt it. Read more into it than fear and panic. She couldn't have that.

Like lycans, dovenatus were a primal species, driven by their more fevered emotions. Emotions like lust.

Shaming warmth pervaded her. He might get it into his head that she *wanted* him to take her right here, like a pair of rutting animals.

"Are you going to quit this stupid game?" he demanded, his voice a hard bite on the air. Hardly the sound of a man driven by insatiable desire . . . and a part of her bristled at that, even as another part breathed a small sigh of relief. Some things never changed. She didn't affect him *then,* and she didn't affect him *now.*

The familiar burn of shame crept over her, re-minding her of the girl she had once been, longing for his attention, craving his love. She had wanted him to be her first kiss. Her first. Period.

She stifled a snort. She was more experienced now. She'd tasted desire and wouldn't fool herself into thinking this man could deliver what no other could. If she had an itch, she would get it scratched by some other . . . as soon as she got away from him and finished her business with Tresa.

"Well," he demanded, "are you going to quit?"

"What? You want me to say 'uncle'?" She sneered at the sudden memory. That had been the only word she could say to get him to stop tickling her as a girl.

His lips twitched and something inside her froze at that. It was like a flash, a glimpse into the past, when she could amuse him and make him grin. "Something like that," he murmured.

Mentally shaking herself, she glanced desperately to the door again. She could still overtake the witch if she escaped now. Although immortal, demon witches didn't possess any of the super speed or strength of dovenatus or lycans. They had their gifts, their magic, but nothing else. Right now, Tresa was a normal woman out there running at snail speed through the tundra. It didn't matter that she'd gotten a head start. Sorcha could track her down in moments.

As though he read her mind, his chest sank ever deeper over hers, pinning her, crushing her achy breasts. "You're not going after her."

"You'll have to kill me to stop me." Bold words, and she meant them.

His gaze narrowed, scanning her face, looking at her, truly looking, probing her every feature as if he was trying to understand this new Sorcha.

"But then you were always good at killing." Her voice lashed out as quickly as a whip finding exposed flesh. The killing had bothered him, then. The bloodshed. He had confided as much. She almost felt wrong to throw that back in his face.

"I don't have to kill you," he drawled in a smoky voice that made her insides quiver. "I can just keep you here long enough for Tresa to get away, put enough distance between her and us that you won't even know where to start hunting for her again."

Her chest clenched as she thought about how long it could take for her to find the elusive witch. How long she might be alone with Jonah. How long before he was satisfied that the witch was well and truly out of tracking range. How long could he possibly trap her in this remote location?

Utterly, wretchedly alone with him.

He glanced away from her face, scanning the large, well-appointed great room. He looked back at her. "I'm certain we can find something to pass the time. Do you still read? I see a bookcase."

She blinked. "Funny." She surged against him in an effort to throw him off her again. Useless. "Too bad I'm not staying."

The light at the centers of his eyes intensified. Suddenly the hard press of his body over hers became too much. Her breasts, her hips, her thighs, everything quivered and ached and softened against his hard lines, melding them, fusing them into one. Her mouth watered, words impossible to form.

"'Course." His voice rumbled up from his chest and into hers. "I'm sure we can come up with more interesting things to do."

FIVE

Sorcha. Jonah reeled, overcome with the reality of her, the incredible sight. The emotion in her outraged expression made her more closely resemble the girl of memory, the Sorcha he thought dead, lost to him forever. The girl he had failed.

He might have celebrated coming face-to-face with her. If she hadn't been the woman he was here to stop—*kill,* if need be. If the press of her body against his didn't send the blood smoldering in his veins.

Except that this was Sorcha. *Sorcha.* Someone he had only ever viewed with tenderness, a little sister he must protect. The desire pumping through him made him feel base and foul. He shouldn't find the press of her body so arousing, even if it was a normal reaction. Physiological. They were of the same species, after all. Naturally drawn to each other.

It was this Ivo had counted on. He had believed the instincts of their kind would eventually force

Jonah to breed with Sorcha. Of course Ivo had been wrong to assume he was a mindless rutting animal.

His jaw clenched. He hadn't been that beast all those years ago.

And he wasn't now.

He was something more. Something better than a hybrid lycan. Something with a conscience.

If he listened to Darby and any other member of her coven, they would have him believe he was their salvation—a demon slayer fated to the task of protecting white witches from demons.

It shouldn't matter that Sorcha was the female he'd come here to stop.

But it did.

He couldn't take his gaze from her face, devouring the sight of her, the face that had changed, and yet was still the same in so many ways. Her doe eyes, her soft mouth . . .

He shook his head. What was she doing here? Hunting Tresa?

Conflicting impulses warred within him. He didn't know whether to strangle her or hug her.

Staring at the fierce creature Sorcha had become, he could only recall his misery as he stared at that building in Istanbul eaten up with writhing flames. He'd hunted down the one responsible for the explosion. Almost killed him. Until he realized it wouldn't fix anything. It wouldn't bring Sorcha back. He'd needed an outlet for his grief, for his helpless rage. He had only ever wanted the best for Sorcha, to protect her from her father . . . from himself. He'd refused taking her to mate because he quite simply wasn't good enough for her. There had been something so pure about her. So innocent despite being Ivo's daughter. Clearly that innocence was gone.

In the end, it hadn't mattered. For all his care and caution, he'd lost her anyway.

He greedily drank in the sight of her, searching for glimpses of the girl he remembered, the girl he mourned, but seeing little evidence of her in the jaded expression of the woman staring back at him. "You've changed." Staring at the hard-eyed female, he recognized the fact that the sweet girl was gone. This wasn't the Sorcha he'd known.

"Yeah, I'm not dumpy Sorcha anymore with the unfortunate acne who trailed after you like a lost little puppy."

His chest tightened. "I never saw you that way."

"Don't worry. I have no intention of picking up where we left off with me stalking you."

"You never stalked me," he quickly inserted even as he admitted to himself that she had come close . . . well, shadowed would be a more apt description.

She snorted. "I was pathetic."

"I always liked you, Sorcha."

Her eyes widened. "Now who's lying?"

He opened his mouth to argue, but from the cold bend of her lips he saw that she did not want him to—nor would she believe him.

Her eyes flickered for a moment, shadows shifting through the brown depths, and for a second he thought he read something there. A hint of the vulnerability that she used to possess. The sight softened him, made him want to fold her in his arms in a comforting hug.

Then, it was gone. Nothing but coldness frosted her gaze now. Where had the girl he remembered gone? It had been so easy to earn her smiles back then. To make her laugh. This Sorcha would just as soon use her sword on him as smile.

He cocked his head, studying her.

She mimicked the motion, watching him as he watched her beneath the choppy fringe of her bangs.

"I don't remember your hair quite so dark." *Or your face so beautiful.* His blood pumped faster as he assessed her.

"Like I said, a lot has changed."

He reached out to touch her face, stroke her cheek.

She jerked back from him, knocking his hand away as if stung. "I'm not yours to touch."

In response, a low growl rumbled in his throat. The old Sorcha would never have slapped his hand from her. Would never talk to him as if she couldn't stand him. The beast stirred in him, intrigued and hungry, excited by the challenge of her.

Her pretty lips curled back, revealing a flash of white teeth. "You may have had that chance once, but that was a long time ago."

Her words burrowed deep, and he knew what she was talking about. He remembered their last night. The night the building blew up. When a fifteen-year-old Sorcha had looked at him with such hope, the hunger for him bright and desperate in her gaze—banked the moment he turned away from her.

He dropped his hand to his side, curled his fingers into a fist. He couldn't explain it, couldn't make her see that he would have been wrong to take her then, would have been nothing more than an animal destroying something innocent and pure. She clearly didn't understand. Only remembered the rejection. "Yeah. A long time ago."

"A lifetime," she shot back.

He nodded. She wasn't innocent anymore. No pure girl's body molded against him. While he mourned that, he also craved her now, as she was.

It was as if looking at her reawakened a missing

piece of himself. A piece he had not even realized was missing.

"Yeah," he agreed, hardly recognizing the tight sound of his voice. "A lifetime in which you've started hunting witches. How did you get mixed up in this, Sorcha?"

"I can ask you the same." Her hands fluttered between them, looking for a place to rest. "Here you are ready to kill me to save some worthless, soulless witch—"

He tightened his lips in a frown. "There's a lot you need to understand—"

"I don't have time for your lies. Get off me." She surged against him and he enjoyed the feel of her breasts beneath their layers of clothing.

"Are you going to run? Promise you'll behave and I'll—"

"In case you hadn't noticed, I'm not a little girl anymore."

"Oh, I noticed."

The pink in her chill-burned cheeks deepened.

He settled deeper into her softness, couldn't resist. "We're going to remain like this for a while, until I have your word."

The light at the centers of her eyes sparked with anxiety, and he knew she was thinking of the passing time, of how each second took Tresa farther away.

"Why are you so determined to kill Tresa? Is it all demon witches or just her?"

"I couldn't give a damn about any other witch. She's responsible for it all . . . for everything!"

"So you want vengeance, is that it?"

She gave a single hard nod.

He stared at her starkly, trying to let his next words penetrate. "You can't do it, Sorcha."

A stillness came over her. She scanned his face intently. "I wish you'd stayed dead to me. Better than what you are now."

Her whispered words stung as they shouldn't have. She didn't understand, but he would make it clear to her, and then everything would be good. Right between them. For some reason, that was important. Meant everything to him.

"Listen to me, Sorcha." He paused, breathed in. "It's not that simple—"

He didn't get the chance to finish. She surged against him with sudden violent force, flipping him over her head.

His back slammed to the floor with jarring impact. He saw stars for a moment, before sitting up and shaking off the stun, cursing himself for dropping his guard. He'd let the sight of her, the memory of what she'd meant to him, distract him.

Whatever she was, whoever she was now . . . Well, he didn't know that person.

By the time he righted himself and looked around, she was gone, out the door and racing through the craggy, snow-whipped landscape. A blur of tan camo, fast as the wind. At that speed, with the instincts of their kind, she would overtake Tresa in no time. He glanced around quickly. The deadly-looking saber was gone. If he didn't catch her, she'd have Tresa's head. And then he'd have a demon loose on his hands.

With a bitter curse, he was on his feet and running out the door after her, sudden fear coating his mouth, sour and metallic as blood.

But not the fear he should have felt. Not fear for the world if that demon was set loose. His fear was for Sorcha if she came face-to-face with a demon that killed and destroyed as easily as breathing.

His jaw locked, hardening with determination. He'd failed Sorcha before—believed her dead.

He wasn't going to let that happen for real this time. No matter the stranger she had become.

SORCHA DIDN'T LOOK BACK. Didn't risk a glance over her shoulder, too worried it would slow her down and trip up her focus.

There were no tracks. The swirling wind had blown whatever trail Tresa left. She could trust only her instincts. She opened her senses, blocked out thoughts of Jonah closing in somewhere behind her. Instead, she focused on the prey ahead of her.

The heavy pounding of her tread echoed in her ears, in perfect sync with the ragged slap of her breath on the dense air.

At last, she caught a whiff. The faint, woodsy, peat-smoke scent of Tresa carried on the arctic wind.

Panting, Sorcha stopped, twisted around, following her nose. Trailing the earthy scent, she slid down an embankment in a spray of snow and landed on her feet. She dragged in a deeper breath and realized Tresa was everywhere, all around her.

Sorcha's gaze swung left and right. Too late, she heard a snap behind her, the crunching of snow and ice beneath the weight of something moving in swiftly.

Everything slowed down then.

She turned, the wind cutting her cheeks. Her ponytail slapped her in the face, so she must have moved quickly, but it all felt so drawn out. Sluggish. As if she moved underwater.

The embankment she slid down hid a den. A shallow burrow from which Tresa emerged, charging Sorcha with an inhuman shriek, her eyes black as tar.

Sorcha dodged the first swipe of her fist and

lifted her sword, ready to strike, but Tresa was too fast. Whipping in a fast circle with the speed of wind, she jumped on Sorcha's back. Like a wild beast, she clung, sharp nails digging into her exposed neck. Sorcha thrashed, trying to fling her off. Her efforts brought them down with a shuddering crash to the frozen ground. Her sword flew wide. With a grunt, she flipped over and scrabbled for it. But Tresa beat her to it. The demon witch stood with the sword raised, her hair a wild black nimbus haloing her pale face, a woman possessed by darkness.

"I told you to leave me be," Tresa rasped, her voice hissing through clenched teeth. Her head jerked side to side as she spoke, clearly under the influence of her dark and twisted demon. "Now I *have* to kill you."

"You don't have to do anything. Why don't you let me end your miserable existence?"

The witch laughed hoarsely, her eyes flashing in and out from black to blue. "Tempting, but I can't let you do that. As bad as I am, unleashing my demon on the world would be far worse."

Crouching low, Sorcha eased forward. "Oh, so you're being altruistic."

Tresa's face contorted in a pained grimace. "Enough," she choked out. "He grows stronger inside me. Soon I'll have no control. He invites my death. Welcomes it, don't you see? He wants you to free him."

"Then let me accommodate him." Sorcha lunged forward but Tresa held up a hand.

It was like smacking into a brick wall. Her body convulsed from the force, shuddered with pain. Gritting her teeth, she tried to move, tried to push ahead.

Her gaze narrowed, and she suspiciously eyed Tresa's poised hand, the fingers that curled in a very deliberate, menacing way. Something else started to happen then. It wasn't just that Sorcha couldn't move anymore. A tingly numbness started in her neck and coursed down her arm. Her chest constricted, each breath an agonized drag from her lungs.

The witch's fingers stroked the air in clawing sweeps, weaving her dark magic. With each pass of her fingers, the tightness in Sorcha's chest grew.

Gasping, she clutched a hand over her heart, pressing at the tightening ache. "What are you doing?" She panted, feeling the slowing thud of her pulse, the sluggish flow of blood in her veins. A cold sweep of fear washed over her.

"Making your heart stop."

No, no, no . . .

Shaking her head, she fell to the ground, her

knees hitting the frozen earth first before she fell to her side.

A heart attack wouldn't permanently kill her. She would recover, but in the time it took her to regenerate she would be at Tresa's mercy, totally defenseless. And that was the witch's plan. Disable her and then sever her head from her body.

As she lay on her side, a cold she had never known penetrated her body, sinking into her bones. Still, she could not rise, could not move, could not stop the unbearable, twisting fist from wringing her heart dry. Her head lolled on the icy ground as she struggled against the dark, killing magic.

Jonah, she thought with her dying breath.

A hazy fog clouded her vision. As though in a dream, she watched Tresa approach. The witch halted before her, the toe of her boot spitting up snow onto Sorcha's lifeless hand.

Sorcha opened her lips, tried to speak, could get out no more than a dry croak. Bleak frustration swept through her. It wasn't supposed to happen like this. *Her death. Gervaise unavenged.*

Her eyes moved, rolled in her head, following the flash of a silver blade on the air as Tresa lifted the sword high over her snow-dusted black hair.

Refusing to be a pathetic witness to her own slow death, Sorcha dug deep inside herself, groping for the barest scrap of will.

Then she heard a shout that didn't belong to her. It was a deep bellow, masculine and rich, stretching over the air like a foghorn.

But then its sound was lost, replaced with another. Air hissed, alive and angry. The wind increased. Silver flashed and sang as the blade descended.

Sorcha willed herself to move even a fraction, just enough to escape certain death—but nothing.

Her beating heart stilled to a stop and her vision blurred, graying at the edges, darkening. Everything dragged to a crawling pace.

She stared out with wide, unblinking eyes, straining to see, to stay awake, even as her heart died in her chest. As blackness crept in, she watched, her dying sight that of a razor-sharp blade sweeping toward her throat.

At the last second the sword was diverted. Swung sideways. A dark shape hurtled past, claiming Tresa. But not before she made contact. Not before Sorcha's body tasted the cut of cold steel.

Not against her throat, but elsewhere.

The blade sliced deeply across her torso. She gasped at the shock, at the stunning pain. Wet blood instantly saturated her clothes, the warmth of it smoking on the arctic wind.

And yet with Tresa distracted, her heart stuttered back to life, renewing its beat. Adrenaline pumped hard through her veins, blocking out the pain and carrying her back to life.

Despite the deep, gaping chest wound, she propped herself up on one elbow, looking around, her pulse striking hard against her neck.

And then she saw him. Realized it had been *his* shout she'd heard. He'd stopped Tresa from taking her head.

Jonah straddled the witch, one arm pressed up to her throat, her arms trapped at her sides. Her black eyes spat fury. She arched her back, her fingers clawing helplessly at the snow, no doubt eager to weave a spell on him.

"Go," he rasped, leaning his face close. "I mean you no harm. Get out of here."

Her black gaze rolled toward Sorcha. "*She'll* kill me, release my—"

"I'll take care of her. Now go!"

Indignant air hissed out between Sorcha's lips. "Take care of me?" she growled, pushing to her feet, blood dripping all around her, staining the pristine white.

"Sorcha," he hissed. "Not now. Shut up. I'll explain later." Hopping off the witch, he edged back toward Sorcha, never tearing his gaze from Tresa.

Tresa rose to her feet, watching them with that

unreadable black gaze that did nothing to conceal its evil.

"Go," he barked, waving an arm.

With Jonah's attention fixed on Tresa, Sorcha moved, shoving aside the pain burning through her chest. She'd heal.

Heart racing anxiously, she picked up the sword, wet with her blood. Before Jonah realized her intent, she flew past him with an animal cry, sword swinging.

"Sorcha! No!"

The witch's hand went up in the air again. Instantly, Sorcha was lifted off her feet and slammed onto her back—as though Tresa's hand was connected to a rope tied to Sorcha's feet.

She barely had time to absorb the sudden cold at her back before a great, jutting pressure stabbed her in the chest, impaling her to the frozen earth. Her ribs cracked in protest, and she moaned, wondering if she could in fact die. The pain was so intense that she felt as if she were dying . . . like it could happen. Like it *was* happening.

She struggled to move. Could only lift her head, gaze in horror at her own sword embedded in her chest, skewering her to the ice-covered ground. She felt the metal blade clink and chafe between her vertebrae. Agony burned through her.

She tried to speak, but blood gurgled in her mouth and she choked, spraying blood.

She swam in the stuff. Warm and sweet-smelling, it rushed over her broken body, running in a steady stream to the snow-packed ground. She turned her face, watched the dark red sinking into the pristine white.

She squeezed her eyes tight, frustrated by her helplessness. She had failed Gervaise. Lost Tresa . . . maybe even lost herself.

Her vision grayed, blurred. Blackness rolled in. Then, suddenly, she inhaled as strong hands pulled the sword free.

Still she could not fight off the darkness. It came for her like a great, thirsting beast. Even a dove-natu could not cheat death. She would endure it, would suffer the full consequences of her injuries before her body could start to mend itself.

Even as the end claimed her, as color faded from her world, one face loomed over her, filling the sweeping dark.

Her lips worked as she tried to speak, tried to say his name. The barest whisper fell. *Jonah*.

Then she lost sight of him. Lost sight of everything but the swallowing black of death.

SIX

Jonah hovered over her for a long moment, scowling savagely as the sound of her voice sifted through his head like sand between his fingers. The whisper of his name on her lips reminded him of the little girl who had always looked to him, needed him.

He stared hard at her now, his hot breath puffing out white fog. There wasn't an inch of her that had been spared blood and gore. Even her dark bangs were matted and stained red on her forehead.

A quick glance over his shoulder revealed Tresa's fading figure. Anywhere else but this freezing tundra, and the demon would have overpowered the witch and let Sorcha kill her to gain corporeal form. This bitter cold made the demon weak. Clearly why Tresa chose to live out here.

Looking back down at Sorcha, he watched her chest sink in a final deep, rattling breath. His own breath arrested inside his chest as he stared, waiting, already knowing he would not see it rise again.

She was dead. For a few moments, at least. Even though he knew she would wake, the sight twisted through him, made him feel slightly ill.

Luckily, she was an unnatural creature . . . like him. They could not be killed through typical measures. Poisoned with silver. Incinerated in fire. Exploded into a million fragments. That did the job. Gutted and impaled with a sword? Not a pleasant experience, but not lethal.

She would breathe again shortly, this woman he knew and yet didn't. This woman he'd been sent to kill and yet couldn't. She'd sip the arctic air and come to life and slowly start regenerating.

He cringed at what she would endure then. That much hadn't changed. He still didn't wish her hurt. Only, unfortunately for her, she would feel the agony of her mangled and shredded body. There was no way to save her from that pain. But he could at least get her out of the subzero temperature and make her as comfortable as possible.

Slipping his hands beneath her lax body, he lifted her dead weight into his arms. He headed back to the lodge, feet eating up the frozen earth. He covered ground quickly, determined to reach the warmth of the lodge before she regained consciousness.

Clearing the threshold, he kicked the door shut behind them. He drove a hard line toward the bedroom, tracking the heat to the warmest room. His boots thudded over the hardwood floor.

With great gentleness, he laid her on a rug before the fireplace, relishing the flames licking heat on his cold-bitten face . . . deliberately forgetting the fact that he was charged with destroying her . . . that Darby had predicted Sorcha would destroy him.

Turning away, he added several logs to the dwindling fire, vowing to stay on guard. Letting her live was one thing, letting his guard drop so she could kill him another. He didn't know this new Sorcha and he would do well not to confuse her with the girl of his past.

He jerked back around at her sudden gasp—like the first sharp breath you take when emerging from a great pool of water. Sorcha's body arched off the rug like a taut bow. Air hissed between her teeth as she resurfaced and ran full force into the agony of her injuries. With eyes wide, her gaze darted wildly within her ravaged face. Then, as if the pain were too much, she squeezed them shut again.

She groped the air with clawing fingers, as if searching for purchase, an escape from the overwhelming pain. He dropped down beside her and grabbed one of her scrabbling hands, cradling it in both of his.

Garbled speech tripped from her feverishly moving lips, the words indecipherable.

"It'll pass," he soothed gruffly, setting to work removing her ruined clothing. What he couldn't remove with ease, he simply cut from the wreckage of her body.

Firelight gilded her, made the blood appear redder, brighter, on flesh as cold as marble. The little skin that wasn't stained crimson glistened as golden as a peach and he muttered an obscenity for noticing, for seeing her as anything other than the child he once knew.

He left her for a few moments, searched the kitchen until he found what he needed. Soon he was back with a basin of water and washcloths. He cleansed the blood from her. As much as he could anyway. The angry red wounds had ceased to bleed, but the ragged flesh still gaped horribly. In places the white of her bones lay exposed.

She moaned against his attentions, fighting his efforts to help her.

He could simply leave her alone and she would heal in her own time. He knew that from experience. She didn't need him to hold her hand. He was charged with stopping her from destroying a demon witch. Charged with killing her if necessary. He'd been prepared to do that. Nothing required that he tend to her.

Nothing except the twinge of tenderness he felt deep in his chest. Nothing except that, years ago, she was the only one who had penetrated the thick walls of his heart.

He told himself that it wasn't that. He told himself that it merely wasn't in him to stand by as someone suffered so horribly. He wasn't a sadist.

He shook his head. Rising to his feet, he wrenched the thick down-filled comforter from the bed and tossed it over her naked body, his movements jerky, angry.

She arched her spine beneath the fabric, fighting her body's torment. Her head tossed from side to side, eyes opening and closing as if she could not decide between sleep and consciousness. Life and death. He smoothed a hand over her fevered brow, hoping to ease her.

At last, her eyes drifted shut and her head rolled to the side. He breathed a small sigh of relief, glad she'd escaped from her pain in sleep.

Frowning, he watched her, studying her face, appreciating her beauty, seeing the Sorcha he remembered in the delicate lines . . . and someone else. Someone he wasn't certain he wished to know.

He was accustomed to beautiful women. He'd

had his fill of them over the years. He was no saint, and at times he needed to lose himself in a woman's heat. He needed that brief moment when he could forget that anything bad or evil existed, when he could forget that he belonged to that unnatural order of the world, where it was kill or be killed. Females flocked to him, drawn to whatever it was his nature emitted. Some sort of animal pheromone, he guessed . . . the animal part of him that functioned as a predator. Lycans possessed the same ability, could almost mesmerize their prey. Victims didn't know what hit them until it was too late.

But it wasn't *him* they wanted. It wasn't *him* they knew.

With a sigh, he propped his arms on his knees and sank onto the floor, settling his back against the bed to wait.

Wait for her to heal.

Wait for the moment when she would wake and he would figure out what he was going to do with her.

SEVEN

They hunted her in her dreams.

One moment grotesque demons chased her, and in the next it was a black-eyed Tresa.

They all spoke, snarling threats and curses. In that they were the same . . . mauling her to shreds with great claws. It didn't end until Jonah arrived. Her girlhood hero, saving her from the agony. Like those many times he'd saved her from her father's cruel games.

At that moment, she forgot her anger with him, forgot the sting of his rejection.

Jonah, Jonah, Jonah.

Warm hands slid up her arms, cradled her shoulders, made her feel safe, protected.

Because it was a dream, she could fool herself, let herself believe in the fantasy of it, let him hold her—and hold him back.

She let herself need him. Want him. Again.

She purred, arching. It was okay. This time he wouldn't turn her away. This time she wouldn't get hurt. It wasn't real. Just a dream.

"I'm here." His voice rolled over her, deep and rich. "Talk to me." She could almost feel the warm breath of his voice on her cheek. She lifted her face toward the sensation.

Jonah, Jonah, Jonah.

She wasn't certain when the dream crossed into reality . . . when she realized Jonah was really beside her, really touching her, holding her, whispering soft words.

She opened her eyes to his face, inches from her own. Her hands gripped his shoulders as if he were a lifeline, the only thing preventing her from sinking back into the hungry dark where monsters hunted her.

His gaze glittered an icy blue. He brushed her forehead with a light touch, delicately fingering her hairline. "You okay?"

She shook her head, darting her tongue out against cracked lips.

"Here." Suddenly, there was a cup. He lifted it to her lips and she drank greedily, stopping only when he pulled the cup back. "Easy," he cautioned.

She stared at him warily, wiping at the dribble of water on her chin. "You saved me," she said, her hoarse voice accusing. She didn't want help from him . . . wished she hadn't needed it.

"Yeah. Imagine that." A smile twisted his lips.

"Why? Why did you help me?"

He cocked his head. "Isn't that what I do when it comes to you?"

"Not anymore."

A shadow passed over his face. "Right. Not anymore."

"So why, then? You're protecting the demon witch I'm going to kill."

His blue eyes flashed. "No. You're not."

She inhaled sharply but bit back the denial that burned on her tongue. Instead, she said, "We're not family, not even friends anymore. Why help me? You could have left me to Tresa."

His stare drilled into her. "Yeah. Maybe. Except you called out for me. Maybe I helped you because you asked me to—"

"No." She shook her head fiercely. "I didn't—"

"Yes. You used that little-girl voice I remember so well and said my name." He shrugged a broad shoulder. "You know me. I was never one to deny you."

"Oh, really? That's not how I remember it." She snorted, nearly choking on the sound, instantly regretting hinting at that long-ago night when he had crushed her.

He cocked his head. If possible, his stare intensified. He remembered that night, too. Embarrassing heat swept over her.

Had she called out for him? Said his name? There at the end? *Damn it*. Did she want his pity again? For him to look at her the way he once did, the pitiable child her father wanted him to mate with in order to breed a grand race of dovenatus? She'd worked hard to put that all behind her. To move beyond the shame of her father treating her like chattel, the heartache of Jonah's refusal. Maybe the worst thing of all was that despite her father's horrible misuse of her, she would have happily given herself to Jonah. She would gladly have gone along with her father's mad schemes. Seeing Jonah again reminded her of that. Reminded her of how pathetic she'd once been.

She had no wish to repeat that humiliation— would not tolerate him looking at her as he once did. She was no longer that girl. For all intents and purposes, that girl died in the explosion.

She shook her head, then stopped, wincing at the lancing pain the movement caused. She struggled up onto her elbows and glanced around the toasty-warm bedroom. Outside the wind howled.

He'd changed since she'd earlier seen him, had removed his outer gear and wore a long-sleeved gray thermal shirt and dark pants. He looked relaxed, refreshed. As if this were a winter retreat and not some reunion from hell.

She moistened her lips, determined to drop the

subject, to move on as if it were no big deal. "How long have I been out?"

He watched her with bright-eyed intensity, assessing. "About a day," he answered.

"What?" Tresa would be long gone by now!

She jerked upright, gasping as air brushed her bare breasts. She made a mad grab for the comforter that had covered her. She glanced down, peeked beneath it to confirm that she was in fact naked. "Where are my clothes?" she hissed.

He shrugged. "There wasn't much left of them."

She adjusted her arms around the comforter to better shield herself. Hard to look dignified wearing a comforter. "I suppose I should thank you for saving me . . . and bringing me back here."

He smiled mockingly, his teeth a flash of white in his tan face. "That would be nice."

"Thanks," she snapped.

A smile twitched his lips. "That's a thank you?"

"Didn't you just hear me?"

"You might want to work on that."

"If it wasn't for you, Tresa's head would be mine. Take what you can get." She glanced around the bedroom again, spying the bathroom through an open door. She tossed her hair, grimacing at the grimy texture. She tested a tendril. It crunched between her fingers with dry blood.

He snorted, looking her over, arching a dark

eyebrow. "Really? You think so? If it wasn't for me, *your* head would have been hers."

She stood, whipping the comforter around her. "I would have managed," she blustered. "And now, thanks to you, she's long gone."

"Good." He crossed thick, muscled arms over his chest.

"No," she choked out. "Not good. I'll have to start all over again trying to find her."

"No. You won't."

Deciding to just hurry up and be on her way, she opened Tresa's closet. A minimal amount of clothes hung there. Sorcha grabbed a heavy black sweater from a hanger. A built-in set of drawers stood at the back of the closet. She found undergarments and a pair of slacks within, all one size too small. Apparently women born two thousand years ago didn't possess much body fat. Still, the clothes would have to do.

Stepping from the closet, she faced Jonah with Tresa's garments tucked close to her chest, a sense of urgency humming through her. To pick up Tresa's trail. To get as far from Jonah as she could.

He'd moved. Stood closer. His breath a soft fan on her skin. Uncomfortably near. She resisted the urge to step back but held her ground.

They studied each other until the air grew charged, electric. She moistened her lips. His gaze followed the movement of her tongue and the centers of his eyes grew brighter, glowed in a way they never had when looking at her before.

The sight disturbed her, made her feel raw and exposed, awakening all those feelings she'd thought buried. Entirely unacceptable considering they were on opposite sides.

Staring down at her with his unnervingly intense gaze, he murmured, "The bathroom might not be up to your usual standards."

She almost laughed. Were they really discussing bathrooms when all manner of unspoken words flowed between them?

"I'll make do."

Turning, she moved into the bathroom, shutting the door firmly behind her with a sigh. She grimaced at the single copper tub. Okay, no running water. She ran a hand through her blood-sticky hair and glanced at the blurred glass of the mirror, grimacing again.

"I've heated water on the woodstove."

She jumped at the low sound of his voice, close behind her. Turning, she gasped. He'd opened the door and come up right on her, as quick as a stalking cat. For a moment she'd forgotten just how fast he could move. How silently.

He was everywhere, it seemed, the pull between them inescapable.

"Can't you knock?" she rasped out, her fingers clutching the comforter until they ached, white-knuckled and bloodless.

He smiled then, the curve of his well-formed lips making her belly clench. That light at the centers of his eyes flickered with amusement and something else. Something dark and sensual that made her blood heat. "I remember a time when you would never close a door to me."

"The years change things," she replied in a strangled voice. "I was just a stupid kid."

His gaze crawled over her face. Desire settled heavily in the pit of her stomach. "You were never stupid to me."

"Yeah? Well, what's a kid know?"

"Sometimes everything."

Having nothing to say to that, she stepped back from the magnetic heat of him, her jaw clenched tight with the strain of his nearness, a ghost from her past, alive and breathing and dredging up impossible feelings.

The corner of his smile twitched. "I'll fetch the water for you."

Before she could tell him that she could get it herself, he was gone and soon back with two steaming buckets. Dumping them in the tub, he moved to the buckets of lukewarm water she had not noticed sitting along the wall. Had he planned ahead for her? The thought made her uncomfortable. Made her remember the way they used to be, the way he'd always looked out for her.

"I can do that," she offered.

He ignored her and dumped the remaining buckets, his biceps rippling against his shirt.

She looked away, releasing a small breath as he turned to leave, glad for a moment to herself.

With one hand on the doorknob, he paused. "Notice," he said with a nod at the bathroom walls, "the lack of windows."

She narrowed her gaze.

"When you get out, we'll eat. I imagine you're hungry."

Famished. Evidently she hadn't eaten in days.

"And after that, I'll be on my way."

His lip curled. "I don't think so."

Her fingers folded into fists at her sides.

"We've got a lot to talk about," he continued. "You're not going anywhere until I'm convinced you won't take it into your head to hunt down another demon witch."

"Just Tresa," she spat out. "She's the only one who matters."

"Whatever the case, we need to be straight on this point or . . ."

Or what?

What did he leave unsaid? That he would kill her? So much for playing hero and saving her.

A sick, wilting sensation flushed through her, dampening her misplaced ardor for him. She trembled with the horrible realization that someone she had admired so much before, respected for being different from her father—compassionate and decent, *better*—would now protect and shelter evil.

His eyes grew chilly, hard as marble as they looked down at her. "You're not leaving until we settle this—" He broke off without saying anything else, but the words were there, the threat hanging in the air. If she didn't relent and give up hunting Tresa, he would stop her . . . keep her prisoner—or worse. She clenched her jaw, ground her teeth together. He could try.

Pressing her lips together, she pressed a hand against his chest and pushed him from the bathroom, fighting to not appreciate the play of muscles beneath her palm. Without saying a word, she closed the door in his handsome face. Turning the lock, she sagged against the hard wood, the slight click making her feel strangely better. For now, it was the only barrier she had.

EIGHT

She took a long time before emerging. Jonah didn't know if it was to avoid him or if bathing in two feet of water presented a challenge. He paced, anxious to see her again, to piece together the enigma she had become . . . starting with why she was so determined to destroy Tresa.

When the door finally opened, he had to stop himself from crowding her, from demanding information, from learning all there was to learn about her. From breathing in her scent. He shook his head. He'd have all the time in the world to learn about this new Sorcha. She wasn't going anywhere.

"Feeling better?" he asked.

Nodding curtly, she wrapped a fist around her hair and tugged on it as if she were readying it for a ponytail, but then dropped the wet strands.

He watched her dark hair fall in a rhythmic sway past her shoulders. The black sweater she wore looked thick, plush. The loose collar was gathered around her neck, revealing an enticing strip of creamy throat. All in all, she looked thoroughly touchable.

"Where's my gear?" she asked, her voice all business.

"I set it by the front door."

She still thought she was leaving? A tight smile curled his lips. Shaking his head, he moved into the kitchen where a pot simmered on the woodstove. "Hungry?" he called out, forcing back a knowing smile when she followed, entering the kitchen, watching warily as he opened a glass cabinet door and removed two bowls.

He caught her uncertain expression as he dished up two bowls of soup. She sat down on a bench at one side of the kitchen table.

He sat across from her, studying her closely. "You need to eat if you want to regain all your strength."

They ate in silence. He didn't mind it. He'd eaten a few times with Darby and her coven and their chatter gave him a headache. They were greedy for him, making certain he knew that slayers commonly married white witches. Covens encouraged it, seeing it as a way to strengthen a particular slayer's bonds to them.

He had no intention of marrying. Ever. And certainly not to some mortal white witch like Darby he would have to bury at the end of her life. And how unpleasant would it be for her to age while he remained forever young? It might tempt her to accept the dark promise of a demon in order to gain immortality.

Sorcha's voice broke the silence as he was finishing the last of his soup. "So. You're dead set on keeping me here."

He glanced at her swiftly. "Did you think I had a change of heart?"

She leaned back and crossed her arms over her chest, her voice mocking as she said, "But we've been playing so nicely together, Jonah."

"Have we?" He cocked his head.

She shrugged one slight shoulder. "We aren't fighting."

"Not at the moment, but if you insist on leaving, we're headed in that direction."

She leaned across the table, her expression earnest and so beautiful he could only stare, marveling at what changes time had wrought in her. Both inside and out. She was hardly recognizable. "She's long gone by now. Why are you doing this?"

"It's what I do—" he started to say.

"Hold other dovenatus captive? Protect evil witches so that they can keep on killing and springing curses that fate millions to death?"

"Yes," he snapped. "And aren't you even a little curious as to why? Because you're right. She's all of that. So don't you want to know why I care to keep her alive?"

She lifted one shoulder in a shrug, her brown eyes gazing at him coldly. "I know why. You're a bastard."

"Come now." He smiled without humor, her words angering him as they shouldn't—as he shouldn't *let* them. "You know there's a reason I'm here and that's not it. You know me. I wouldn't protect her unless I had reason to."

With a snort, she propped her elbows on the table and stared at him intently, her expression tough and vulnerable at the same time. God, if the look didn't affect him . . . didn't send the beast prowling through him, searching for release. "You keep talking as though I should know you. It's been what? Over ten years? We don't know each other, Jonah. I'm not sure we ever did."

"Then why are *you* here?" he asked abruptly. "Since you won't hear me out, why don't you explain what you're doing here."

After a long moment, she confessed, in a near whisper, "She took someone from me . . . Tresa, her demon, whatever. I want them both gone."

He cocked his head, reading the bleakness in her gaze. "Who? Who is this someone?"

She swallowed, the tendons of her neck working. Rising, she took her bowl to the sink, moving away as if she couldn't stand his gaze, or the reminders his question provoked. "I won't talk about him," she murmured. "Not with you."

Him. Her answer only inflamed him. As if Jonah weren't good enough to know about her special *him.* His hand rolled into a tight fist where it sat on the table. "Then is it my turn now?" he began. "Are you ready to let me explain my reasons?"

"Not really," she replied casually. "There can be no justification for protecting the likes of Tresa."

"You won't even listen? You're right. You have changed. The Sorcha I knew had more sense. She wasn't mule-headed or blind to the truth."

"The Sorcha you knew was a fool!" Dishes clanked in the sink and she whirled around on him, her doe eyes bright. "She thought you were honorable! Worthy of respect and love." Hot color stained her cheeks and she quickly bit her lip, looking away.

Ah. So she wasn't as immune to him as she pretended to be. She remembered him as well as he remembered her, for all that she appeared unaffected by him.

Her gaze turned back to him, cool and distant as the stare of a stranger. "You're just the mercenary dog you always were."

He inhaled sharply the sting of her words. The air smelled different, adrenaline-laced, and he knew she was braced for a fight again.

He swallowed a growl, not eager to knock heads with her once more. There were other things he would much rather do. Other ways he could distract her and make her forget her vengeance for a demon witch he could never let her kill.

His gaze roamed over her slowly, assessing, enjoying the way her too-tight slacks hugged her legs. "We don't have to fight at all, you know. We can be friends. Again."

She studied him, wariness bright in her eyes. "Friends?" She uttered the word as if it were the most ridiculous thing she had ever heard and not where they had once been in their relationship. Her hands held the edge of the countertop behind her, knuckles white and bloodless where they gripped.

Without a word, he rose and rounded the table, walking in a hard line toward her, stretching out his arms and caging her between himself and the counter.

"Friends," he murmured, watching the light in the centers of her brown eyes start a steady smolder. He cocked his head and breathed in the scent of her neck, marveling at how easy, how natural it felt to have Sorcha back in his life again. Even if the way he was feeling toward her was decidedly new and *more* than friendly.

NINE

Is this your plan, then? Subjugate me through seduction?" Sorcha asked breathlessly, squeezing past him and moving out of the kitchen and into the larger living area. Much-needed space. Distance from him.

Outside, the wind howled, gaining force. Snow fell past the living room window in thick, white sheets.

He stared after her with a hungry look in his eyes. The way she had prayed for him to look at her as a girl, so that he might sweep her off her feet and run away with her. That had been an especially favorite fantasy following any unpleasant encounters with her father. A foul taste coated her mouth. Yes, she'd come a long way from those days. She was not about to go back.

He shrugged one shoulder. "I'd hardly call it subjugation."

"No? What would you call it? Rape?"

His head jerked back, eyes changing, glittering like ice, colder than the arctic winds outside.

"Don't be dramatic. We are what we are." He flipped a hand in the air. "I'm only saying that there are more enjoyable ways to spend our time than fighting, Sorcha."

"Pleasant for *you*."

"And you, too." He leaned closer and sniffed near her neck, as if he smelled her even after her bath. "Even you see that. You're not a little girl anymore. You must feel it between us . . ."

Her breath locked in her lungs. She had craved such attention from him years ago. And the way her heart beat a little faster, she had to admit that maybe she craved it still. Just a little.

"I'm sure you're a real stallion," she mocked, "but I prefer the human variety."

He blinked and she knew she'd surprised him. It took him a moment to reply. "I suppose they're easier for you to manipulate."

She laughed lightly.

His eyes narrowed.

"Is that the reason, you think?" she asked.

He stepped nearer, until his chest brushed against her. She tried not to shrink back from the contact, the imposing size of him, the overwhelming maleness. "Yeah. That's what I think. Being with someone like me requires trust. Both in me and in yourself. Clearly, the years have robbed you of that. Too bad."

Her smile slipped as his words sank in, too close to the truth.

He continued, "How about taking on someone who can give as much as he takes? Someone you can't dominate? Or is that too risky?"

"No. I simply want a man with a soul."

"You think I'm not in possession of a soul?" His jaw hardened. "I'm not lycan. I've not—"

"You're no better . . . just someone who values the life of a demon witch like Tresa."

His gaze raked her up and down, his scorn palpable, something that reached out to slap her. "You have no idea the hell that will break loose if you kill Tresa. Killing her sets her demon loose."

"I'm aware of that."

He blinked, then looked at her as if she had lost her mind. "And you don't care?"

"I fully intend to kill her demon."

"You couldn't even kill the witch! What makes you think you could destroy a demon once it takes form?"

She swallowed down the hot thickness in her throat. Her anger was too great. She felt that. Recognized the swarming heat in her face. He was nothing to her, and she should act that way.

She shook her head and took several steps away. "You don't know me anymore, Jonah. And I don't want to know you."

He stepped closer. His gaze flicked over her. "Really? I don't believe that. You know I'm speaking the truth. You're just afraid to hear it, though. To find out your mission is over. To accept that you're out of your league here."

"It's not over," she hissed, thinking of when the demon had possessed Maree. He'd told Sorcha he'd been warned that she could destroy him. Clearly, there was a way. She could do it. She *would.* "You've delayed me, sure . . . ruined my plans. For now."

He moved before she could even register his intent. Hard hands seized her by the arms. "Get over it. She's gone. Move on to something else." His eyes glowed brightly, twin torches dancing at the centers where dark pupils should be. Her heart pounded against her chest.

"You mean *you*?"

His gaze swept over her face, clearly digesting her words. "Why not? Like I said, you're not a little girl anymore, Sorcha. You felt something for me once."

"Yeah," she spit out. "*Once.*" She struggled in his arms, amazed—even as she knew his strength rivaled her own—that she could not simply break free. It had been years since she'd been around anyone like herself, someone who could physically overpower her. The realization both terrified and exhilarated.

His head descended, inching toward hers. The old insecurities rose inside her. Even now she wondered if any of this was genuine. Was Jonah truly interested in her, truly attracted to her? Or was this his way of distracting her from her purpose?

She jerked her head out of the way and cut a swift circle out of his arms. He grabbed her and hauled her back, colliding them chest to chest. Seizing her by the back of the head, he held her still, his face so close their noses almost touched.

They glared at each other, chests heaving hard. She tasted his breath then, his lips so near hers. When his eyes dipped toward her mouth, her stomach clenched. She bit her lip to keep a sigh of longing from escaping. It was too much.

In that moment, she could think only that this was Jonah. Jonah, whom she'd wished for, dreamed of, all those years ago. Who made her smile when her father made her cry. Jonah, whom she'd wept for when she thought him dead.

While she was trying to summon the strength to push him from her, he made the final move.

He kissed her.

The strong hand at the back of her head slid to her face, his palm rasping her cheek as he swallowed up her cry, drank deep of the sound.

His lips burned, a scalding shock in the cabin's pervasive chill as his mouth devoured hers.

She was not inexperienced, had not lived as a nun. Even though she and Gervaise had a platonic marriage, men had passed through her life, through her bedroom, since his death. She'd hoped a lover would end the loneliness. Or at least offer some solace from it. Of course it hadn't worked.

Jonah's kiss felt new. Like the first. The brush of his warm lips robbed her of all struggle, weakening her knees. Like an easily awed virgin, she clutched his shoulders, clinging, fingers curling into the hard muscles of his body so she wouldn't drop. She held on for dear life, the mere texture and taste of his mouth completely devastating her.

This. This was what she had been missing. What she'd never had.

After a moment of shocked stillness, she kissed him in return, giving back with all the fervor that he treated her to. She couldn't help herself. Her body burned, skin pulling and rippling, overcome and ready to shift. For the first time she didn't have to worry about that. She didn't have to fear liking a guy too much, responding so much that she shifted without thought or control.

With him, there was no secret to protect. She could let go.

Her lips moved over his, nibbling the top lip first, then sucking on his bottom lip, moaning when he slid his tongue inside her mouth. He skimmed his hands down her back, grasped her and lifted her off the ground.

She wound her legs around his waist, her arms around his neck. Weaving her fingers through his hair, she deepened their kiss, not even minding when he strode across the lodge with her locked in his arms, his each step jarring. In the bedroom, his full weight fell hard over her, sinking her into the soft mattress.

Her legs parted, instinctively inviting him to settle into her body. He ground down against her. Her core clenched in need, for more of his hardness, more of his driving heat. More of him.

He held her head, kissing her thoroughly, biting at her lips in sharp nips. His fingers pressed into the tender flesh of her cheeks, holding her face in place for him.

Growling, she struggled to move her head, to sample him as he sampled her, but he held her, trapped her for his enjoyment . . . a delicious torment.

It wasn't enough. None of it was enough. Her body burned. She wanted to lick him, bite him, kiss him all over. She whimpered in protest at the barrier of their clothing. When he slid a hand between their bodies and palmed her between the legs, she cried out against his lips, surging into him, into that pushing hand. Hunger burned a fiery trail to her core.

Her zipper sang out, and his hand dove beneath the waistband of her jeans, slipped inside her panties and touched her. His fingers parted her folds, played in her wetness and found that small nub of pleasure.

She screamed, her cry echoing off the wood walls as he rolled it with increasing pressure. A sob shattered from her lips. She arched, tearing her lips free. He dragged a blistering kiss down her throat, his tongue tracing the tendon there.

His mouth lifted from her neck. Cool air caressed the exposed, wet flesh.

He stared levelly at her, eyes glittering, his hand still on her, pressing against her intimately. She gasped as he traced her opening, her gaze devouring the perfect beauty of his face, the hard-etched lines and masculine angles. The eyes that could see right through her. She marveled that this was Jonah. With her, touching her. Doing such delicious things to her.

For a heartbeat, she saw his face flash in and out, the beast a shadow there, hovering just beneath the surface. In response, she felt her own face do the same, flicker in and out, and was struck with how perfect they were for each other. Two of a kind.

That thought echoed through her with dangerous familiarity, striking her like a slap to the face. As a girl, that was what she'd constantly told herself . . . what she'd believed, why she let her father convince her that they were each other's destiny.

But this wasn't her destiny. Fate had *not* brought them together. Life had taught her that she alone controlled her fate. Not her father, not forces beyond her power . . . no matter how close they lurked. Always close. Dark shadows creeping near.

She was a dovenatu who must forever pick her steps carefully through a roomful of broken glass. One misstep and she falls, loses her soul, loses herself.

She'd convinced herself Tresa would be an end to all of that. Killing Tresa would bring her the peace she craved. Now Jonah had ruined that dream for her. Her face grew hot, ears burning, eyes stinging. He was good at that. Excellent at ruining dreams.

"Get off me," she hissed, clawing his hand free from between her legs.

His expression darkened, glowering down at her. Seizing both her hands, he forced them on either side of her head, on the bed. "Why do you fight it?" He pushed his erection against her, and her body reacted, clenching with need. "When we both want it? Maybe your father was right," he charged. "Maybe this is the way it should be between us."

If her hands had been free, she would have struck him. "My father was wrong about everything. Especially us. For one moment of insanity I let common animal lust cloud my head."

"This isn't insanity. It makes perfect sense. It's there. It's what we are, why would you deny—"

"I'm more than an animal eager to rut with one of its own kind on the first encounter. Maybe that's all *you* are, but I'm more than—"

"Better," he spit out. "You think you're better than I am."

"I didn't say that."

"Yeah, you did." He flung himself off the bed and away from her. "You know the difference between you and me, Sorcha?"

She scrambled to a sitting position, zipping up her slacks and ignoring the throbbing pangs at her core that begged for satisfaction. For him. "Oh, there's a difference? I thought you would have me thinking we're the same lust-driven animals perfectly suited for each other."

"The difference is that I know what I am. I accept it. I don't *play* at being human."

"I'm not playing at being human!"

"You take only humans to your bed," he

charged. "You said as much. You're afraid of what you are. Afraid of what I am and what might happen if you let yourself go with another dovenatu."

"Don't psychoanalyze me. You don't know me at all." That much was true.

And yet he'd hit unerringly close to the truth. Being a dovenatu was like living in a cage. Never getting out, and never letting anyone inside.

He cocked his head, his lips curving in a cruel smile. "So why don't you tell me who you are now, Sorcha? Besides someone who lets vengeance fool her into thinking she can take on a demon witch."

She clung to anger, let it mask her unease at how he seemed to delve beneath her exterior and doubt herself. "Why don't you go to hell?"

He smiled, but there was nothing friendly about those curving lips. He prowled close, climbing back onto the bed, forcing her back, caging her in. She inched away, pulling herself along with her arms. He followed, his arms twin bands of muscle straining against the fabric of his shirt.

She fell back down on the bed, her head landing on a soft down-stuffed pillow. She inhaled and caught a whiff of earthy woods. Tresa. The smell of her lingered, surrounding her. A bitter reminder of what brought Sorcha here—and how she had failed.

Resisting the urge to close that hairsbreadth

distance and taste his mouth again, she reminded herself that he was her enemy now. That maybe he always had been. She'd just been too young and naive to know it.

"Go to hell, huh?" He stared down at her, his expression more perplexed than offended. With a soft voice, he whispered, "I still see you in there. You haven't changed that much."

"Please get off me."

A long moment passed before he finally moved, rolled off her.

For a while neither of them moved. They both lay looking up at the ceiling, side by side but not touching.

Lacing her fingers over her stomach, she struggled to even her breathing . . . to stop herself from rolling over and pouncing on him as every fiber of her being screamed at her to do. Damn dovenatu instincts.

He flung an arm over his forehead and released a heavy sigh. "You're determined to make me the enemy."

She inhaled shallowly. Before she said anything more that she might regret, she shoved herself off the bed. Looking down at him, she tried not to let the delicious sight of him, with his rumpled gold hair and wild eyes, entice her.

He might not serve her father anymore, but he

worked at some other foul purpose now. She'd left the shadow behind and had stepped out into the light. Clearly, he had not.

"I'm going to get my things together and leave. Don't try to stop me, Jonah."

He stared at her, his expression hard as concrete, the white flames twisting at the centers of his eyes telling her he wasn't going to go along with that. "It's not that simple."

"You pointed out that we're practically invincible." She nodded once before striding away from him, calling over her shoulder, "*Practically.* Don't make me put it to the test with you."

TEN

Sorcha . . ." He drew out the sound of her name, his voice heavy with warning.

She stopped and looked over her shoulder, sending him a slanted look, her brown eyes peering out beneath a fringe of dark lashes.

"You're not going anywhere until we reach an understanding." And even then, even if she did see reason and agreed to give up hunting Tresa, he struggled with the idea of letting her go. Letting her walk away as if he'd never seen her. As if he'd never learned she was still alive. "Don't take another step."

A sudden stillness came over her. Her eyes intent, deep and fathomless as any he'd ever seen.

His nerves tightened, squeezed dry. He watched her, devouring the sight of her. Something rippled across her face. Confusion maybe. Or maybe something else. Something more. The light at the centers of her eyes arrived, burning bright and clear, eclipsing the dark irises.

He lifted his hand to scratch his jaw. The move flared her to life and ignited her in a way he had not anticipated.

She bolted.

With his heart in his throat, he sprang after her, vaulting through the bedroom door. His fingers snatched a handful of her ink-dark hair.

They crashed onto the floor in a tangled pile of flailing limbs. Her strength was no match for his, especially after her recent attack. He flipped her over. Straddling her, he pinned her to the ground, his hands locked down on both her shoulders. "Sorcha! Enough!"

She thrust her chin out and shouted, "Get—off—me!"

Not the sign of surrender he was looking for. He shoved his face close, staring into the hard glitter of her eyes. "What's wrong with you?"

Her eyes raked him as if he were the lowest sort of vermin. "Right now the only thing wrong is that you didn't die in that explosion," she hissed, surging up from the waist, trying to buck him off her.

Her words continued, lashing him like a whip. "Now you'd rather see me dead, hold me prisoner to protect some—"

"Sorcha," he growled, staring at her flushed face for a long moment before the rest of his words exploded from his lips in a rush. "You think I'd kill you now? I still see that explosion when I close my eyes. I see *you*!"

The hostility faded from her eyes. Tension ebbed from her. She felt soft, yielding beneath him. He remembered those moments on the bed together and grew hard again. He'd never allowed himself to think of her in that way before, when she'd been alive to him. It seemed disrespectful when he cared for her the way he did . . .

"I'm a demon slayer," he began. "Well, in a way. It's not like I wanted to be . . . it's just . . . what I am. I can detect witches and demons, the goal being to protect white witches from demons . . . to keep demons from possessing them and turning them into demon witches."

"A demon witch like Tresa."

"Like Tresa," he confirmed.

"Then why are you trying to protect her? She's already possessed. Already a demon witch."

"You can't kill a demon witch without releasing her demon. And you can't handle this particular demon."

Her tension returned. She stiffened beneath him. "I'm no weakling—"

"Do you even know how to kill a demon?" he challenged. "What it involves? It's not easy. Practically impossible."

"But *possible*," she stressed. "That's good

enough for me, then. I'll take the chance. I want Tresa dead." Her jaw locked, a muscle feathering the delicate flesh.

He glared down at her, not sure if he wanted to shake her or take her in his arms. He still couldn't get over the sight of her . . . the knowledge that this was *her*. His Sorcha.

No, not his, he quickly amended. She'd never been his. And yet, this close to her, his blood pumped hard in his veins, eager to possess her.

At that moment the wood floor began to shake beneath them, vibrating as if the earth itself had just awakened, hungry and roused with temper, ready to devour all and everything.

"What's happening? Is it an earthquake?" she called over the breaking of glass.

A roaring beat filled the air, accompanied by a whistling wind. He shook his head, realizing at once what *it* was. Grabbing her hand, he pulled her to her feet. He opened his mouth to answer, but he never got the chance.

The door burst open, shattered off its hinges, breaking into splinters as a dozen armed men flooded the room.

SORCHA'S NOSTRILS FLARED AGAINST the sudden crowd of strange men. All armed to the teeth. Instantly her flesh rippled and burned, crawled with an awareness of the sudden danger. Her core vibrated, smoldered.

Jonah took position before her like a great barrier. *Her protector.* The gesture both rankled and comforted her. She'd done without a protector for over ten years. *Too little, too late.*

One of the men spoke into his mouthpiece. "Two subjects located."

A scratchy response crackled back, "Status on the witch?"

Suddenly another chopper arrived outside, beating the wind and whipping freezing air inside the house. Icy snow sprayed through the busted door and broken windows. Even with the mounting heat inside her, the subarctic temperature was difficult to tolerate. Rising back to her feet, she fought to hide her shivering, hating the idea that they might read her shaking as fear.

She pressed closer to Jonah's hard back, exhaling cold breath on him. Tossing her bangs from her eyes, she surveyed the group of mercenaries. "Um, friends of yours?"

"Not that I'm aware of."

"Quiet," one of the dark-clad men barked, jabbing a weapon in their direction.

The pounding chopper blades slowed outside, then stilled to a stop. In the sudden quiet, a new figure emerged, walking through the door as if he were strolling into a dinner party and not into a cabin in the Alaskan tundra.

His booted feet thudded on the floor, crunching over glass. A dark floor-length coat brushed his ankles as he stopped in the middle of the room. A hissing breath escaped Sorcha's lips. Even before he removed the dark sunglasses from his eyes, she knew, she felt it, smelled it on him. *Lycan.*

Jonah's hand reached behind him to seize her arm, and she knew he felt it, too.

The dark-haired stranger cocked his head, the motion predatory. His silvery eyes narrowed on both of them. Like pewter ice, able to freeze, to kill with a glance. He was old, maybe even ancient, despite his youthful good looks. She got that at once. Inhaling, she smelled death from his every pore. It curled its tainted tendrils around her.

"Two lycans?" he murmured with a deep inhalation, scenting them in turn. His hard features gave nothing away, not pleasure or concern at finding them here. "Didn't expect to find a pair of my brethren—" His nostrils flared sharply, a muscle rippling across his square jaw. "No." He stepped forward, looked over Jonah's shoulder, directly at her, blasting Sorcha with the full intensity of his cursed stare.

She tried not to flinch beneath his pewter gaze, letting her father's hated voice roll over her . . .

taking courage from the memory of his words—the only thing she had ever agreed with him about. *Lycans are dogs. They have not our strength, nor our intelligence. They lack all will, all control. They're fit only to be our slaves.*

Well, maybe she didn't agree with the last part. That had been her father's madness talking, after all. In her mind, lycans needed to be destroyed, wiped from the earth.

Yet somehow her father's words failed to ring true gazing at this lycan. He hardly smacked of weakness or stupidity. No, surrounded by gunmen, he looked very organized. Deadly and systematic. Not an opponent to underestimate. Unlike any lycan to cross her path before.

"Not lycans," he murmured, clicking his tongue as he realized just what she and Jonah were. "Dovenatus." He laughed then, the sound dark and deep. "How interesting. Fifteen years ago I did not even know dovenatus existed, now I seem to run into them everywhere." He sobered, tilting his head to allow his gaze to slide over her.

She shivered beneath that stare. There were few men who could inject her with fright. Well, no *man* really. There hadn't been since that night years ago when she'd first transitioned . . .

She was in danger here. She knew that at once, read his unhealthy interest in her.

A lycan was a formidable opponent, but mostly during a full moon. Their inability to shift at any other time put them at a disadvantage against a dovenatu . . . that's what made them so easy for her father to enslave.

But this one . . . he was different.

He wasn't your average lycan. He made her feel decidedly unsafe even in the absence of a full moon. She looked him up and down, fought to hold his icy stare, to show courage. This one her father could never have taken.

Her skin rippled, burned, ready to fade out. Ready to give way to the beast. Her best shot at protecting herself was in full shift.

She reached up, gripped Jonah's shoulder, forgetting that moments ago she had considered him her enemy. Now he was the lesser evil.

The lycan angled his head, assessing her over Jonah's shoulder. "Don't worry. I'm not here for either of you. You're safe. Why don't you come out here, sweetheart, so that I can better see you?"

Jonah made a growl-like noise in the back of his throat. His arm shot out around her, stopping her, holding her in place behind him in case she decided to comply. "She's not going anywhere."

"Ah, yours, is she?"

"I'm not anyone's!" she hissed. "Would you mind getting these guns off us?" A bullet might not kill her, but it was no less unpleasant. She'd already endured enough pain and wasted time regenerating.

"You heard her," Jonah commanded. He motioned to the mercenaries. "Find somewhere else to point those rifles before I unleash myself on your thugs here."

"Easy," the lycan soothed in a voice that did nothing to put her at ease. He strolled a short path back and forth in front of them. "I'm not here for either one of you. As interested as I am in what the two of you are doing here, I'm more interested in where the witch is."

Sorcha's fingers dug into Jonah. They were here for Tresa.

The lycan glanced around, as if she was hiding behind a piece of furniture. He inhaled and, if possible, his eyes glowed brighter. "She was here. Where is she now?"

"Gone," Jonah bit out. "You missed her by a couple of days."

"Hmm." The lycan approached, stopping beside the gunman nearest Jonah. "Now why would she have left? Anything to do with either one of you?"

Jonah and Sorcha exchanged glances.

The lycan continued, "Because that annoys me. Very much. I've invested a great deal of time and energy into tracking her down."

Sorcha nudged out from behind Jonah, tired of hanging back. She wasn't about to start hiding behind someone now, after years of being on her own. "Yeah? You and me both."

"Sorcha." Jonah's voice rang heavily with warning.

She spun to face him. "Don't say my name like you know me or something. We're nothing to each other." Spinning back around, she glared at the lycan. "You want to know what happened to Tresa?" She jabbed a finger in Jonah's direction. "Ask him. He's the one who ran her off."

She stormed back into the bedroom, found a heavy coat in Tresa's closet. Shrugging into it, she snatched up her gear. Sword in hand, she strode back into the living room. All guns swung back on her.

"Take it easy, fellas." She gave her sword a little shake in the air. "I'm not planning on using it on any of you. Just passing through on my way out."

The lycan lifted a dark eyebrow in mild surprise and flicked a glance toward the door. "Out there?"

"Don't worry. I've got a ride."

"Sorcha." Jonah grabbed her wrist. Each of his fingers left an invisible mark on her. "What are you doing?"

"I'm going. I don't have any reason to stay here.

Not now." She paused, the words oddly thick in her throat at the thought of leaving Jonah. Never seeing him again. *Stupid*.

She shook her head, reminding herself that this was never about him. This was for Gervaise. For her own sense of peace. She'd have to start over again. Figure out a way to track down Tresa, to finish her off—and her demon. Then it would truly be over. Gervaise would be avenged.

And that wasn't going to happen with Jonah around.

"We're not finished," he growled, his gaze feverishly bright.

Why should Jonah care whether she stayed or left? He had a purpose. A calling. It had fallen into his lap without his even asking. Whether he wanted it or not, he was a slayer. "Good-bye, Jonah."

He surged in a step toward her, indifferent to their observers. "Sorcha, wait."

She hovered on the threshold of the broken door, a dozen plus eyes trained on her. Cold air stirred behind her like the burn of swirling steam. "What for?" She smiled, felt the cruel turn of her lips.

"Yes, don't rush off," the lycan said in his gravelly voice, a faint accent underlying his words. His pewter eyes mesmerized, their pull undeniable, and she wondered how many he had lured to their deaths with those eyes, that voice . . . He walked toward her, each step a measured thud that resonated through her. "I'm enjoying you far too much. I'm disappointed to have missed Tresa, but I must say that I'm not sorry to have found you here."

Sorcha laughed hoarsely. "You think I give a shit?"

He smiled then, a seductive pull of his lips. He was much too handsome, she noted dispassionately, but it didn't touch her, didn't affect her. His beauty was a deceptive poison. A lycan could never be trusted, never be saved.

"Sorcha," he murmured with an approving nod. "I'm not nearly done with you yet."

You're done, she could only think, not liking the gleam in his eyes, and cringing altogether as he lifted his hand to brush her bangs from her forehead. The cold at her back surrounded her, and she shivered uncontrollably. At least she told herself it was only the cold.

He frowned and took her arm. "Come, let's get you warm by the fire. You can tell me more about Tresa . . . and yourself." This last he said with dark satisfaction. As if it were already decided, as if they were enmeshed with or without her consent.

She dug in her heels, resisting, but it did little

good. Her shoes were simply dragged along the wood floor. "No—"

He slipped a hard arm around her waist, practically lifting her off her feet. She brought a fist down on his rock-solid shoulder. He didn't care. Didn't even flinch. He was steel. Ruthless stone.

An animal growl rumbled on the air and she knew without looking that it was Jonah. He charged, burst forth in a flash, shifting in an instant, his human skin rippling and stretching into his beast.

The lycan released her to meet him, shouting at his men as they lifted their guns to Jonah. "He's mine!"

Sorcha stumbled back, staring wild-eyed, transfixed, *horrified*.

"Sorcha, run. Run!" Jonah roared in a thick, garbled voice moments before his body made contact with the lycan.

She hesitated, unsure, unwilling to abandon Jonah. Then her gaze collided with his face. He glared at her over the lycan's back, his eyes twisting flames of ice. "Don't stand there! Go! Go!" he snarled.

Turning, she fled, the sound of smacking fists and crunching bones sharp behind her. She dove out the door into the hard bite of the tundra, telling herself that Jonah would be fine. He could handle himself. He always had. Without the full moon, the lycan was no contest for him. And she needed to get away. Not just from the lycan with his hungering gaze, but from *him*—Jonah. In many ways, he was more dangerous to her than the lycan.

Heedless of the cold, she raced into the blistering freeze. She hardly felt it. Glancing over her shoulder, she was half afraid the lycan or his crew followed her, and half afraid that she would see Jonah, pursuing her. Mingling with that fear was the deep worry that Jonah would *not* be there, right behind her, that he would not follow and find her. Again.

The glance over her shoulder revealed only the lodge, shrinking in size amid the barren snow-swept landscape. No Jonah. She paused for a moment, ready to turn back around. Then she heard his voice in her head shouting for her to continue on.

Facing forward, she forced her legs to keep up their swift pace, working them hard until the tears froze to ice on her cheeks. As she pushed through the swirling arctic gust, she told herself it was the cold that made her eyes tear, and not leaving Jonah behind.

Eleven

A gunshot exploded on the air, lifting Jonah off his feet. The impact dropped him to the floor twenty feet from the lycan he fought.

"I told you not to fire," the lycan snapped, clambering to his feet with a grunt.

"Looked like you needed some help," one of the mercenaries replied, stepping forward to deliver a swift kick to Jonah's ribs.

Jonah hardly felt it, huddled into a ball, hissing against the fiery pain in his shoulder. His burning muscles worked, squeezing and contracting around the bullet, his body rejecting the small chunk of lead, pushing it out of him, but with no amount of ease.

"Look at that," the mercenary said with a whistle as the blood-soaked bullet clattered to the floor. As if Jonah were some sort of circus freak.

"She's gone," one of the mercenaries panted from the doorway. "Damn, she's fast. Can't even see her anymore."

Relief swept through him. At least Sorcha got away and wasn't stuck here to be some lycan's plaything.

"Of course," the mercenary nearest Jonah replied. "She's a freak like this one."

Jonah felt the air shift as the bastard pulled back his leg to deliver another kick. He lurched up and met the swinging leg, catching the booted foot in both hands and with a snap twisting it viciously. The mercenary landed hard on his back with a shrill shriek.

Another bullet struck Jonah in the chest. He groaned, staggering back from the force.

"Enough!" the lycan bellowed. "The next man to fire his weapon will be left here to freeze to death." He snapped his fingers at the fallen mercenary. "Move him somewhere else. His screams are most distracting and I wish to question our friend here."

Friend. Jonah snorted.

"Rise. I have much to ask." The lycan spoke with the formality of an age lived and lost, and Jonah wondered precisely how old he was.

Gasping against the pain of his bullet wounds, he struggled to his feet, watching the lycan stroll into the living room. He stood before the fire, hands stretched out to soak up its warmth. After a few moments, he glanced back over his shoulder. "Better yet?"

Grunting, Jonah dropped down on a chair, snapping, "What are you doing here?"

"Hunting the witch."

Jonah sighed, wondering how many were on the trail of Tresa. "You can't kill her."

"That's to be decided. I've been looking for her for some time now." The lycan strolled around the living room, picking up the odd knickknack and examining it as if it interested him . . . a link to the witch who had lived here. Whom he hunted.

With a sigh, Jonah began to explain. "You don't understand—"

"Oh, but I do. I know all there is to know. Kill a witch, release her demon." He nodded as though bored. "I know. And then some." He squared off before Jonah's chair. "Probably even more than you."

Jonah stared up at him, one hand pressed to the sucking wound in his chest. "You know how all this works, and you're still prepared to risk it? To free her demon?"

"She's not just any demon witch, is she? I've been around a long time . . . I'm willing to risk just about anything to get my hands on the witch who started it all."

Jonah shook his head, muttering beneath his breath, "You sound just like Sorcha."

"Maybe you're in the minority for a reason, then."

"I don't want to free some demon so that the son of a bitch can enslave me and—"

"Aren't you a slave already? To the curse? Perhaps not as I am. Moonrise doesn't own you in the way it owns me." He shrugged a broad, muscled shoulder. "As far as I'm concerned, Tresa is worth capturing. There has to be a way to end this. Through her. I believe that."

Jonah stared hard at this lycan, speechless, able to forget Sorcha for the moment. He had never before met a lycan who regretted his existence, who wanted to be anything other than the voracious beast he was. He shook his head slowly, marveling. "Who are you?"

"The name is Darius."

"How long have you been around?" he asked because he sensed a timelessness to this lycan.

A shutter fell over his pewter eyes. "Too long. Now." His tone turned brisk, businesslike. "Will you tell me what you can of this Tresa?"

"So I can help you find her? No. I won't risk you unleashing her demon. I can't do that."

Darius sank down onto the sofa across from him, throwing one arm along the back. As if they were having a friendly visit. As if armed men did not surround them, their weapons trained on Jonah. As if bullet holes did not riddle Jonah's body.

Darius motioned to one of the men. "Fix the door, will you? Find a tarp at least. I'm starting to get cold." Two mercenaries moved at the command. Another dark-clad soldier stoked the fire. Darius leveled his chilly gaze back on Jonah. "I will find her anyway, you know. I've made it my business to learn all I can about her. She can't evade me forever."

Jonah nodded tightly. Inside his head, he heard Darby whispering at him to kill this lycan, destroy him. To put an end to the threat against Tresa. Funny how he hadn't heard that whisper around Sorcha. Or he'd chosen deliberately to ignore it.

Incredible as it seemed, something in this Darius reminded him of Sorcha. His hard-carved face echoed the desperation he read in Sorcha's face . . . the cold determination in her eyes to end the curse was the same. He couldn't kill this lycan for that same reason. For simply wanting his humanity back. However misguidedly he went about it.

Flexing his fingers over one gurgling-wet bullet hole, he muttered, "I can only hope you'll come to your senses before you do damage to us all."

Darius smiled, motioning to the door. "I guess you'll want to be moving on. Before she gets too far. Good luck to you and your . . . *female.*"

"She's not mine," Jonah gritted out.

"No? Could have fooled me. Perhaps I should

go after her myself, then. She was certainly easy on the eye. And she can hold up better than mortal women. That's the misfortune in dealing with human females, isn't it? They're so fragile. And lycan females are always too blood-hungry for my taste. Now that female, Sorcha was her name?" He tapped his chin. "She might be just the thing to warm me on a cold night like this—"

Jonah lurched up from his chair and lunged forward in one angry step. A mercenary lifted his weapon, but caught himself, pulling back. Jonah did not relish another bullet. Clenching his teeth, he ground out, "Put her out of your head."

Darius laughed, low and dark. "I'll leave her to you, I'm not one to squabble over a female. I've learned to live without. Some of us are destined to be alone."

Jonah opened his mouth to dispute Sorcha's being anything to him, but he'd already shown that she was. Why deny it? The lycan wouldn't believe him. Hell, he didn't even believe himself.

He glanced at the broken door. In one blow, he'd found and lost Sorcha. But then, she had never really belonged to him. She could hardly have known what she wanted when she offered herself to him at the age of fifteen. And now she looked at him with such scorn and aversion that he wondered if the Sorcha he knew was in there at all.

Perhaps she had died in that explosion after all. Lost to him forever. All that remained was her shell.

Whatever the case, he wouldn't go after her. He would trust that Tresa was wise enough not to get caught up in Sorcha's path again. She hadn't survived this long being easy prey.

He would return home and do his best to forget that he'd ever seen Sorcha again. Just as he shoved everything else—anyone else—from his life, he would shove her out as well. Darius was right. Some people were meant for solitude.

TWELVE

So Tresa is safe, right?" Darby demanded the moment he entered his condo.

Lounging on his couch in a pair of pajama bottoms and a tank top, she looked up at him. She tossed aside a magazine, sat up and stared at him with expectation bright in her hazel eyes.

Dropping his bags near the door, he glanced at the boxes of Chinese food littering his coffee table. "Save anything for me?"

"She's alive, right? Tell me she's alive. If not, I can't even return home. My aunts will go ballistic . . ."

He shrugged as he picked up a carton of sesame chicken. "Last time I saw her, she was alive and well."

Darby stabbed her chopsticks back into a carton of lo mein. "That doesn't sound very heartening. You were supposed to make sure she lived."

"I did my part. I made certain the *female* you sent me to stop didn't actually kill Tresa."

Darby frowned. *"Female?"*

"It just would have helped if you had given me a bit more information about her."

Darby wrinkled her brow. "Why do you call her a *female*? And what did you need to know about her other than that you needed to stop her?"

"I call her a female because she's not human. She's a dovenatu. Like me. That would have been good to know."

"No way!" Darby shook her head. A small smile played about her lips as she resumed working her chopsticks in the noodles. "That must have been a fun surprise." Her smile slipped and she looked up again with a sobering expression. "Wait, now my vision makes a bit more sense . . . seeing her kill you. Well, it wouldn't be such a challenge for her, right? I mean, if she's like you." Darby motioned at him up and down with her chopsticks. "Same abilities, strengths and all that."

"No worry. I'm alive, and I don't think she'll kill me—or try to. Turns out we've got history."

Darby shook her head, clearly uncertain. "My visions are never wrong . . . I saw her pull a sword from your back."

"A sword wouldn't kill me."

"Well, maybe it wasn't a typical sword. Maybe it's dipped in silver nitrate . . . or enchanted or something." She shook her head, her expression helpless. "You looked dead to me."

"Look, she was kind of a sister to me. I don't see that happening."

Did he actually just say that? Equate Sorcha to a *sister*? Maybe once. Long ago. Only the woman he'd kissed and touched and held in his arms in that cabin was in no way a sister to him.

"So she understood everything when you explained that she couldn't kill Tresa?"

"Let's just say she accepted it." His lips pressed in a hard line as he thought of her escape into the tundra.

"Hmm." Darby plucked a shrimp from her carton and chewed thoughtfully. "That's a weight off my mind. I couldn't return home and tell the coven that—"

"Now, I can't promise the witch won't be killed," he said, thinking of the lycan Darius.

"What?" Darby lurched up on the couch.

"It appears Tresa has more than one enemy in the field."

"Who?"

"Some lycan is hunting her."

"A lycan?" Her face reddened. "What is it with you dovenatus and lycans wanting her dead?"

"Tresa is the origin of the curse. She's the key." Even he could see there was sense in that—that maybe there was some way to break the curse that the covens didn't know about.

Darby flung both hands up in the air. "Great. I can't go back and tell them she's alive for now, but who knows about tomorrow."

"Whoever knows about tomorrow, Darby?" He dropped down on the chair across from her. "There are no guarantees. Why don't you head back and take care of your aunts the best you can? What will be, will be."

"Spare me the fatalistic bullshit." She leaned forward on the couch, resting her arms on her knees. "You're supposed to be our slayer. It's your job to help determine what *will be*. Why do you think you found me that day? It was destiny—"

"Do I have to hear this again?" He groaned.

"Yes—"

A brisk knock on the door silenced her before she could say anything more. He glanced at the table littered with takeout. "Did you order more food?"

"No."

He moved toward the door, his steps cautious, his skin snapping into hyperalert. He never had visitors. One would need friends for that.

Before he could look through the peephole, a familiar voice called out, "Jonah, it's me. Open the door."

Sorcha. Here? His heart hammered furiously in his chest.

"Who's that?" Darby hissed.

Without answering, he pulled the door open, schooling his face into impassivity. "What are you doing here?"

"Nice to see you, too." Her dark hair gleamed with healthy shine, falling sleekly past her shoulders. She looked so good his mouth watered.

"How did you know where I lived?"

"It wasn't that hard. You mentioned Seattle and it seems you leave an impression everywhere you go." Had he mentioned where he lived? He couldn't seem to recall much of their conversations—much of anything but her. "The female staff at the airport definitely remembered you. Once I was close enough, I just followed my nose." Tapping a finger to her nose, she strode past him, into his condo. She pulled up at the sight of Darby on the couch.

"Oh, I didn't know . . ." For a moment, she looked uncomfortable, her features tight. Her fingers clutched the strap of her bag. "I thought I would find you alone."

He crossed his arms and glared at her, not bothering to explain Darby's presence. Sorcha's being there was too dangerous to him, far too enticing. "I'm still trying to figure out why you're here at all."

She tore her gaze from Darby to him again.

He sighed. "It's all right. Darby knows about us."

"Does she?" Her perfectly tightened lips barely moved as she spoke. Her eyes narrowed beneath her arching eyebrows. "How nice." She circled the room, the heels of her boots clicking over the wood floor, her gaze trained on the other woman.

Darby eyed her with something akin to awe. Sorcha's black leather jacket hung open above her snug-fitting jeans and silk blouse. She looked sexy as hell.

"I thought you'd be on a plane home," Jonah said. She'd sure been in a hurry to leave him the last time he'd seen her.

"I thought I'd pop in on you. Learn a bit more about what it is you do."

"And what is it I *do*?" He frowned, not sure he even knew.

She swung around, leaning her back against the tall marble counter, hands buried deep in the pockets of her leather jacket.

"Yeah. I'd like to know that, too," Darby piped up.

Jonah cut her a glowering look.

"Demon slaying," Sorcha explained. "I might be interested in learning about how that works. How all this demon and witch stuff works."

"Why? Still looking to take Tresa's head?" Darby asked, a touch of anxiety in her voice.

Sorcha merely shrugged.

"No," he bit out. "Forget it. You're not a slayer. I'm not even going to pretend I can train you to be one."

Her eyes drew to slits, the brown almost black.

"No," he repeated, his voice hard. "You're either chosen to be a demon slayer or you're not. It's cut and dry. Black and white. Supposedly I've been chosen."

"No supposedly about it," Darby objected. "You have been."

Sorcha crossed her arms. "Who *chose* you?" Her dark arched eyebrows seemed to say that choosing him had been a mistake. He couldn't disagree with that. He wasn't a particularly religious man. Not because he doubted God's existence or anything. He believed God existed. Kind of hard not to. Whenever he stepped on consecrated ground he felt slightly ill. That was no coincidence.

He simply believed God wanted nothing to do with him. He was a cursed dovenatu. According to the covens, God was involved in choosing slayers. It had to have been some mistake selecting Jonah as one of his holy assassins. Only humans had been chosen as slayers before. Why him?

"God," Darby readily supplied, butting her

nose in as usual. "God chooses slayers. Or more specifically, the angel Gabriel."

"God," Sorcha said, the skepticism rich in her voice, "chose Jonah?"

He pressed his lips in a thin line, trying not to take offense. She only echoed his thoughts. Still, it rankled that she thought him of so little worth.

"Yes. Jonah is God's instrument. He and all other slayers are charged with fighting Satan's minions who would have influence here on earth."

"Jonah?" Sorcha repeated—again. "You do know he's led a fairly wretched existence? Ten years ago, he was the right-hand man to my father." Her lips twisted and she joked dryly, "My father, who may or may not have been Satan."

Jonah smiled despite himself. Her assessment of his life at that time was accurate. He had led a wretched existence in service to her father. The sad thing about it all was that he would *still* call his life wretched. Ever since he'd lost her . . .

He cut off the thought with a swift shake of his head. Sorcha had never been his. And you can't lose something you never possessed in the first place.

"It's not our place to question God's decisions," Darby pointed out, somehow managing not to sound sanctimonious.

Sorcha gazed unflinchingly at the witch, assessing her from the tip of her fuzzy socks to the top of her wild red head. "Who are you, anyway? How do you come to know so much?"

"I'm a witch. Jonah's a member of my coven. Not that he'll have much to do with me or my aunts. I keep chasing him down, hoping he'll answer his calling and move in with us."

"I don't need to live with you and sign my life away to act as your slayer," he ground out.

He glared at Darby, tired of this conversation and even more bothered that he was having it in front of Sorcha. He felt bare, stripped and exposed beneath her intense gaze.

"I'll do it," Sorcha announced.

"What?"

Darby cocked her head. "Do what?"

"I want in. He doesn't want to move in with your coven and protect you all? Fine. I'll do it. You can teach me everything I need to know—"

"There's nothing to get *in*." Jonah stalked closer, reached for her arm. "It's not the army. You don't simply join."

She eased her arm out of his reach and strolled to the stretch of glass that faced the night. The skyline winked up at her, a thousand white and blue lights.

"Sorcha," he growled, trying to keep his voice controlled and even. His patience was running thin. "You heard Darby. Slayers are chosen . . . you haven't been chosen."

"I can be useful—"

"You don't get it," he growled. "I can see them. They're shadows that only I can detect. You can't. And you can't fight what you can't see."

"It's not an unreasonable offer. Something to consider. I can train her." Darby rose and approached the window. "You're a dovenatu, right?"

Sorcha gave a single nod.

"We could use your talents."

"No." Jonah shook his head. "She won't even be able to see what she's fighting. She can't see demons. She won't know where to strike to kill them."

"We can train her. I can work with her . . . help coach her."

"This is insane. You're not taking her home with—"

"I'll go," Sorcha announced.

"Great." Darby looked at him. "If you don't like it, Jonah," she added with an evenness that set his teeth on edge, "then why don't you help train her? Make sure it's done right."

"Yeah, Jonah," Sorcha said, her voice faintly mocking. She crossed her arms. "Train me. If I can do your job, then maybe they'll quit harassing you to move in with them."

Muttering, he glared out the window. "You can't see them." It was the one point he couldn't get around. She'd be helpless against them.

"Teach me to see them," she whispered, stepping close, her voice so soft he doubted Darby could hear her. "You owe me, Jonah. Give me this."

He inhaled, the heady scent of her filling his nose. He winced, closing his eyes. This was Sorcha. Little Sorcha. She was right. He did owe her. He'd always felt protective toward her. The thought of taking her to mate at the tender age of fifteen and using her for the purpose of procreation had sickened him. Protecting her had been one of his life's overriding ambitions. And he had failed. He'd failed her.

"All right," he agreed even as he wondered if he wasn't making a mistake. Training her to fight demons, to fight what she couldn't see . . . did she even stand a chance?

But he couldn't say no. Not when she looked at him with such desperate hope in her eyes, even if she tried to hide it. Thrusting out her chin, she almost passed for a hard-ass. Except for the eyes. Her eyes pleaded with him, and he was reminded of the last night he'd seen her in Istanbul, eavesdropping on him and her father discussing when he was going to take her to mate. She'd waited for him in the corridor, and put the question to him directly. She'd bared her heart to him in that moment, offered herself to him body and soul, and he rejected the offer. Rejected her.

That look in her eyes was his last memory of her. Standing here now, she looked at him with the same hunger in her gaze. Only the hunger wasn't for *him*. It was for what he could do for her. He couldn't say no. Not twice. He'd do this for her, and then call it quits with Sorcha. Any obligation or responsibility he felt for her would be relieved then.

"Thank you," Sorcha said, her voice louder. With a wobbly smile, she sent Darby a nod.

"Just don't get yourself killed," he growled. "I don't want that on my head."

Her glossy lips curved. "I'll do my best."

"Well," Darby said as she settled back down with her box of lo mein. "Not an official slayer, but you have to be better than nothing. Hard to kill, that's for sure. I think my aunts will be pleased."

"Heartening," Sorcha murmured dryly, all the while looking at him, peering intently, as if she could read his mind. He didn't look away either, kept staring at her face, her lips . . . imagining that mouth tasting its way down his body.

He jerked his head from such thoughts. This

was Sorcha. He couldn't think of her like that. What'd he'd done to her in that cabin could be forgotten as long as he didn't repeat the mistake.

What he did with women was never sweet or gentle. The idea of doing those things with Sorcha stabbed him with guilt . . . and lust. Except the guilt was more powerful. At least he told himself that. He told himself guilt would keep him in check.

"So, where do we begin, Jonah?" Darby asked. "I've never tried to find a demon. Actually, I spend most of my time hiding from them. How does one go about hunting one?"

Jonah tore his gaze from Sorcha and smiled at the witch he'd come to know so well. "With bait, of course."

Darby's smile slipped as she looked uncertainly between him and Sorcha. Stabbing her chopsticks into her box, she leaned back on the couch, her gaze sliding uneasily to Sorcha. "I'm not going to enjoy this, am I?"

THIRTEEN

So," Darby began mildly as Sorcha selected things from her luggage that she would need for her shower. Sorcha glanced at the younger woman where she lounged on the bed with a familiarity reserved for old friends. Jonah had given up his room for Sorcha. Darby already occupied his one guest room, so that left the couch for him. At least it answered her question regarding his relationship with the redhead. "Jonah's like your brother?" Darby finished.

Sorcha's head snapped up at that question.

The moment Sorcha had first seen Darby she'd felt a hot flush of jealousy. Horrible considering she thought all feelings for Jonah dead. All softer feelings anyway. The soft, warm kind that led to emotions like jealousy.

"Brother?" Sorcha echoed, mulling over the word, letting it sit like bad food on her tongue, a foul bite she resisted swallowing. She'd never viewed him as a brother. Not even when she was five. Especially not when her father reminded her every day that she and he were destined for each other in order to increase their race. "Not exactly. Is that what he said?"

"Something like that."

She wouldn't characterize the things Jonah did to her in Alaska as brotherly.

Maybe that's why his eyes looked so coldly at her. Like frost over a darkened lake. Maybe he saw only the girl he'd turned away from all those years ago. A girl he never wanted in his bed then. Or now.

She slammed the lid of her suitcase shut. "We grew up together."

"Huh," Darby replied, looking at her speculatively. "I bet that was interesting. Jonah's kinda tight-lipped about his past."

"I suppose," she replied, feeling that familiar stab of jealousy. Clearly the witch was attracted to him. It was written all over her and in the drip of every word. Sorcha didn't miss the slight hitch in her breath or the skip in her pulse when she mentioned his name.

"I'd like to hear about that someday."

Sorcha frowned. "What?"

"You and Jonah . . . as kids."

She didn't bother explaining that Jonah's youth hadn't been hers. She doubted Jonah had ever really been a kid. At least she hadn't known him when he was. "You'll have to ask him about that."

"Yeah." Darby snorted and lightly punched at the pillow balled up under her elbow. "Because Jonah's all about letting it hang out. He's a real open book."

Sorcha pulled open the bathroom door, wondering why it bothered her so much that this female appeared to be half in love with Jonah. It wasn't as if Sorcha had any claim on him. It wasn't as if she wanted that. Those feelings had died long ago. She wouldn't travel that dark road again, fantasizing that one day the two of them would live out their own fairy tale. Fairy tales didn't exist. She wouldn't let herself believe in what wasn't real ever again.

WHEN SORCHA EMERGED FROM the bathroom later, her only thought was of falling into bed and sleeping off the last several days.

Rubbing a towel against her wet head, she jumped at Jonah's deep voice rolling across the air. "What are you doing here, Sorcha?"

Clutching the towel close to her silk pajama top, she faced him with as much composure as she could manage.

"Where's Darby?" she asked, scanning the room for the redhead, suddenly eager for the sight of her.

"She went to sleep." He sat on the bed, hands dangling off his knees as though he had been waiting for her for some time.

She wadded up the wet towel in front of herself. "Don't assume that because I'm staying in your home you can walk in on me whenever you choose. I realize this is your room, but I expect my privacy."

He rose in one swift motion and approached her with the slow stealth of a jungle cat. "You're the one who barged in here uninvited. You're in no position to place requirements on me. You don't know what you're getting involved in here, Sorcha."

"Should I be so scared, then?" She tried for an edge of mockery, but her voice gave out at the last minute and shook a little. He was just too damn close. So overwhelming. So big. So male. So . . . *everything*.

"You should be," he said in a voice like smoke.

She crossed her arms, hugging the damp towel to her body, letting it soak into her silk top.

He stared at her for a long moment, standing closer than she wanted him to. His eyes flickered, roved over her hurriedly. "What are you doing here?"

"I have to *do* something."

"So it's let me train you or else . . . what?" His

eyes scoured her. "You still want to hunt down Tresa, don't you? That's what this is all about. Why should I train you to go after her?"

She shrugged. "*You* don't have to train me. I can go home with Darby. Learn from her . . . help her coven. You won't, after all."

"Darby is none of your affair."

Her throat tightened at what she imagined she heard in his voice. Possessiveness. "What? I think she's a nice girl. Why don't you marry her?" She spat the words out, surprised at how they stuck in her throat.

He scowled at her. "Funny. Darby and the others . . . the witches in her coven—" He stopped and dragged a hand through his hair, feathering the strands back from his forehead. "They're not my responsibility. I don't want anyone needing me."

"Afraid you'll fail them?"

He inhaled sharply, and a grim look crossed his face. "They expect too much from me."

"C'mon, Jonah." She shook her head, her chest tight with envy for what he had. "Don't be a fool. At least you're needed, wanted. They know the real you and still want you. Do you know how lucky you are?" The only person who ever knew her, loved her and accepted her was dead.

"I like it alone. Like living alone." He punctuated each word, his eyes distant.

"Well, I don't. So I want this. I'll take the life you don't want. A life with purpose."

He studied her thoughtfully, angling his head, as if wondering whether to believe her. Moonlight slanted in through the window. Even in the dim light of the room, his hair gleamed a lustrous dark gold. "Is that what you've been looking for, Sorcha? What this whole Tresa thing has been about?"

"At least I'm living and not hiding." She stared at him pointedly.

"I don't hide," he replied quickly. "I'm simply a realist. I'm not human."

"Darby and her coven need you."

"And I've helped them. I simply prefer not to mingle with them as though I'm an average guy. I'm fine with hunting and slaying demons." He laughed harshly. "What would you expect of me, Sorcha? A house in the burbs? A nine-to-five job? Minivan?"

"I don't expect anything of you." She paused, bit her lip. "But what would be so wrong with any of that?" It sounded a bit like heaven to her. A slice of normal, forever unattainable for her. Something she'd had for a too brief flash of time with Gervaise. God, was she back to dreaming about fairy tales again?

"Is that what you've been doing? Trying for

normal?" At her silence, he pressed, his voice hard and intent, an unforgiving lash. "How does hunting down Tresa do that exactly?"

"I lived a normal life." Her lips twisted, pain stabbing her heart. She glared at him, the emotion hot in her throat as she thought of her life with Gervaise. "As normal as I could get. I married. I lived the dream, had the great house, companionship, dinner parties . . ."

For a moment, something passed over Jonah's face. A flicker of emotion she could not identify.

"You married?" he asked, his eyes distant.

She paused. His voice sounded strange. Subdued. "I was."

"You're divorced?"

She lowered her gaze and walked across the room to her luggage. "He died. Tresa took him from me. For that, I will end her life. And her demon's."

He didn't acknowledge this. Instead, he asked, "He was human?"

She nodded, wondering at the tightness in her chest. It had been a long time since she'd wept over Gervaise. She wouldn't do it now, in front of him. She'd show no weakness.

He sighed heavily. "Sorcha. I'm sorry."

"Yes, well, that's what humans do." Finding her robe, she tugged it from her suitcase and yanked it around her. Facing him again, she added, "They die."

He nodded grimly, his mouth hard. "You loved him."

"Very much." For some reason, she resisted adding that she'd loved him like a father. Like the father she'd never had.

Jonah looked her up and down before glancing to her Louis Vuitton luggage. "It appears that he left you with a comfortable living."

"Gervaise was a wealthy man. Quite a bit older. I doubt I could spend his money in several lifetimes."

A muscle rippled in his jaw and he suddenly didn't look so sympathetic. "How fortunate for you."

"It's given me freedom, true. Before I met him, I was barely surviving on the streets."

He arched a dark gold eyebrow, his expression smug, as if he understood, knew why she had married Gervaise, which of course he didn't. He couldn't understand. Couldn't understand their relationship, the connection they shared. "I'm glad for you. Hope the price of marrying some old man made it all worthwhile."

Anger rolled through her. "Gervaise taught me a great deal," she defended hotly.

"I bet."

Heat fired her cheeks. "About life, and the arts . . . how to dress and comport—"

"I get it. You were a rich man's toy—"

Her hand itched to slap his face. She curled her fingers inside her palm. "Get out."

He shrugged. "I never thought you would give yourself so cheaply."

She opened her mouth to deny the charge, to convince him, to explain. She stopped, shaking her head. He would believe whatever he wanted to. Let him.

"Why not?" She thrust out her chin. "I gave myself to you. Offered myself freely. Remember that, Jonah?" Even as she asked, she hated herself for mentioning it. Still, the dam had opened and she couldn't stop the flood of angry waters. "In exchange I received only heartache. Why not make sure the next time I put myself out there for a man, I get something out of it?"

His eyes glowed, pale light twisting at the centers. "What's happened to you?"

"Life." Her lips curled. "I've grown up."

"I liked you better before."

She laughed hoarsely. "Yeah. Well, I couldn't tell. You certainly didn't show it. Not that I care what you think of me anymore."

Then something came over her. A bold, brazen part of her she'd never thought to expose to him.

Tossing her towel to the floor, she untied the sash of her robe and shrugged it off her shoulders.

Cool air rushed over her. Her nipples pebbled against the damp silk of her top.

She approached him slowly, with measured steps and a seductive roll of her hips. "Really, Jonah? You don't like what I've become?" Looking down at him where he sat on the bed, she brought her hand between the vee of her breasts, brushed her fingers down her silk-covered belly. "Don't you want me? Men do."

"And you love that." His lip peeled back from his teeth in a snarl.

She stepped between his splayed thighs and dropped her voice. "C'mon, Jonah." She stroked her hand back up her belly, slowly, palming her breast, gratified to feel her nipples crest against the silk. "You didn't expect me to stay fifteen forever, did you?"

His eyes grew brighter, more intense. "I thought you were dead. In my mind, you were always fifteen. I could never have imagined you like this." His gaze deepened, clung to her, the bright flame writhing in his eyes.

Her fingers moved to one thin strap, sliding it down her shoulder so that her left breast lay exposed, peaked and wanting. He angled his head, studied her, stared hard, devouring.

"You liked me well enough in Alaska."

"Yeah. Well, that was before you moved into my place and declared yourself a demon slayer in training."

"Why should that matter?" she demanded, feeling an unreasonable flash of anger. Would he reject her again?

With determination burning inside her, she sucked a finger into her mouth, intent on proving him wrong. On breaking him, ruining him for any other.

Locking her gaze with his unflinching stare, she slipped her wet finger from between her lips and rolled it over her bared nipple.

"What are you doing?" he rasped, his voice quick.

Trying to show him she wasn't the inexperienced girl he had brushed aside before.

Trying to prove to him that he wanted her. *Her*—Sorcha.

Words weren't needed. Sucking her finger into her mouth again, she repeated the process, laving her nipple until it stood glistening wet and engorged.

Her breath fell faster, the sound ragged and wet. From his hard stare or his presence or the simple act of arousing herself, she couldn't know for sure.

He lifted his hand toward her. Not quickly but not slowly either. She held her breath, waiting for his touch.

His fingers grasped her bodice, clutching the flimsy neckline in his curling hand. In one move, he ripped the silk clean down the center.

FOURTEEN

Sorcha stood before him, naked from the waist up. She fought the urge to cover herself. She knew men liked her body. They'd told her before. Being a dovenatu gave her a certain advantage . . . provided her with the kind of body women visited gyms and plastic surgeons to achieve.

She was all lean lines and hollows with curves where they should be. High-tipped, swelling breasts and flaring hips that had eluded her at fifteen.

He looked her over slowly, leisurely.

"Do you like what you see?" she asked in a voice that sounded far more confident, far more seductive, than she felt.

His gaze snapped back to her face. "Who wouldn't? You're perfect."

Men had said that to her before, too, but from his lips the words sounded different. Hoarsely deep, he sounded as though he meant it. As though he had never seen anything as lovely. She shivered.

Flattening her hands on his warm chest, she pushed him back on the bed. He dropped easily, willingly, watching her intently with his unblinking gaze.

She stared at him for a moment before turning toward the cracked bedroom door and closing it.

Facing him, she advanced, strolled through the soft moon glow. She climbed into bed, working and moving her body in a way that she knew showed it to advantage.

Back dipped and ass thrust out, she reached around him and pulled back the covers. She didn't want to talk, wanted only to satisfy the deep burning ache that Jonah had awakened in her from the first moment she'd seen him.

Maybe that was the real reason she'd come here. Not to learn the tools necessary to avenge Gervaise. Maybe she wanted Jonah to finish what he'd started when he kissed and touched her in the tundra. He was like her. He could satisfy her in ways a human man never could. A few had scratched the surface but never penetrated the deep ache, never gave her true sexual fulfillment.

Rolling onto her back, she wiggled herself out of her pajama bottoms, all the while feeling his hot stare on her. Swallowing her nervousness, she flattened her feet on the bed and bent her knees.

On her back, she dragged her thighs open, splaying herself wide for him.

There was no part of her not exposed to his view. It was an explicit invitation. A call to mate.

He stood up from the bed and circled around to look down at her, his gaze roaming, missing nothing, not a bare inch of her. His eyes glowed as bright as the moon watching them through the window. Finally, he spoke. And when he did, it was just one word.

"*No.*"

She jerked. A slap in the face. Just like those years ago.

Propping herself up on her elbows, she hissed at him, "Can't handle one of your own kind? Thought it might be an interesting experiment after all . . . to fuck someone with no fear of breaking him."

"And I thought you preferred humans," he shot back in a voice just as furious.

She gazed at him, bracing herself for when he would turn away from her. Walk away like before. Her body wept, ached with need. His nearness tormented her. Cool air rolled over her naked body, a dragging kiss. She needed satisfaction. *Needed him.* And maybe that was it, maybe he sensed that need in her. He'd told her he couldn't stand to be needed, after all.

The longer he stood there, staring down at her, unmoving as a giant rock, the hotter her body burned . . . and her rage. He would do this to her again. Reject her. Humiliate her. *No.* Not without suffering for it.

With a curse at him, she slid her hand down her belly and into herself. She played in her moist folds as he watched. "What's wrong? Afraid you'll disappoint me? Afraid you can't measure up to other lovers?"

"I don't want to hear about your other lovers," he growled.

"No? What *do* you want, Jonah?" she demanded, her voice a purr as she slipped a finger inside herself. She gasped. His eyes sparked brighter and his nostrils flared, scenting her. As she stroked herself she imagined it was him inside her, dragging against her tightening flesh. Moving with her, against her.

Her channel clenched around her finger, and she rolled her hips.

Furious at his stillness, at his absolute composure in the face of her surrender, she whimpered, "What do I have to do?"

Still he did not move, only watched her as she shook with desire.

He was immune. Nothing could entice him. He didn't want her to talk about other lovers?

Well, she would do just that. There had only been a couple. Never anyone close, no one she could let in. But he didn't need to know that. Let him think that after Gervaise parted, she had to install a swinging door in her bedroom.

"Sometimes I have two, three men in one night. However many it takes." She thrust her pelvis against her hand. "Maybe you can satisfy me, Jonah. Maybe I won't require anyone else."

He growled low in his throat. The sound was decidedly inhuman and a little frightening, and nothing she'd ever heard from a man she was about to give herself to, but still she continued, pushing him toward the breaking point. "I like it hard, Jonah. And fast. Can you do that?"

With her free hand, she cupped her breast, squeezing and kneading, rubbing her nipple between her thumb and forefinger.

His eyes narrowed, impossible to read as he watched her.

"I love it when I feel out of control. Problem is, I can never do that. I have to stay the one in control . . ."

That much was true. Explained her lack of orgasms. Impossible to achieve an orgasm when you're focusing on staying in control.

With Jonah, it would never be that way. He was just as strong, stronger even . . . the one capable of hurting her. Being with him was complete trust. The prospect terrified her. A dark road never traveled. But she desperately wanted to go there.

Only he still hadn't spoken, still hadn't made a move.

She whimpered in frustration and was about to give up her efforts when he broke.

He was so fast, a blur on the night she could not have escaped even if she wanted to. He grabbed both her ankles and slid her down the bed until her ass balanced on the edge of the mattress.

"Is this what you've become?" he hissed in her face.

He released one ankle. She heard the slide of his zipper and her heart seized, the pulse skittering in her throat as she gazed up at his hungry face, his expression stark and pained. She nodded mutely, the sheets cool against her bare back.

"You want me to use you? Treat you like a whore?"

His hands moved back to her ankles. He forced her thighs wide, positioning her feet apart. Her bent knees quivered with anticipation. She hungered for his hands to touch her, glide up from her ankles and explore her aching body, her heavy breasts.

"Touch me," she pleaded.

"You're not in control anymore, remember?"

he bit out. "Isn't that what you wanted? No more men to play with like toys, fuck and toss aside?"

She opened her mouth to answer him, to admit she had exaggerated that, but all thought fled, the words lost as he buried himself deep inside her with a single shocking thrust, locking himself inside her to the hilt.

Sensations overwhelmed her. She arched, threw back her head and screamed at the force, at the pulsing thickness of him buried deep, at the pleasure bordering on pain.

He buried his lips in her hair. "I don't even know you anymore." Clutching a fistful of her dark hair, he pulled back to look at her face. She had never thought eyes so bright, so alive with hunger, could appear so dead. So hateful.

"Did you ever?" she choked out.

"Oh, I knew you. Maybe better than you did."

She was beyond words, unable to disagree.

His hands circled her ankles like manacles as he worked himself over her, splaying her wide for his pleasure. And hers.

Her body bounced up and down on the bed from the force of his thrusts. Pressure built, twisting tighter and tighter. A strange, new heat rose until the throb at her core burst open.

She cried out, splintering apart, but still he thrust himself inside her, invading her so fully, so totally, that he brought her right back to the edge. Tension coiled tightly in her again, rising and building.

She jerked and clawed against him from his repeated thrusts, desperate for more, faster, harder. He released her ankles and grabbed her by the hips. His fingers dug into her tender flesh. The sensation of his hands gripping her, anchoring her for his assault, reduced her to a boneless mass. Limp as a doll, she fell back, could do little more than surrender, letting him ravage her body as he would.

As his movements became fiercer, the twisting pressure low in her belly exploded again. She arched, pressed her mouth into his chest and bit down. The impulse to bite him was primal, instinctive. It had never happened before and it horrified her. Still, she couldn't have stopped herself.

He hissed and grabbed her by the hair, pulling her back to glare hotly into her wide eyes. She felt his blood trickle down her chin and swiped at it with the back of her hand, disgust with herself at an all-time high.

She thought she had gone too far, had pushed him too far, but he only stared at her as he continued to pump in and out of her. As if he couldn't stop even if his life depended on it. As if someone held a gun to his head and demanded he move, work himself over her until he spent every last drop of himself inside her.

As the pressure built within her yet again, she arched her pelvis, writhing and pumping her hips against the clasp of his hands, hot and eager, pushing and pulling at his cock with her body.

She didn't know how long they went on like this. Only that it was longer than any man had ever lasted with her before. Time blurred. Colors spun before her eyes.

It felt unreal, too overwhelming, too intense, as if she were out of her body, floating above herself and watching.

She told herself it was because he was a dove-natu. Like her. Not because he was Jonah. Not because he was someone special to her.

Suddenly his thrusts became deeper, jarring her to her very bones. Even in the gloom, she saw his face shift, blur before her eyes, flash in and out, cheekbones sharpening, becoming more angular, his flesh more bronze.

He dropped over her then, his blunt teeth biting down on her shoulder as he came inside her, spilled himself deep. She felt him break her skin, mark her as he reached climax. Warmth gushed over her shoulder.

She joined him, shrieking out her release. Grabbing a fistful of his hair in her hand, she twisted the ends as he wrung yet another orgasm from her.

Gasping as though he'd finished a marathon, he rolled onto his back beside her.

"Wow." He spat out the word, more like a grunt than actual speech.

"Yeah," she breathed, dragging a hand down her perspiring cheek. *Wow.* How was she ever going to have sex with a normal man after this? Nothing could compare. It'd be liked eating canned soup after tasting lobster bisque from her favorite bistro.

He rolled his head to study her. She was already watching him. Something she read in his eyes told her he was thinking the same thing she was. There was no going back after this.

"Have you slept with a dovenatu before?" she asked, couldn't help asking. She wanted to know. Needed to know.

"No. Haven't come across too many of us."

Their gazes clung, words passing without being uttered. Suddenly he stood and removed the last of his clothes.

"What are you doing?"

He picked up one of the pillows that that fallen to the floor and tossed it back to the head of the bed. "Getting ready for bed."

"I thought you were sleeping on the couch."

His mouth gave the barest twitch. "Now what would be the point in that anymore?"

She swallowed, feeling suddenly vulnerable. Sex was one thing, but sleeping together? Side by side? "Is this a permanent arrangement?"

"As long as you're here," he answered. "I don't see us going back now, do you? Now that we've had each other?"

"No," she murmured, snatching up her garments. "Not much point." Only it would be harder to leave once he finished training her. Harder to walk away from him and his bed. Pulling on her pajamas, she gave her head a small shake and slipped back beneath the cool sheets. Turning on her side, she tried not to roll into him when the bed dipped from his weight. Instead, she reminded herself that she had initiated this. Begged for it, lied and taunted him until he had no choice.

She winced as she recalled that they weren't alone in the condo. "Guess Darby knows what we've been up to."

"I think the people in the penthouse above us know."

She bit back a giggle. Just nerves, she mused. None of this amused her. Nothing humorous about the fact that she just slept with Jonah.

"Does it bother you that she knows?" Jonah asked.

"A little," she admitted, and a little *not*. "She's in love with you, you know."

"She's in love with the idea of me as her coven's slayer. It would make it easier if she and I hooked up . . . easier to keep me tied to the coven. She's the youngest member. The other witches are older . . . they place a lot of responsibility and pressure on her."

Was that pity in his voice? Admiration? Sorcha didn't like it, whatever it was. She didn't like knowing he felt anything for Darby that he didn't feel for her.

Great. Was she really so jealous? Really still so infatuated with him? She hadn't come here to start something between them. She had come here because she wanted to know more about demons and witches . . . because she still intended to find Tresa.

"Tell me about your husband." His voice rolled over her in the gloom, tugging her from her jealous thoughts.

"Gervaise?" She flexed her fingers on the crisp cotton pillow beneath her head. "I met him when I was hiding in his carriage house about a year after I escaped Istanbul." She winced at the memory of that night, the night she'd killed Gervaise's groundskeeper and taken her first life.

Cold and starved, she'd broken into the carriage house, hoping to find some food . . . and a place to crash. Instead she found a man happy to abuse a defenseless teenage girl, a female he thought he could rape without reprisal. And if she hadn't transitioned that night—at long last—he would have succeeded.

Jonah shifted, rolled a little closer. "Did your husband know what you were?"

"He knew. It would have been hard for him not to." She sucked in a breath. "He found me standing over the corpse of his groundskeeper." She laughed, the sound broken and hoarse. Why was she telling him this? Still, she heard herself continue. "It wasn't a pretty sight. Not me. Not that body."

"What'd the groundskeeper do to you?" He breathed these words against the side of her face as his hand closed around her arm, gripping her as though he would never let go.

She closed her eyes and sighed, moving into his lips, savoring the brush of them against the side of her face. It shouldn't have comforted her that he automatically knew the murder had been justified, that she wouldn't have killed without reason, but it did. It mattered that he knew her that well.

"The groundskeeper attacked me. I reacted thoughtlessly, instinctively, to protect myself. Gervaise walked in and saw me in full shift. He didn't call the police. He seemed to understand the situation at once. He was so . . . *kind*. Hard to imagine. For all he knew, I was a monster."

"Christ."

"It was the first time I shifted. Some Initiation, huh? I'd begun to wonder if it would ever happen . . . like Ivo feared." She shook her head at the cruel memories of her father trying to force her to transition.

Jonah's hand slipped through the dark to grip her arm. His thumb roved in small circles on her skin. "How did you end up married to him?"

"He took me in, fed me. Put me in an elegant room, cleaned me up. He offered to marry me after only a few days, and I accepted." She lifted one shoulder in a shrug. "He was fascinated with what I was, and he wanted to help me, too. He was old, had a weak heart. I think he was searching, hoping to make his final years matter. For whatever reason, he thought they would matter with me in them. He didn't have any family and neither did I. We became that for each other. He brought me back to life. Gave me the world, art, music, society—when we chose it. Beautiful clothes, travel. We discussed science and politics—"

"And in exchange, you warmed his bed." His voice cut like a whip. His grip on her arm tightened, became less comforting and more punishing.

"No." She couldn't continue that lie. "It was never like that between us. That would have soiled what we had. Even if Gervaise could have performed his husbandly rights, he would not have tainted our relationship."

"You mean you were married and you never—"

"No. I took my first lover after he died. Even though we were not intimate, I could not bring myself to break our vows while he lived. It seemed disrespectful."

"So since Gervaise died you've been sowing your long-suppressed oats, is that it?"

Sighing, she studied the hard lines and angles of his face. "I might have exaggerated on that. There've only been a couple of men. Two."

He was utterly still for a moment. His naked chest hardly moving, hardly drawing breath.

She continued, "I lied to make you mad. If you were angry, I knew you couldn't keep control. You'd stop looking at me as little Sorcha and give in."

He slid a hand around her waist, pulled her closer. "And you wanted me that much?"

Her breath caught in her throat. "Like I said, I've only been with two men and neither really knocked my socks off—"

"How could they? They were mere men." She heard the smile in his voice as he said this.

"But you've taken women to your bed." She winced at the accusing ring in her voice.

"And none have been as good as you. Isn't that what you want to hear?"

Her breath released in a shuddery gasp. A smile fluttered on her mouth.

"It's what we are," he added. "Two sides of the same coin."

"So it's like my father said. We're meant for each other." Her lip curled, fighting the idea that her father had been right about anything. Even something she might want him to be right about.

His hand stilled on her waist. "We're not getting together to breed dovenatus to create a new world order, Sorcha. Get that out of your head. This is just about sex. Satisfying a need. If you have to put a name to it, call it friendship."

She flinched, stung in a way that she shouldn't be. She wasn't in possession of many friends. She should be glad for one, glad that she and Jonah had moved past fighting.

Still, she could not stop the thickness from entering her voice as she said, "Of course. I wasn't saying we're going to spend the rest of our lives together." That would be too much like the dreams belonging to the stupid girl she used to be. Now she had dreams of vengeance. Dreams of serving long-needed justice. *That* warmed her as no lover could . . . even Jonah. "Don't kid yourself. I didn't think we were talking about happily ever after. I'm going to learn all you and Darby have to teach me."

And from there, she would track Tresa down again. Sorcha couldn't forget about her, or the fact that she'd created so much misery for everyone, for thousands . . . millions, maybe.

His hand slipped, gliding down her stomach. She forced herself to relax, told herself that he was right. This was just sex.

"You'll have to do everything I say," he warned. "You'll have a hard time fighting what you can't see. I'm not sure it's possible."

"I have confidence in you. You'll teach me." She swallowed a yawn. Rolling onto her side, she spooned herself into him and tucked a pillow close to her front, locking one thigh around it and forcing an emotional barrenness to sweep through her, hollow her and push everything else out. "It's possible." Anything is possible. Even ghosts you thought long dead returning to face you.

"Tired?" he asked at her second stifled yawn.

"Yes. The last few days have been . . . a lot."

He chuckled low and deep. The sound made the tiny hairs on the nape of her neck prickle. "Yeah. They have."

"Good night," she murmured, slipping into sleep's waiting embrace.

FIFTEEN

A week later, Jonah followed Sorcha and Darby into his condo, removing his sword and then sliding off his long trench coat. He hung both on the steel pegs near the door, fighting back a weary sigh.

A weariness that had everything to do with Sorcha. Being around her was taking a toll. Having her, holding her and enjoying her while knowing it could never last . . .

Sighing again, he dragged a hand through his hair. It had to end. Hunting for demons was a joke. Tonight had proved that. He was humoring her so he could have her around. He admitted that to himself. He craved her like a drug. This girl he had never thought to have. The idea had been reprehensible to him. And now he was here, taking her at every opportunity, sinking into her heat, fusing himself to her body. Countless times. Countless ways. Ivo must be having a good laugh in hell.

"Figures," Darby announced, plopping down on the couch. "When you want a demon to make an appearance, it's a no-show." She kicked off blood-red pumps and flexed her squished-looking toes. Curling her long legs beneath her, she ran a hand through her perfectly arranged red hair, loosening the smooth style that brought back memories of the thirties.

Sorcha moved to the window, arms crossed. She stared out at the night, silent, her expression pensive. He watched her, wondering at her thoughts. He sensed her disappointment. Was she ready to quit? End this game and leave? The thought of her leaving, moving on, made his gut clench. Like the way he'd felt in Istanbul when he stared at the blazing inferno he'd thought to be Sorcha's funeral pyre. His jaw hardened and he pushed the sensation down. Well, he would just have to get over that. He'd moved beyond before. He could again. He'd have to. This arrangement with Sorcha wasn't permanent. She wasn't a pet to be kept.

"Okay. So. What's next?" Darby asked carelessly. "Can we try a different venue? I'm really not into spending another night hanging out in a smoke-infested club and being hit on by another loser who wants to know if I'm a *natural* redhead."

"Demons hang out around negative and intense

energy," he reminded her. "There's plenty of that at the Dungeon Room."

"Yeah, well, there was plenty of negative energy there tonight and no demons," Darby muttered. "Can't imagine more meth heads or bikers in one place. Your girlfriend there nearly started a riot with that skirt. She stirred up plenty of intense emotions, and guess what? No demons."

Sorcha shot Darby an annoyed look, clearly not appreciating the reminder of the brute who'd grabbed her ass. Of course, it could have been Jonah beating him to a pulp—and his sorry-ass friends who jumped into the fray—that she wanted to forget.

"What else attracts demons?" Sorcha sat down, lowering herself carefully to the couch in her short skirt.

Darby spread her arms wide. "Me. Witches. Demons flock to us, eat up whatever pheromone we put out like bees to sugar and honey."

"That's it?" Sorcha frowned. "Well, then, you would think tonight would have done the trick." She shook her head. "There's gotta be something else we can do." Arching a dark eyebrow, she looked back and forth between them.

Yeah, give up, he thought, but said nothing.

Darby bit the corner of her lip. "If a witch is in the process of using her powers, that's usually a red flag a demon can't resist. Whatever it is we emit is stronger then. Many witches give up their powers altogether for fear of attracting demons." She frowned, her forehead creasing. "Unfortunately, it's not that simple for me."

Jonah leaned against the bar and settled his gaze on Sorcha. She hadn't looked at him since the fight and them being tossed out of the bar. Even now, she stared at Darby, ignoring him.

"What are your powers exactly?" Sorcha asked. "Can't you just use them . . . summon them or whatever . . ."

"I have visions. Usually in my sleep, in my dreams. It's not something I can summon." Her red-glossed lips twisted. "Useful, I know. My aunts keep telling me I'll eventually learn to manipulate my visions." She shrugged. "Until then, I'm at the mercy of my power."

Jonah moved toward the bedroom, finished with talking about demons. They'd done little else in the last week. It grated on him to see Sorcha dragged into the mire, too. He hadn't found her alive all these years later just to lose her again fighting some demon she was ill equipped to battle. "Let's call it a night."

"You two go ahead." Darby slipped off her shiny bracelets and pulled the cream-colored mohair throw from the back of the couch. Snuggling into the blanket, she grabbed the remote control and punched a button. The flat screen gleamed to life with a soft chime.

"'Night, Darby." Sorcha walked toward Jonah's darkened bedroom, her miniskirt fluttering around her thighs as she moved. It was a sight that had tormented him all night.

She'd just cleared the door and was reaching for the light switch when he shut the door abruptly behind them and swung her around in the dark. Aligning his body with hers, he pressed her to the door. "All night I've watched you. Watched other men stare at you, imagined having you . . ."

Her eyes were wide and dark as any animal's, the light at the center burning low. He fought the sudden tightness in his throat and buried a hand in her hair, dark and sleek as a seal's pelt. "When that bastard touched you—"

"You nearly killed him," she cut in.

"He's lucky I didn't."

"We were working tonight," she reminded him. "You shouldn't take any of it personally. You got us kicked out."

He laughed roughly. "When it comes to you, it's personal." He tightened his grip on her hair and forced her head back. "It's always been personal, Sorcha."

Her gaze roved over his face, dropping to his

mouth. His gut tightened, cock hardening with anticipation. "From the first moment you stepped out in this fuck-me skirt, I've been imagining getting you home. In my bed."

Her breath escaped in a flutter of air. The look in her melting brown eyes . . . Shaking her head, she wet her lips and spoke. "You're going to have to stop getting so distracted. We have a job to do."

His hands skimmed up her thighs, beneath her skirt. Reaching her panties, he ripped the thin strings at her hips. When he slipped a hand between her thighs, he found her ready.

Their gazes clung, locked with a deep hunger.

"Right now," he rasped, "we have only one thing to do."

With a single hop, she locked her legs around his hips.

He wedged his hand between them and freed himself. In one move, he buried himself in her clinging wetness. It was still as good as their first time. Too good. So good it scared him to think of letting her go and never having this anymore.

She gasped and bit his earlobe with a ragged moan.

He carried her to the bed and fell down over her, pumping and moving inside her with feverish intensity. Her hands seized his shoulders. She forced him to roll over so that she could straddle him.

His hands squeezed her thighs, so slim and warm and giving beneath his fingers. She placed her hands on either side of his head, lowering her face so that they were nose to nose, eye to eye. Her hair fell like a curtain on either side of his face.

She kissed him, devouring his mouth as she moved over him slowly, working her hips in deep, sinuous drags. She prolonged their pleasure, moving her body against him when he wanted it hard and fierce and fast. Every time with her was like that, bringing out the animal in him.

He cried out her name, a strangled sound that sounded like death in his throat. Like life. Perhaps for the first time he truly lived.

He came then, shattering apart as she pushed down on him, burying him deep in her clenching warmth, her fingers claws on his shoulders.

He ran his hands deep into the silk of her hair, his fingers curving to the contours of her scalp. He pressed his lips to the side of her throat in a breathy kiss, the taste of her skin sweetly addictive. Potent and alluring, weaving a spell on him.

With a sigh, she nestled against his chest, so trusting, so natural and easy, that his throat thickened.

Because it couldn't be. This was beginning to feel dangerously good . . . something he wanted to make permanent.

Her breath deepened and slowed, fanning warmly against his chest. She was asleep. Sprawled in his arms, their bodies still joined, it didn't get any more intimate. Any better.

Any more desperate for him to end.

THE SHADOW ENTERED THE condo, slipping beneath the door and crawling like a slow-slithering snake through the silent space, searching, hunting its prey through each still room.

It found what it sought at last, asleep in one of the bedrooms. Her hair spilled a dark red around her on the mattress, a bloody beacon in the deep of night.

It hovered above her, a shape darker than the night, floating, flexing, pulsing heat on the air.

She felt the sudden warmth. Uncomfortable, pulsing heat. Kicking off her covers, she whimpered the moment before the shadow swooped in, vanishing inside her body, rooting and burrowing deep in her vulnerable shape.

SORCHA OPENED HER EYES, her skin tight and snapping, pulling with an alertness born of the beast.

Murky night surrounded her. She blinked and glanced around, wondering what had woken her. She wasn't in the habit of waking suddenly in the middle of the night. Especially after thorough and body-shattering sex.

She held herself still, her gaze flicking left and right, nerves stretched, reaching, feeling for whatever it was . . .

Jonah slept soundly beside her, on his stomach, one arm disappearing off the edge of the bed.

Her skin rippled and she shivered. Lacing her fingers over her stomach, she listened to the silence. Nothing. If she'd heard something, if there was anything to worry about, Jonah would have woken, too, she reasoned. He was like her, hypersensitive to sound and movement.

Sighing, she closed her eyes, determined to reclaim sleep. Tomorrow would be another long night of scouring the city.

Eyes closed, she tried to sink back into darkness, lose herself in the swirling dark, shapeless black.

Then she felt it again, whatever sensation had torn her from sleep moments ago. Her skin shivered.

Her eyes flew back open, and she gasped.

Darby stood over her. Still as a statue and silent as death. Only it didn't look like Darby. Something was different. Her eyes weren't hers. They looked darker, deeper, motionless black space.

Sorcha opened her mouth to ask her what she was doing in Jonah's bedroom when she noticed the pillow in Darby's hands. Before Sorcha could speak, Darby swooped in faster than she'd ever seen a human move. As fast as a lycan or dovenatu.

Sorcha opened her mouth to scream, but no sound escaped before the pillow slammed down over her face with surprising force.

Writhing, she inhaled, but couldn't draw breath through the heavy press of cotton. She clawed at Darby's hands, her nails scoring the flesh.

This wasn't right. Darby shouldn't be this deadly strong. She shouldn't be capable of such an act.

And why should she *want* Sorcha dead?

Suddenly, the pillow lifted and she tasted air.

She knew it could only have been a moment with that pillow on her face, but it felt like forever. Her lungs filled with sweet oxygen and she knew, felt in her core, in the stretch of flesh over her expanded bones, that she had fully shifted. She had turned and still been unable to fight off Darby. How was it possible that Darby had overpowered her?

Gasping, she jerked to her side and glanced wildly around.

Darby collapsed to the floor, shuddering, holding herself tightly as she convulsed.

Jonah dove out of the bedroom, a streak of movement.

Trembling, Sorcha gave Darby a wide berth. Still unsure if the woman was out to kill her, she staggered after Jonah.

With one hand pressed to her heaving chest, she leaned against the bedroom door, gasping, struggling to catch her breath. Bewildered, she watched Jonah tear through the living room, vaulting over furniture as if he was being chased.

He looked like a madman racing naked around the condo. Possessed.

He clutched his sword, wielding it like some kind of warrior of old, swinging it through the air. At first it appeared he struck nothing, stabbing into empty space.

And then, she realized what was happening. She understood.

He wasn't being chased. He was chasing . . . something.

Squinting, she detected the cloudlike shadow twisting through the room, over furniture, around objects. *A demon.* Jonah followed it, slicing furiously and stabbing with his sword. He'd turned, too. His body was huge, his skin a tawny bronze, rippling with muscle and sinew.

She tried to follow his quick movements, but he moved so fast he looked almost as blurred and hazy as the demon's shadow he chased.

The croaky voice at her side made her jump.

She turned, snarling, on Darby, remembering that moments ago her *friend* had tried to kill her.

"Oh, God," Darby managed, clinging to the door jamb, watching in horror. Her lips trembled.

"What do you see?" Sorcha snapped. "What's it look like?"

Whatever Darby saw as she gazed at that shadow must have been terrible. She didn't even flicker an eyelash at Sorcha in full shift beside her. She rubbed her arms and shook her head fiercely, gawking at the demon shadow. "It's horrible," she whispered. "He . . . *it* took me in my sleep."

Sorcha released a slow, hissing breath, understanding at once. A demon had used Darby to try to kill her.

SIXTEEN

Sorcha dragged a shaking hand down her face, her own heart hammering with a frenzied beat. Steel clanged loudly on the air as Jonah's sword made contact with a lamppost.

Darby shook her head, her fiery hair a floating nimbus around her head. "It's never happened to me before. They've never invaded *me* and made me do things—" Her voice ended with a choke. "They're not supposed to do that to a witch. Not without the witch submitting, giving consent . . ."

Sorcha grabbed Darby's arm and forced her forward, pointing to the living room. "What do you see?" she demanded, her voice thick and garbled in her mouth.

Darby shook her head again. "I've never seen a demon like this. He wears his bones on the outside, stretched over this horrible, gross"—her fingers worked on the air—"black flesh. I see the mark of the fall on him . . . Jonah sees it, too . . . it's right near a horn that's sticking out of his back."

Sorcha absorbed her words, tried to imagine the scene described as she stared at Jonah chasing the shadow and plunging his sword into it again and again. "The mark of the fall . . . what's that?"

"The only place he's vulnerable. Jonah has to stab him there to kill him." Darby yelped suddenly. "There! He almost got him!"

The shadow took a sudden dive toward the front door. Jonah dove after it, landed on top of it. For a moment it looked as though he were riding the air. The great shadow billowed up around him, swallowing him in a cloud of smoke and char.

Jonah lifted his sword high in both hands and plunged. The sword embedded itself in the carpet with a heavy *thwack*. Sorcha watched, her eyes aching, wide in her face.

Darby shouted, the sound exultant.

The demon cloud grew then into a great billow, rising, twisting up, up, up, until it reached high in the air, where it faded, evaporated like fast-fading smoke.

"Is he gone?"

Darby nodded. "Yeah." She released a breathy little laugh. "He did it. Sent it back to hell."

Jonah rose and yanked his sword from the floor with a vicious pull, indifferent to his nudity. His bronze-hued flesh rippled like a beautiful animal as he moved. He stared up at the last curling wisps of shadow. He swallowed, the tendons in his neck working. "What the hell happened here?" he spat out.

Eager to reclaim some semblance of calm, of normalcy, Sorcha forced her heart rate down into an ordinary range and shifted back. Her bones tugged, pulling into place with a faint crackle. The heat at her core ebbed.

Jonah pointed a finger in the direction of where the demon had once been and glared at Darby. "Explain how that demon took possession of you."

Darby looked at Sorcha uncertainly, apology all over her face. "I don't know. He must have sensed me when I was having a vision . . ." Her voice faded, her hazel eyes bleak.

"In your sleep?" Jonah barked. "How in the hell did he take possession of you and force you to stuff a pillow over Sorcha's face?"

Darby waved her arms. "I—I don't know! I don't remember doing that! The dream realm operates at a different level. I guess as long as I didn't wake, he could guide me—"

Jonah advanced on her, his expression furious enough to make Sorcha cringe. "And why didn't you just wake up?"

Darby's eyes sparked. "I never wake during my visions. I'm practically catatonic in those moments. Look, I wasn't trying to smother your girlfriend! And can you shift back, please! You're terrifying yelling at me like this!"

Jonah inhaled a deep breath, the muscles of his chest undulating.

Sorcha stepped between them. "Jonah," she said in a low voice. "Get hold of yourself. It's not her fault."

Darby moved to the bar counter, and sank down on a stool, shaking her head in slow torment, inhaling deeply, as though she was fighting tears. "This has never happened to me," she muttered softly. "What if it happens again . . ."

Jonah drew in a deep breath. His body turned back then, shifted in a blurring flash.

"It can't . . . if it does, then anyone with you is at risk," Jonah snapped.

The color bled from her face, and Sorcha knew what Darby was thinking then. Her family. Her friends. Any future family. A lover, husband, children . . . She could never have any of that and keep them safe from her.

"Sorcha." Darby looked at her then. "I'm so sorry."

"Of course," Sorcha cut in. "Do we have to talk about this now?" she asked quickly, her voice almost shaky. "I . . . think I need a shower."

"There's plenty to talk about," Jonah growled,

marching into the bedroom. He was back in an instant wearing a pair of boxers.

Facing them both again, he took his time glaring between them. "You," he said, pointing to Darby. "Go home. You're going to have to figure this out . . . talk with your aunts. You can't be around us, trying to hunt demons, when you're a ticking time bomb."

"Home? What about training Sorcha? You need bait to—"

"That's over." His gaze settled on Sorcha, intent, hard. "It was a bad idea from the start. We're finished."

Sorcha felt his words like a punch to the gut. She held her ground, masking the impact the words had on her.

"I can't train you anymore," he announced.

"You mean you won't," Sorcha corrected.

His eyes stared down at her, cold as ice. "Whatever. This isn't going to work. I've been kidding myself, kidding you."

"Jonah," Darby pleaded. "After what just happened, I need to be around you." Her face flushed, as though it embarrassed her to admit this. In that moment, Sorcha could not recall any of the jealousy she'd harbored toward the witch. She felt only pity.

She remembered Jonah telling her that this was

what he hated, what he could not tolerate. Someone *needing* him. Still . . .

She stared at him expectantly, waiting, certain he could not refuse Darby when she was in such desperate straits.

Jonah dragged his hand through his hair as if he would pull it out by the roots. "Don't you hear me? I just want to be left alone." Releasing his hair, he swung around on Sorcha, leveling on her a blistering glare—as if she was responsible for all this mess. "You need to go home, too."

"No." She shook her head slowly, wondering what had happened to him tonight. Why was he so angry? She was the one Darby had tried to smother. Where had the tenderness she felt whenever he touched her gone? She had grown accustomed to it. Craved it.

"Did you see what just happened?" He swiped a hand savagely through the air. "If I hadn't been here, that demon would have used Darby to kill you."

Indignation burned down her throat. "She wouldn't have killed me." She wasn't certain of that, but she felt the need to argue the point. She'd survived this long without Jonah, after all.

He pointed at her. "You're not a slayer. You can't pretend to be one. Go home." Something quivered deep inside her, a jagged, shuddering pain at the ring of finality in his voice, at his flat, dark stare. He was finished. Finished with her. "Just go. Pretend you and I never met up with each other again."

She drew a deep, wounded breath, getting it at last. Understanding. He was afraid. Afraid to get involved, afraid of being needed. And failing. "I took you for many things," she whispered, "but never a coward."

He jerked back, flinched as if she had reached out a hand to slap him, but then he changed direction, came at her, an angry light in his eyes.

"Jonah!" Darby's voice rang out, stopping him cold.

He inhaled sharply and looked at Sorcha, standing there as if he didn't even know her. With a shake of his head, he growled, "Go to your room, Darby. Start packing."

For a moment, they all held still, emotions swirling thickly around them.

Then Darby finally moved, her voice tight and small, her eyes suspiciously bright. She looked like such a little girl that Sorcha felt a surge of protectiveness toward her. But before Sorcha could do anything, Darby was gone, vanishing into her room.

Alone with Jonah, Sorcha looked down, glared at the wood floor as if she saw something there in its swirling pattern, something that made sense out of why he was sending her away.

She shook her head in frustration, her hands curling open and shut into fists at her sides. It was happening all over again. *Damn him*. "Why can't I stay and train?"

"This isn't for you. I know you're looking for purpose, meaning . . . but this will only get you killed."

She laughed brokenly, inhaling through her nose and catching his scent in the shirt she wore—his shirt. She'd put it on sometime during the night, cold in bed beside him.

"Look," he bit out. "I want us to part knowing that I didn't set you on a course that's going to get you killed."

"You, you, you," Sorcha hissed. "We're discussing my life. I'm not a little girl anymore whose fate is in someone else's hands . . . it's not in *your* hands anymore, Jonah." Bitterness filled her as she glared at him, absorbing the tiresome truth of that statement.

He stared at her steadily for several moments, his gaze cool and unflinching. "You know, when I first saw you—when I realized it was you—I was so glad, so relieved that you were alive." He blinked long and hard before reopening his eyes, settling them brightly on her.

Their gazes clung. She held her breath, not wanting to ruin this moment. He had shared so little with her. Just his body. Never any other piece of himself. For once, she felt that she was seeing the real him.

"I'm not sending you to your death now," he finished at last, his voice as resolute as she had ever heard it.

Crossing her arms, she thrust out her chin, determined that he not slip away, that she not lose this moment, this closeness . . .

"Maybe I like it here too much to go." Dropping her arms, she pushed out her chest, letting the hard points of her breasts pebble against the cotton of Jonah's shirt. "Maybe *you* like me too much to let me go."

He moved before she could blink, grabbing her by both arms and nearly lifting her off her feet. "Can't you see you're making a fool of yourself? Staying here when I don't want you?"

She flinched. His words drove dangerously near the old wound. Her cheeks heated with the stinging memory of her sisters, quick to tease her for trailing after him. Or watching him. Or inventing excuses to talk to him.

His voice continued, sharp as a whip. "This thinking you can be a slayer when you're not is pathetic, Sorcha." He shook his head. "Go. Just leave me alone and go. I never wanted you here. I never asked you to come knocking on my door."

"Then you'll have to let go of me," she hissed between her teeth, certain if he didn't unhand her in that moment, she would do him harm, come at him with teeth bared and fingers clawing. *I never wanted you here.* Who knew he could be so cruel again? She would never have thought it. "It looks like my father taught you well after all. You're an expert at being a real shithead."

His gaze burned her up. "Yeah." He nodded, the motion jerky, fierce. "You won't be alone for long. Enjoy your money. Why don't you find a boy gigolo?"

"Bastard." Her hand whipped up, fingers curled, ready to claw his face. He caught her hand in a crushing grip, jerked her against him with an angry growl.

The tiny hairs on the nape of her neck tingled and she knew she had provoked him too far. His face flickered, blurred, his eyes flame-bright.

The air changed subtly, thickened, grew electric. He snatched both her wrists and pushed her back into the bedroom. Shoving her on the bed, he pulled her hands above her head.

"What are you doing?" she demanded as he pressed the hard length of his body down over hers.

His unsmiling face stared down at her, watching her intently as his head dropped. She dodged his mouth.

His eyes narrowed to slits, mouth thinning into a grim line. Releasing her wrists, he flipped her over on the bed, crushing her beneath him. His breath warmed her neck, puckering her flesh. A small, tantalizing shiver rippled through her.

He grasped her hips in rough hands, pulling them up slightly from the bed. A gasp escaped her as he nudged her thighs apart. She wore nothing except his shirt. Nothing barred her from him.

"What are you—" Her voice froze, trapped in her throat as his hands slipped beneath her, up and under her shirt to fondle her breasts. The hard bulge of him prodded at her ass.

His fingers rolled, tweaked and squeezed her nipples into rock-hard points. Desire pooled low in her belly. A keening moan escaped her. She turned her face and rested one cheek against the cool sheets, unable to move, unable to resist the delicious assault.

Then his hands fell away.

She moaned in disappointment. Until she felt him yank her shirt higher. Cool air caressed her. His hand traveled over the backs of her thighs, her ass. A hissing cry escaped her when he slid down and nipped at her quivering cheeks. His hand slid between her legs, fingers probing, pushing deep inside her from behind.

She came out of her skin, sobbing into the bed as his fingers worked inside her, in and out in erotic drags. Then his touch vanished. An anguished whimper ripped from her throat, swallowed up in the pulsing night. She bit her bottom lip, waiting, desperate for what was to come, what she had thought she would never have again because he'd just told her to get out of his life.

Her body burned, ached, trembling between the hard press of him and the bed.

Strong hands grasped her hips, fingers digging into her softness, lifting her to accept the sudden, hot push of him sliding home inside her. He penetrated her deeply and a scream welled up in her throat.

His hands shifted, hauling her up almost to her knees, angling her for deeper invasion, anchoring her for each of his thrusts. She clawed the mattress, fighting for a handhold, leverage. Her knees felt like water. Only his hands on her hips kept her from sliding flat on the bed in a shuddering, boneless pile.

Cries tore from her mouth at the slick heat of him working over her. He lifted her higher. His breath came hard and fast in her ear as he ground into her.

One of his hands skimmed her hip, sliding around, dipping to find that spot between her thighs begging for attention. He knew her body so well. She gasped as his fingers worked, moving in fast little circles against her clit until she broke, shattered, convulsed beneath the man who had become her entire world. *Again.*

A few more powerful thrusts and he stilled, buried to the hilt. A mixed sense of elation and horror grabbed hold of her heart, squeezing tightly. A bitter wave rolled over her. He'd just told her he wanted her to leave, so what the hell was this? A farewell screw?

Feeling used and not a little unclean, she lifted her cheek from the bed and gazed dully at the headboard, the ceiling, anywhere. Moonlight washed the walls, tingeing the plaster blue.

He brushed the back of her neck, and she shuddered. "Sorcha—"

"No," she choked out, loathing for herself—for him—burning up her throat as she squeezed out from beneath him, wrestling her shirt back down. Her hands shook as she rose to her feet beside the bed. "Don't even talk to me. Don't speak!"

Something flickered in his gaze but he didn't say a word.

She looked away from his face. That's what got her in trouble. That damn handsome face made her knees go weak.

She stalked to his closet and pulled out her luggage, trying to ignore the wetness between her thighs.

"What are you doing?" He hadn't moved from the bed.

"You're talking," she snapped.

"Sorcha." He said her name with a ring of warning.

"I'm leaving. Just like you told me to do." Tossing her suitcase onto the bed, she swept what belongings she could find into it. "You just had your last bit of fun with me. Now strikes me as a good time to go."

"It's three A.M. I didn't mean you had to leave right now. You can leave in the morning."

"And spend one more moment with you? Or are you hoping for another roll in the sheets with your *pathetic* little fuck buddy?"

"Don't be irrational—"

"I'm not. The airport's open." She moved about the room with long strides, changing clothes and tossing the last of her belongings into her suitcase, careful never once to glance his way, too afraid of what she might see. Of what *he* might see if she looked him straight in the eyes.

After several moments of being ignored, he left her and moved into the living room. She breathed easier and took a moment to collapse on a chair near the window and pull herself together so that by the time she emerged, she would be as calm and composed as any woman ending an affair would be.

Could she even call it an affair? Didn't an affair need to last longer than a week?

He sat on the couch, facing the window, studying the night as if something held his attention out there. She pulled her suitcase to the front door and hovered there for a moment, wondering whether to speak. Was there anything left to say? It seemed he had said it all.

With a grimace, she reached out a hand for the door.

"Sorcha." It was Darby.

She turned at the soft voice, almost eagerly, even though it wasn't Jonah who had spoken her name. Still, it was something. A reason to linger in the same room as him for another moment. This might be the last time she ever saw him.

Darby stood in the doorway of her room, clutching the hem of her nightshirt. She looked pale, her red hair a stark contrast to her wan, oval face. "Where are you going?"

Sorcha smiled and felt a stab of compassion for the white witch. She just might have it worse than Sorcha. Darby had a hard road ahead of her. What did you do when demons invaded your dreams and took over your body? What *could* be done?

"Away from here."

If possible, Darby's expression grew more pitiable.

"Good luck, Darby. I hope . . . You're going to be all right."

With a parting glance for Jonah, Sorcha opened the door and stepped out into the hall.

Darby's voice was muffled through the door. "Jonah! Stop her!"

Idiotic, but Sorcha hesitated before walking away for good, hoping that he might change his mind, that he might say something to indicate remorse. She would take that. Any crumb. Anything not to feel so bitter right now.

Several moments of silence passed before it sank in and she accepted it. He wasn't coming after her. *So get over it and stop acting like a fool, Sorcha.*

It wasn't as though she'd ever expected this to go anywhere with him. They'd both been up front about that from the start.

So why did she feel this deep ache in her chest? A gnawing pain that mirrored nothing she had ever felt before. As if he were dead to her all over again.

SEVENTEEN

Jonah! Stop her!"

It was several moments before he answered Darby, long after he sensed Sorcha had left the building. He knew the moment she was gone. It was as if all the energy had been sucked from the room with her. All the enlivening warmth, all life.

Darby glared at him, hands propped on her hips.

"Stay out of it, Darby." He drummed his fingers on the arm of the chair. The bay loomed far below and beyond that, a thousand winking lights. Somewhere, Sorcha was out there, hailing a cab, on the way to the airport. Away from him. Safe. All this crazy demon-hunting business firmly behind her. That was best. *Right*. No matter the ache in his chest.

Darby snorted. "I'm supposed to buy that you're okay with her leaving?"

"I don't care what you think. Tomorrow, you're leaving, too. And I'll have my life back."

"What life?" she hissed.

"My life. The one I want."

"You want *her*."

He flinched, then remembering, demanded, "And why should you care so much? You're the one who prophesied that she would kill me." For a moment, she looked perplexed, her brow wrinkling. "Did you forget that?" he demanded.

"No. Of course not." She shook her head. "Only, any fool can see she cares about you. My vision couldn't have been right. The course isn't set in stone."

"You're always right," he reminded her. "Never been wrong before about what you see."

She shrugged uneasily. "Things change . . . choices . . . my visions can be averted."

He shook his head and dragged a hand down his face, noticing that his skin felt cold. Far colder than when Sorcha had been here.

He wasn't worried about Sorcha killing him. That was not why he'd shoved her out of his life, why he'd said those things. Treated her like such shit. Even if she was still here, he couldn't imagine her harming him. Not deliberately. Her heart was too big, too soft. A lot had changed about her, but not that.

"You'll regret this," Darby murmured. Her voice carried an ominous ring.

Scowling, he watched as she disappeared back

into her room. He wouldn't regret it. Because it had been the right thing to do.

For years he'd thought Sorcha dead . . . and held himself partly to blame. He wouldn't go through that again. Tonight put it all in perspective. He wouldn't train her to fight demons she couldn't even see to target. He wouldn't lead her into certain death. He had failed to protect her the last time. This time he wouldn't fail. No matter how much he wanted her.

Sighing, he nodded once, decisive and satisfied despite the wrenching in his gut. She'd been ripped from him before and he had survived. He would survive this, too, he vowed. "Good-bye, Sorcha."

SEVERAL STORIES BELOW JONAH'S condo, Sorcha lifted her face upward in the misting sky. "Good-bye, Jonah."

And this time, she meant it. For once, finally, she would bury him in the past.

His words echoed through her. *Go. Just leave me alone and go. I never wanted you here.* Those words permanently laid him to rest.

The future yawned before her. Even if it was devoid of Jonah, it was far from empty. She had purpose, a goal.

Tresa was still out there. And Gervaise still deserved vengeance.

EIGHTEEN

Sorcha wrapped her cashmere scarf around her neck twice and burrowed her head low against the brisk evening wind. "I think I would like to walk home from here, Richard." She winced at the hollow sound of her voice. She couldn't even seem to sound . . . *alive*. Not since Seattle, not since Jonah. Back in New York, she couldn't shake off this melancholy. Blinking suddenly burning eyes, she forced a smile for her date.

The blond, blue-eyed Adonis at her side pulled a pretty pout and mock-shivered into his coat. "Sorcha, darling, it's much too chilly to walk. Besides, I thought we'd go to the theater."

Sorcha shook her head. "Dinner was lovely, but I'm still tired from traveling. A bit jet-lagged, I think."

"But you don't go out very often." True. She'd emerged from her loft in Soho hoping for distraction while she waited for the private investigator she'd hired to contact her with information on Maree.

Since their last dealings, the witch had mysteriously vanished, packed up all her things and abandoned her apartment. Clearly, someone or something had gotten to her, leaving Sorcha without any leads on where to find Tresa.

She usually avoided going out this close to a full moon, as lycans grew more aggressive then, but she couldn't stand the silence or endless space of her loft. It felt too lonely, and her thoughts echoed loudly in her head. Thoughts of Jonah thousands of miles away, on the other side of the country and quite happy to be rid of her. His cruel words reverberated through her head in a terrible litany.

The city, activity, people, had seemed like a good idea, a good escape from the noise in her head. Only it wasn't working. It was as though Jonah's memory burned brighter, the echo of his voice rang louder, rising over the city's restless purr.

Richard seized her hand, lacing their fingers intimately. Before, she wouldn't have minded the gesture. Before, she would have taken whatever comfort his body could give her. Only now his touch made her feel faintly ill, heightening the empty feeling inside her. She slipped her hand from his.

His pout turned into a genuine frown. "I'm sure you're starved for company. All your friends miss you. I still don't understand why you had to sell your penthouse." Jonah's face flashed across her mind. She was starved only for him—damn his soul.

Richard arched his eyebrows and used a coaxing tone. "Good times. Good theater. And afterward . . ." His eyes darkened to a deeper shade of blue. *Afterward, good sex*. That was his clear suggestion.

She stifled a sigh. What else would he think? He was one of the two men she'd let in her bed. Gervaise's estate attorney, he'd been invaluable to her. After Gervaise's death, she'd accepted the invitation that had always been in his eyes. She knew he would like nothing more than to take their relationship to the next level. She'd entertained before the notion of them in a more permanent arrangement. But she knew it could never last even in those fleeting moments when she'd played with the idea. They could never have a future. She could never have a future with anyone.

Her life loomed ahead of her . . . a string of empty encounters and empty relationships. She swallowed against the sudden thickness in her throat. At least she still had her mission. Tresa was still out there.

Sometime in the next year she would have to relocate, move far away, hire a new firm to handle the estate. She was twenty-six, but looked more like twenty. She couldn't stay any longer, couldn't raise suspicions. She had to start over. Maybe this time out west. Nowhere near Jonah, of course. He wanted nothing to do with her. She would not be desperate enough to chase him around like a starved little puppy.

"The night's still young. And so are we, Sorcha," Richard coaxed.

She stepped back, edging away and laughing lightly. "Well, tonight I feel old."

"Oh, that's tragic. You can't call it quits after such a glorious dinner. Let me take you out. It doesn't have to be the theater. There's a wonderful new club in the East Village." His eyes glinted and he leaned his golden head toward her. "Or we can be alone. Go back to my place. Let me make you smile again."

To oblige him she smiled, the curve of her lips brittle on her face. She reached out a gloved hand and stroked his cheek fondly, wondering why she couldn't love someone like him. Someone handsome and uncomplicated. Kind and flirty. Then she remembered. Not that she ever forgot. He was human. She was not.

He'd be terrified at the truth of her, at the sight of her in full shift . . . at what she was beneath her pretty, shiny exterior.

"Good night, Richard. Another time."

He held his hands over his heart. "Please let me at least take you home in the car."

She buried her hands in her coat pockets. "Thank you, but I want to walk. It will do me good." She blew out a gust of frothy breath. With a small wave she turned and left her blond Adonis standing alone outside the restaurant.

Crossing the street, her booted heels clicked over the sidewalk, skillfully skirting grates as she weaved through people out for the night. She paused a moment outside the salon Gervaise had first taken her to when she was seventeen, shortly before they married.

She sniffed and rubbed at her cold nose, determined not to cry, not to feel sorry for herself. There was nothing wrong with being alone. Plenty of people were alone. They led perfectly contented lives. And who was to say it would be like this forever? She shook her head, disgusted with her forlorn thoughts.

Gervaise had thought her amazing, beautiful, in any shape or form. He'd insisted that she keep herself open to the possibility of love. He didn't think it necessary for her to hide what she was, but then Gervaise never could see the existence of evil in others.

She dare not expose herself. Ever. Mankind had a history of persecuting anyone deemed "different." She couldn't bring herself to trust a human. She couldn't bring herself to trust *anyone*. She'd stumbled upon Gervaise quite accidentally. She didn't count on that kind of tolerance from anyone. Hell, she hadn't even found it with Jonah.

Moving away from the salon, she hurried from the familiar sights that reminded her so much of Gervaise, eager to return to her loft.

The waxing moon followed her, peeping out between bony tree branches.

She thought about the tundra again, about Tresa's comfortable lodge there, a haven nestled within that hard, relentless ice world.

She'd lost her chance to kill the witch. And her demon. Jonah believed the risk of freeing Tresa's demon was too great. He was wrong. Still living, she wrought her evil at the behest of a demon. How was that any better?

Suddenly Sorcha stopped, stared ahead unseeingly in a sudden moment of clarity. Maybe she hadn't lost her chance entirely. Surely Tresa would return there. She'd left her life there. Her clothes, her belongings, everything. And she felt safest in the cold, where she had more autonomy from her demon. Even if Tresa didn't return, maybe there were clues. Something that indicated where she might go next.

Sorcha's pace quickened, her heels clicking

sharply, matching the sudden racing rhythm of her heart. A renewed purpose flowed through her, fortifying, heartening her as nothing else had since she'd left Jonah.

She knew exactly what to do.

NINETEEN

If possible, the tundra seemed even more desolate the second time around. Sorcha's wind-chapped lips twisted in the cold-burned air. But then, it hadn't been too desolate the last time. She'd confronted all manner of life: Tresa, Jonah, a lycan and his mercenaries.

She approached the lodge slowly, her boots crunching over dead, ice-singed earth. Subarctic wind whipped over the ground in curling drafts the color of smoke. She bit back the guilt rising inside her. She owed Jonah nothing. He'd sent her packing with no thought. So why did each step she took toward Tresa's lodge feel like a betrayal of him?

Shaking her head, she cleared it of thoughts of Jonah. This was for Gervaise.

A tarp covered the lodge's broken door. Pushing it aside, she entered the dim confines and saw that the fabric had done little to shield the structure from the harsh elements. Ice covered almost every surface. Even snow had managed to gather and pile up in the forgotten corners.

"Guess Tresa didn't come back," she muttered to herself, disappointed even though the hope had been slim.

Undefeated, she walked into the deep shadows, determined to unearth something, some clue that would lead her to the witch. Her tread rang hollowly in the house as she strolled over the hardwood floor. She eyed her surroundings, looking at everything with fresh eyes, trying to see the house as a home, as Tresa had seen it.

In the bedroom, she inhaled and caught a faint whiff of the cursed witch, a lingering earthy aroma, woodland grasses and fresh-tilled earth. The wind howled outside, a forlorn sound, like the howl of some beast haunting the snow-craggy terrain. She approached the bed, brushed her gloved fingers over the bedside table, leaving a streak in the layer of icy frost. Shaking her head, she forced herself into action. She lifted the small pile of books on the bedside table and examined them, flipping through the pages of each one. Tresa was a reader. Mystery, nonfiction, the occasional biography.

Sorcha slid open the drawer and thumbed through two journals, each written in a language she was not familiar with. She tucked them into her large coat pockets for later dissection. From there, she moved on, searching the rest of the bedroom.

She was rummaging in the closet when she stilled. Cocking her head to the side, she listened. Nothing. Not a sound. And that was the trouble. Even the wind seemed to have slowed to a stop. She dropped the clothing in her hands and turned, facing the open door. Slowly, she stepped over the threshold.

Had Tresa returned, tamed the winds with her corrupt magic? Or could it be Jonah? Her lips wobbled, tempted to smile if it was him. Heart hammering in her too-tight chest, she peered into the dark bedroom.

The empty bedroom stared back at her. Bit by bit, the tension eased from her shoulders. No Tresa. No Jonah. Something closely resembling disappointment settled in her stomach. Still, the quiet was oppressive. She walked through the bedroom and into the living room. No howling wind.

Shaking her head, she turned to finish searching the bedroom and stood face-to-face with a total stranger. Beyond him loomed three others, dark-swathed figures with an aura of menace, of barely leashed violence. Their pewter gazes drilled into her, marking them instantly.

She held herself perfectly motionless, shoving down the rising tide of panic. Her skin tightened and her core heated, vibrating. She smelled them then. A subtle, distinct odor, as coppery as fresh-spilled blood. The blood of their kills coursed through them. They smelled of evil.

Alone, facing the four lycans made her feel small and weak. Defenseless. They were big, well-fed males who dominated the room, ate up all the space.

"What do you want?" she asked in a surprisingly steady voice.

They exchanged looks.

"We've come for the witch," a gravelly female voice announced. A woman stepped forward, her voice ringing with authority. "Where is she?"

Sorcha turned, eyeing the older female. With gray-streaked hair, she looked more like a librarian than anyone who hung around these killers. Inhaling deeply, Sorcha immediately picked up on the fact that while she wasn't human, she wasn't lycan either.

"I'm looking for her, too," Sorcha said, hoping to position herself as an ally—not an enemy. They outnumbered her. Her best chance of getting out of the situation unscathed was to let them think she was useful.

The female looked around again, assessing, her keen eyes missing nothing. The motion stirred the air, kicking up a pungent aroma of loamy woods. "Appears she hasn't been here for a while."

"You mean we came all this way for nothing?" one of the lycans griped.

"She was here not that long ago," Sorcha began. "I can—"

"Not for nothing," the witch announced, looking at Sorcha in a way that made the hairs on the back of her neck stand up. Angling her head, she gazed intently at Sorcha. "There's you."

"Me?"

"A dovenatu is a rare find. That's what you are, isn't it?" She didn't bother to let Sorcha confirm before continuing. "Even if we didn't find Tresa, we'll not return empty-handed. We'll have you."

Sorcha swallowed, her muscles tensing, readying for battle. "And what do you want me for?"

The witch smiled then, her lips pulling back in a slow stretch over her teeth. "You'll see." She flicked her fingers toward Sorcha. "Gentlemen, escort our guest to the vehicle." They moved in as one, a great menacing wall.

Sorcha focused her attention on them, kicked the one nearest square in the gut, sending him from her like a launched missile. Spinning around, she kicked the next one.

The final two charged, closing in.

"Leave her be." They stopped abruptly at the terse command.

How was it she controlled them? She approached Sorcha with a benign smile on her sun-browned face. "We want to bring her home in good condition, after all."

Curious and bewildered, Sorcha looked the female up and down. "Who are you?" *What* was she that she could command a group of lycans?

She lifted a hand, the motion unthreatening, almost elegant. "You'll be a wonderful addition. He'll be very pleased, don't you think, boys?"

He who?

The lycan Sorcha had launched across the room limped to her side and rasped in her ear, "Yeah. She'll be great in the arena. Excellent bait."

Arena? Sorcha shook her head, uncomprehending. "What are you talking about?"

"We may not have Tresa, but we have you." The woman flashed a bright smile, her teeth white as plaster. Then she lifted her hand higher, stopping it before Sorcha, curling and uncurling her fingers as if she were grasping something on the air. Something invisible to Sorcha, but it was there. Sorcha felt the change in the air current. A tinny thinness. Her skull began to pound, a twisting pain squeezing at her temples. A warning buzz filled her head. Enough. Time to get out of here.

She jerked back a step, willing her feet to move, run . . . speed had always been her ally before—

Nothing.

Her gaze slid down. Her arms wouldn't move. Her body had issued the command, but nothing. The buzzing grew, centering in her forehead.

She tried to move again, concentrating on making her limbs cooperate. Her lips moved silently with fervent words. *Go, run, go . . .*

She moistened suddenly dry lips. "What—" The word came out a croak. She stopped and swallowed. Tried again. "What are you doing to me?"

"Relax, pet," the female soothed, her voice far away against the incessant buzz in Sorcha's head. She stroked a hand down her cheek. Sorcha lacked the will even to flinch from the abhorrent touch. "I'll take care of everything."

Then, Sorcha saw it. The endless deep dark she'd seen in Darby's eyes the night she had tried to smother her with a pillow. The same blackness she saw in Tresa's gaze. The woman was a witch. A demon-possessed witch with the power to immobilize her prey. And Sorcha was that prey.

The buzzing in her head eclipsed all else. Gray edged her vision, thickening . . . thickening. Her limbs grew heavy, leaden, until two lycans moved to her sides to support her. She hung between them. She clung to consciousness, swimming hard toward the light.

The witch's voice reached her, a distant whisper.

"Relax, pet. Relax. And sleep. When you wake, you'll be in your new home."

ON A RIDGE FAR above the lodge, Tresa sat on the craggy snow-swathed earth, the cold seeping into her bones unpleasant, but a comfort nonetheless. The cold was the only thing keeping her demon at bay, the only thing that gave her any freedom, any protection. For her, subarctic temperature was as warming as any fleece blanket and roaring fire.

She watched her house, her disappointment deep and sharp, a cutting pain in her chest. She'd liked it here. She'd actually managed to stay here for quite some time before she'd been found. More fool she, she'd come to think of it as home. *Home.* As if such a thing would ever exist for her.

She grimaced and shook her head. Over two thousand years old, she should have known better. Known never to feel too comfortable, too secure. Peace and comfort were not part of her existence.

The lycans emerged into the swirling wind, a demon witch at the helm, and in their midst, the female. The dark-haired dovenatu Sorcha. Strangely, she didn't fight, didn't resist as she was hauled from the cabin. Tresa suspected it had something to do with the witch and her particular power.

For a moment, Tresa wondered what they

would do with Sorcha, but then familiar indifference crept back in. She couldn't afford to care.

It was enough to stay one step ahead of her pursuers. She was always hunted. For different reasons. For whatever they thought she could do for them, *bring* to them.

The group grew smaller, heading toward their vehicles, parked several miles away. Tresa smiled humorlessly. As if they could have hidden their approach from her, as if she didn't know when someone was near. How else had she lived these many centuries unscathed?

She released a heavy exhale, something akin to pity filling her chest as the unfortunate female was led away to her fate. Tresa doubted she would see her again.

Hopefully she would break free from whatever enchantment the witch had trapped her within and escape, but whether she did or not, it was her problem. Tresa no longer had room in her heart to care. It was enough to evade her demon and keep herself out of the wrong hands. That was all she could do to try to make things right.

Turning, she walked full force into the wind's teeth, embracing the cold, the loneliness that stretched before her for generations more.

TWENTY

His phone rang in the kitchen, the soft, lilting ring tone echoing in his condo. He didn't bother moving to answer it. With a beer bottle in his hand, he sat on his sofa and stared out at the city, alive and breathing far below him as he sat apart, distant, watching it as a spectator.

He finished his beer and rose, idly picked up his phone from the bar. Glancing down, he expelled a heavy breath. One missed call from Darby. He hadn't heard from her since she'd left, since he'd told her to go.

Holding the phone to his ear, he waited for her voice to flood over him and with it the reassurance that Darby was okay—that he hadn't thrust her out into a cold, hard world in which demons invaded her dreams and laid claim to her.

He'd thought about her almost as much as Sorcha, which only drove him deeper into a bottle.

Jonah, call me back when you get this. I had another vision. Sorcha's in trouble, Jonah! Real trouble. Jonah, she . . . Well, just call me back and I'll explain everything.

He folded his phone in his clenched hand, squeezing it so tightly the metal creaked, threatening to snap.

Sorcha's face flashed across his mind, her expression the exact moment he'd told her to get out of his life. That last sight of her had not ceased to plague him. He'd vowed to let her go, had believed saying those ugly things necessary to drive her away. All for the purpose of keeping her safe. He couldn't live knowing she was in danger somewhere . . . that he had released her into that.

Relaxing his grip around the phone, he punched in Darby's number.

SORCHA WOKE SLOWLY, WITH great effort, as if swimming upward from a pool of thick, gelatinous water.

The floor beneath her burned ice-cold into her body, penetrating her clothes, burrowing deep into her very bones. She lifted her cotton-stuffed head, peeling her cheek off the floor, wondering vaguely if she was still in Alaska, and then wincing with the sudden memory that, no, the witch and her lycans had taken her far from there.

She had vague recollections of jostling rides in the back of a van, and then, later, being transferred to a jet. Whoever this witch worked for had gone to great lengths to claim Tresa. Hopefully, he didn't have a fit when he learned he'd gotten only Scorcha.

Her last memory was being secured in a seat, the witch's voice lulling and mesmerizing in her ear, commanding her to sleep. Evidently more intoxicating than a tranquilizer.

Wincing, she opened her eyes a bit. The muted light felt like knives attacking her pupils. Her skull throbbed, pain jabbing from the top of her head down into her forehead.

Moaning, she sat up fully, reclaiming herself. With a deep breath, she assessed the small room she found herself in. Colorless and gray, no windows, a single cot propped against the far wall. A utilitarian toilet and sink that looked like they needed a good scrubbing. She tilted her head back and stared up at the single fluorescent light buzzing far above her head. A tiny chain dangled from it in the airless room. Dropping her head back down, she focused her attention on the steel door. A prison door, without a handle or latch.

Her shoes were missing, her feet and calves filthy, as if she'd been dragged over the ground. She wouldn't put it past the lycans who'd grabbed her, or the demon witch in league with them.

Standing, she approached the door, patted it all

over as if she might find a latch or a knob—or she might manage to budge it somehow. Impossible. A small square was located high in the door. A window, but it couldn't be opened from her side.

"Hello!" She beat her fists against the door until they grew numb. "Is anyone out there? Open this door!" After several minutes, she stopped, her arms aching and quivering. Turning, she slid her body down the door and buried her face in her hands. She rubbed her knuckles against dry eyes. A normal woman might succumb to tears at this point. But she'd never been normal. Hell, she wasn't even a woman. Not a human woman, anyway.

Lifting her face from her hands, a broken laugh swelled from her lips and spilled out, rusty and raw on the air.

"Ah, Jonah."

It was comical in a sad, twisted way. He thought she was putting herself at risk by training to hunt demons, and here she was, stuck in some dungeon at the mercy of lycans and a demon witch. Life was dangerous. Anywhere she lived it, anything she did. Too bad Jonah hadn't realized that. Of course, she was assuming that if he had, she would still be with him, warm in his bed. She was assuming he'd only sent her away because of her determination to hunt demons. Maybe if she had simply focused her energies on him—on *them*—he wouldn't have run her off.

Too late to wonder *what if* now. She dragged her hands down her face just as the bolt on the other side of the door lifted with a metallic clang.

She flew to her feet and turned, feet braced apart, ready for whatever emerged from the other side.

JONAH WAS ON THE verge of kicking in the door when it finally opened to his insistent knocking.

"Jonah?" Darby blinked groggily.

"Took you long enough," he growled.

"It's two in the morning." She rubbed a hand over her flattened hair.

"I got your message." He strode past her into her house. "Of course I'm here."

She dropped her hand from her head and looked at him tiredly, anger slowly arriving in her hazel eyes. "Well, yeah. Guess I wasn't too sure whether you cared. You did send Sorcha packing after all."

He stopped in the center of her living room and glanced at the suitcases waiting at the bottom of the stairs. He arched an eyebrow. "Going somewhere?"

She crossed her arms over her chest and shrugged.

"Darby," he prompted.

She dropped her arms. "Well, I can't stay here.

I talked it over with my aunts and we decided I needed to relocate someplace . . . safer."

Deep shadows were smudged beneath her eyes. She didn't look as if she'd been sleeping well, and he wondered if she'd slept at all since the demon had taken possession of her in his condo. "Relocate where?"

Her voice sounded tired, resigned, as she answered him. "I hear Greenland is pretty cold year-round."

"Greenland?"

"Well, what else should I do? Wait for the next demon to find me in my sleep?"

One of her aunts shouted down, "Darby! Who's here?"

"It's Jonah, Aunt Mel."

"Does he know what time it is? Put him up in the rose room. Tell him I'll make him my famous waffles in the morning."

She called back up to her aunt, "I'll do that. Go back to bed, Aunt Mel."

"Darby," he snapped. "Just tell me what you saw. Is Sorcha alive?" Because that was the only thing that mattered, the only thing that drove him right now. Finding Sorcha. Saving Sorcha.

"She's alive. I had two visions. One of her surrounded by snow, white winds. There was this old-looking cabin—"

A curse blew past his lips. "She went back after Tresa."

"I thought she was over that."

He shook his head roughly. He should have known Sorcha wouldn't let that go . . . that she wouldn't let Tresa go. Not after the witch murdered her husband. Not after Jonah shoved her from his life.

"What was the second vision?"

"In the second one she was in a city, far from the snow. They were speaking French. Paris, I'm pretty sure." Her smooth brow wrinkled in thought. "I didn't understand everything they said, but I understood . . . I knew their intent. They walked past a patisserie with a red door, turned into an alley, and then . . . darkness."

"They *who*?"

"Lycans. I recognized the silver eyes. And there was this demon witch. They took Sorcha—have her in some kind of . . . prison." She worked her fingers on the air, as if she were groping for something. "It's beneath the city. I think I can find it."

"What do they want with her?" He grabbed Darby by the arms, pulled her up from the couch where she'd dropped.

"They weren't looking to kill her. She's alive for now. How much longer, though, I can't say."

Nodding, he turned for the door.

Darby's voice reached out to stop him. "You won't find her. Not without me."

He turned slowly. As much as he didn't want to bring Darby along—she was a target for demons everywhere and he had to concentrate on saving Sorcha—he recognized that she was right. He needed her right now. He could track Sorcha down that much more quickly with her help. "Okay." He glanced at her luggage. "At least you're already packed."

THE STEEL HINGES CREAKED as the door swung inward. Sorcha took a quick step back as the witch from last night entered her cell.

"I thought I heard you awake down here."

"Where am I?" Sorcha demanded.

"Paris."

Sorcha glanced over the witch's shoulder, checking for lycans. Nobody. The demon witch was alone.

She poised herself on the balls of her feet, preparing to bolt. A vague sense of helplessness crept over her. Even if she could escape the witch's dark magic, Sorcha didn't know what waited for her outside these doors. But she couldn't stay here as a prisoner. That much she did know.

The witch clucked her tongue and wagged a finger at her. "Be careful. You don't want to run. Not unless you want more unpleasantness. I only gave you a taste of what I can do."

She forced herself to relax her stance. Or at least *appear* relaxed. Defeated.

How would Jonah handle the situation? Somehow the thought of him right then gave her strength. Maybe it was because he was safe, far from here. He lived. He would manage to survive. And so would she.

Reaching behind her out the door, the witch grabbed a bucket of water by its handle and set it inside the room. "Here you go. Make yourself presentable, and wear these."

Only then did Sorcha notice the bundle of clothing in her arms. On top of the pile rested a pair of leather boots.

She thrust out her chin. "What if I refuse?"

The witch smiled with those brilliant white teeth. "You don't want to do that. It will only hurt your chances."

"My chances?"

"In the arena."

"The arena," she echoed dumbly, remembering then what the lycan had said in Alaska about her being great in the arena.

"Yes. You're scheduled to compete tonight, and I think you've got a good chance despite your opponent's winning streak." The witch cocked her head. "There's something about you. You're strong. You're not the prize Tresa would have been, but you're nothing to sneeze at either."

Sorcha shook her head, bewildered. "I don't understand."

"You all say the same thing. Really, though, when you think about it, it's not that difficult to comprehend."

A sinking dread began to take hold, clenching Sorcha's stomach into knots as suspicion took root. She sniffed, smelled the stench of lycans on the air. And others buried deep beneath the earth with her. Others, but not humans. All of them close, nearby.

"I see you're starting to get the picture." She turned back to the door.

Sorcha lunged, intent on escape. The witch turned suddenly, her hand raised high. As if she were some mesmerist, she curled and uncurled her fingers several times, working them over the air. A familiar buzzing filled Sorcha's head.

Without the witch saying a word, Sorcha heard her, felt her silent command seize hold. As if she were nothing but a puppet to be led and controlled, she began undressing. In front of the witch she removed every stitch of clothing until she shook, naked in the chill room. Her skull pounded, and the twisting pain in her temples made her want to weep.

She glared into the witch's demon-dark eyes,

despising her for her power, her *gift*. Whatever demon possessed her must revel in her talent. A talent that held Sorcha hostage, that she couldn't even attempt to fight.

"Is it worth it?" Sorcha asked, relieved that she still possessed the ability to speak. Powerless to resist, she moved toward the bucket of water and began washing herself with the sponge, wincing at the bite of icy water.

"Is what?"

"Selling your soul," Sorcha bit out.

"Ah." The witch tilted her head thoughtfully. "You know how it works, then. No surprise, I guess. I did find you at Tresa's." She fluttered a hand. "My demon loves this little operation, so he leaves me to my own devices."

Sorcha sneered. "You must be pretty sadistic when your demon can't come up with anything worse for you to do than what you would want to do anyway."

The witch laughed, the sound grating. "That's about right. My only regret is waiting this long to contract with a demon. I could have been immortalized at twenty-two instead of fifty-two. I held out much too long. And for what?"

Damp and shivering from her cold sponge bath, Sorcha quickly donned the pants, top and armored vest. "The matter of your soul, I suppose," she retorted. "That's what keeps most witches from selling out."

"Who needs a soul or God's favor if you're going to live forever?" The witch angled her head. "I hope you make it in the arena. Half the scum down here can't do much more than grunt their names. *You* I can talk to. You'd be nice to have around. For a while anyway."

She turned toward the door again, and the tightness in Sorcha's skull began to ebb. "Wait." Sorcha took a struggling step forward, desperate for some idea of what was to come. "What's this arena you keep talking about?"

"I'll return for you later," the witch called over her shoulder. "The gamekeeper likes to meet every competitor before they enter the games. He'll tell you what you need to know."

"Wait!" Sorcha called out. "Who's this game-keeper? What games?"

As the door clanged shut, the pain in her head stopped completely and she was able to move, to surge forward and pound out her frustration on the door.

After several moments, it became clear that she was only exhausting herself. The witch was not returning. Sorcha collapsed on the cot, feeling drained, spent. In a matter of moments, she sank into sleep.

TWENTY-ONE

Sorcha rolled over on the bed and stretched long and slow, feeling the pull deep in her muscles. Gradually, she blinked her eyes open. Stared at the bright fluorescent bulb dangling at the center of the room. The nape of her neck tingled, kicking her into alert. She was not alone. Frowning, her gaze darted around.

With a gasp, she sprang into a sitting position, rubbing the last of the sleep from her eyes and glaring at the witch. "You again?"

"Did you sleep well? Excellent." The demon witch nodded as though Sorcha had answered. "Follow me. It's time." And then she was gone and the door yawned open.

Sorcha remained on her cot for a moment before rising and stepping out into the eerily silent corridor. The demon witch was still there, waiting for her, a vacant smile plastered on her face.

Sorcha crossed her arms over the stiff armored vest she wore. Sometime during the night, when she woke briefly, a peace had settled over her. Calm, cool resolve. She had little power against the demon witch. She needed to stay sharp, needed to watch. Learn and observe everything . . . play by the rules of her enemies until she learned their weakness. Then, she would make her move. Break and escape . . . or strike and kill. Whatever was necessary.

"Where are we going?" she asked.

"It's time for you to meet the gamekeeper. He evaluates all the new recruits before putting them in the field. He prefers to assess your worth so that he can best decide your role in the games."

Sorcha bristled at the thought of anyone judging her worth . . . like some slave monger. "And who's this gamekeeper?" Really, she was asking *what* he was. After coming face-to-face with both lycans and a demon witch, she couldn't imagine a human commanding such a crew.

Above them, a train roared. Sorcha braced herself, her legs apart. For a moment, it appeared the very walls shook.

"All you need to remember is that the gamekeeper is someone very important. He's in charge. You'll only help yourself if you make a good impression."

"Why aren't you in charge?" Sorcha looked the deceptively frumpy woman up and down. "You're certainly powerful enough—"

The witch slid her a sly glance. "I don't choose to be. Let's just leave it at that." Turning, she vanished down another corridor. After a moment of hesitation, Sorcha hurried after her.

"Why not?" she persisted, following close on her heels. Their steps fell flatly on gray concrete.

"You're full of questions."

"I like to be informed." All the better to learn about her enemies.

"You're just nosy . . . looking for a way out of this. You all are. Full of questions in the beginning. I'll tell you what all the players come to realize: there is no way out of this. The only thing left is to survive. Remember that. If you want to make it, train, study your opponents. Just don't die."

They cleared a door and passed through a wide room with benches bolted into the floor. In several spots chained manacles extended from the walls, the bracelets wide open at the moment, dangling. Empty. But waiting. She rubbed her wrists as she passed, almost imagining herself chained and sitting on one of those benches.

"This is the holding area." The demon witch waved to the room. "You'll spend plenty of time in here. Unchained if you behave. Or chained." She shrugged as if it mattered little to her.

"What's your name?" Sorcha demanded, desperate, digging for a connection, an advantage, something, anything to hold on to.

The demon witch glanced back at her, her smile revealing a flash of white teeth, a stark contrast to the coppery, well-lined skin of her face.

"Ingrid," she answered. "Not that it's important for you to know. The only thing you need to be concerned about is following the rules. And winning in the arena."

Several doors lined the room's walls. Ingrid took one that led up a winding set of stairs.

"This will be the most important meeting of your life," Ingrid continued. "Let your attributes shine. You're attractive. Clever. Play it up. If he thinks you're an asset, he'll strive to keep you around longer."

Around longer . . . She meant alive. With cold clarity Sorcha understood that at once. Just as she acknowledged that she would do whatever she had to. *To make it.* To see Jonah again. Because now she got it. Now she realized she wanted that more than anything else. She wanted *him.* Even more than revenge on Tresa.

The stairs ended. Ingrid stopped before a door. "Here we are. Any questions before we go in?"

"Yeah." Sorcha lifted her chin. "Tell me, Ingrid. Do you give everyone this little pep talk and do they actually believe you give a shit about whether they live or die?"

Ingrid smiled, pushing the door open. Instead of answering, she said, "Don't be nervous."

The room on the other side of the door was nothing like what she had seen since waking up in this nightmare. It had all the elegance and prestige of a prized private suite at a stadium. A bar and buffet were set against one wall, a uniformed waiter standing, ready to serve. Buttery leather chairs and couches sat in the middle of the room, arranged with precision on a Persian rug.

On the far side of the room gleaming glass stretched in lieu of a wall. Clean, pristine glass, winking and shining with light. She had forgotten that anything clean existed in this world.

On the other side of that glass a balcony extended out into the air. From where she stood, she couldn't appreciate the view. A half dozen cushioned chairs occupied the area. In one chair a man sat, his back to her. A thin cigarillo extended from his elegant hand. Her heart sped up, her pulse quickening in her throat. *The gamekeeper.*

He didn't move, although he must have been aware of their arrival. She recognized the beast in him. And he had to have recognized it in her. Scented it. Felt its arrival a few feet behind him.

A dovenatu ruled this little world?

He was like her. A dovenatu in charge of his very own little corner of hell. Why not? Her father had been a dovenatu and half mad, driven to all kinds of depraved schemes. A dovenatu wasn't always like her, like Jonah. She swallowed the painful lump in her throat at the thought of Jonah. Now wasn't the time . . .

It stood to reason some dovenatus were as rotten as their lycan brethren. *Worse*. Because at least a dovenatu had a choice. He wasn't ruled by hunger, possessed by moon fever. A dovenatu possessed free will. This dovenatu's free will led his goons to capture her and hold her hostage in a rotting little room. All for his pleasure.

Ingrid put a hand on her elbow. "Come. We don't want to keep him waiting. He hates that."

The nape of her neck shivered, scraped her flesh with a familiar dread at this comment. She shoved the sensation aside. Despite her anger and fear, her thoughts burned in a straight path, determined to make a good impression. Whatever that was. Until she managed to escape, he held her fate. She'd follow Ingrid's advice.

Ingrid slid the glass balcony door open with a *swoosh*. In the air, the clang of weapons rang out harshly. The balcony looked out over a small stadium of maybe three hundred seats. Far below, in the center of the arena, a barren stretch of sandy earth served as some sort of fighting grounds. Three men and two women practiced, ran through drills in full armor, putting forth an impressive display of skill.

Far below, six lycans stood guard at the single entrance into the area, a steel-barred gate between them and the practicing fighters.

Ingrid motioned for Sorcha to wait. The witch moved to stand beside the gamekeeper, waiting to be acknowledged as he clapped vigorously at the antics below.

The blood rushed in her ears, everything slowing to a crawl as he turned, still clapping, to face them. She gazed at his profile, a sick feeling slithering through her.

No. No, no, no.

He turned to face her, and she realized she had spoken aloud.

The gamekeeper stared at her, and she couldn't deny it. Not with those horribly familiar brown eyes drilling into her, so cold, dead and utterly mad. A madness she had seen before. Had lived with all the days of her youth.

A time, a life, she had fled and never thought to see again stared her in the face.

"Sorcha." Her stomach plunged and a hard

shudder racked her body. The breathy sound of her name on his lips brought a surge of bile to her throat. *No, no, no, no . . .*

Her father said her name again, stronger, firmer, full of delight. "Sorcha, my dear!"

Even though she had no possible chance of escape, she turned, a strangled cry choking from her lips as every horrible memory of the man bombarded her. She ran back into the elegant suite, intent only on escape.

The wild thought occurred to her, flitting like a frenzied moth through her head: *Again, again I'm running from my father, running for my life.*

As that awful, familiar buzzing filled her ears, forcing her legs to lock and wait for Ingrid's bidding, she knew. This time there would be no escape.

TWENTY-TWO

Stop.

The word wasn't uttered aloud, but she might as well have heard it spoken. Ingrid might as well have yelled it for all that Sorcha heard it and was forced to obey.

Without a sound, Ingrid pulled at something inside her, some force that Sorcha could not resist. She stopped. Her muscles locked tight and frozen, waiting for a command.

It was a terrible sensation. She couldn't move forward. Couldn't turn around and flee. She could only wait for Ingrid's bidding.

Ingrid's smoky voice rolled over the air. "Come here."

And like that, her muscles loosened, liquefied. She wasn't even certain if Ingrid spoke the command aloud or if she just heard it inside her head. Whatever the case, Sorcha moved, rotated on her heels. The control the demon witch wielded was total and complete. Sorcha might as well have been physically bound. She felt like one of those marionettes, only guided by chains instead of strings.

"Let me go!" she hissed between her teeth.

Ingrid shook her head, her look disgusted. "You know what I can do, so why do you even bother? You can't run. You can't escape. Why would you even think to try?"

How can I not? How can I stay and endure him? How can I share even one breath in the same space with him?

"I'm afraid that has everything to do with me." The voice rolled over her like liquid, terrible in its familiarity even after all these years.

There were some things one never forgot: faces, voices . . . the man who had given her nightmares for so long, who'd bred fear in her heart from an early age. She'd never forget him. Finding Jonah, he'd been in her head, lurking in the darkest corners. Because, face it, if Jonah was alive, she had wondered if her father could be, too. Now she knew.

Here she was. Here *he* was, his face unchanged. Handsome. All sharp angles. High cheekbones. The brown doe eyes like her own . . . down to the twisting light at the centers. A horrible beauty, unwanted, reviled. Lethal.

He moved forward with long-legged strides and

grasped both her shoulders. "Sorcha." He beamed at her as if they were long-lost friends enjoying a reunion. "You look lovely. I hardly recognize you . . . you look so like your mother when I first met her." He brushed her hair, fingering her bangs with a light touch. "She once wore her hair like this."

A shudder of revulsion racked Sorcha. She wanted to look nothing like Danae. Staring into his eyes, she knew it would be useless to deny her identity. Her reaction to him alone only served as confirmation. She shook like a leaf so close to him, gripped in his hands. Feeling like that frightened little girl all over again, she wished only to run.

Air hissed from her lips in barely suppressed loathing as he pressed a kiss to each cheek. She marveled at the warmth of his lips, that a man so cold could feel warm in any way.

Pulling back, he looked at her with delight brimming in his dead eyes. "I should be surprised, I suppose, but I'm not. I never believed it. Never thought I could have lost all of you in the explosion." He assessed her up and down. "You look well. Strong. Come, don't you have anything to say to your father?"

"Father?" Ingrid blinked, looked between the two of them, her mouth a small dark O against the tips of her blinding-white teeth.

"Yes. Sorcha is my eldest daughter. The others, my daughters, sons, my mate . . . all are dead." He said this so unfeelingly that she knew he hadn't cared when he'd learned of their deaths. If he'd suffered remorse at all, it would have been the loss of what they could bring him—not *them* specifically. He'd never loved them. "Maybe the others will turn up yet, hmm." His eyes gleamed with a faraway light and she recognized the madness there, still running strong. Maybe even stronger. "I do miss your mother," he murmured, as if reading some of her thoughts. "She was a comfort to me."

Sorcha felt little sorrow for the mother who had looked right though her, who had only ever been distant, aloof, indifferent to anyone except Ivo. She cared nothing for the children she gave him, nothing except that she made him happy providing him with offspring.

He drew Sorcha to a plush leather couch. "Good work, Ingrid. I take back all those nasty things I said to you when you didn't return with Tresa. We'll still find her, I've no doubt." He snapped at the waiter tucked in the corner. "Fetch another drink. Sorcha, what will you have?"

"Nothing. I'm fine."

"Nonsense. Are you hungry?" His lips twisted in a self-deprecating grin. The kind she'd seen politicians use on television. He could be that way.

All smiles one moment, then dangerous snarls the next. "I imagine the fare we provided you with earlier was merely palatable. Well, that's at an end now. What do you like? We have a wonderful pâté. Oysters on the half shell? Didn't you love seafood?" That had been her sister. Sorcha grimaced, remembering her sister flicking shrimp tails in her face and her father laughing.

"Nothing. Thanks."

He frowned at her and pinched her chin as if she were still ten. "Still difficult, I see. You always were a petulant little sourpuss."

She jerked her chin from his fingers and stared him straight in the eye. "Let me go. I want to go home."

"You are home. At last." He spread his arms wide.

She shook her head and edged back a step. "I have a life—"

He scowled. It was an expression she remembered well. She resisted pulling back in a flinch. "You're not striking the proper tone with me, Sorcha. A little gratitude, a little excitement at seeing me again, might be in order."

She sucked in a breath and glanced around. Anywhere but at him. "So. You're running . . . this enterprise."

"Yes, impressive, I know. Quite an operation.

Not what I originally planned for myself, but after Istanbul I count myself lucky to be alive. Hunters captured me, EFLA, the Federation—but I convinced them not to destroy me. That I could be useful to them. It wasn't easy, but I finally convinced them of my use. Eventually we came to this arrangement. I'm quite content. For now. It's marvelous—you'll see. The last games we could hardly fit everyone in the seats. We may need to expand soon. Open a second—"

She nodded toward the arena. "Who are the spectators?"

"Who else? Lycan hunters. They need their fun, too."

She faced him again. "It's disgusting. You deal in death, torture . . . and make it a grand game."

His smile vanished. And she was reminded of his fire-quick temper, the flashes of rage that would send her hiding in corners. "Still a judgmental little prig, I see. I had hoped that with age you might grow out of that. Grow and accept what you are. Pity."

"Apparently, I haven't."

He scowled. "If this is what you are, you might as well be dead to me."

"If it helps for you to forget me, then go ahead and do that. Think of me as dead." She stepped toward the door again. Ingrid inched closer, ever ready to rein her in, to work her cruel, will-robbing magic.

Her father held out a hand, stalling Ingrid, keeping her from intervening.

"You're right," Sorcha snarled, waving a hand about the elegant room. "I want no part of this. Or you. You haven't changed. You're as horrible as before. As mad."

A muscle flickered in his jaw, the only sign that her words affected him. "Sorry to hear that, Sorcha. Especially as you *will* have a great part in all this." A smile twisted his lips. "One way or another."

The nape of her neck prickled with warning.

"What do you mean?"

"You're my daughter, my legacy. Either join me and be a true daughter to me or . . ."

"Or . . ."

He motioned toward the arena. "You'll have a starring role."

She blinked. "You can't mean . . ." Her voice faded. Of course he could. Had she thought that because she was his daughter he might spare her? The way her father looked at her, she knew he meant every word.

"Take her to her cell." He looked at her, steady and intractable as a stone column, unmoved that he'd just resigned her to a ten-by-ten concrete cell. And beyond that, a fate in his damned blood games. "When you decide to be my daughter, just say the word, and I'll move you into more comfortable quarters. You're all I have left, Sorcha. I'll never release you."

His gaze shot back to his demon witch. "Get her on the fight schedule."

Surprise flickered across Ingrid's face. "You don't want to run her through practice for a few weeks first?"

"A daughter of mine won't need such preparation. She'll fight in the arena tomorrow."

With those words, Sorcha felt the noose settle firmly about her neck. Turning, she followed Ingrid from the suite. She didn't have a choice, after all.

In the distance, clanging swords and shouts filled the air from the arena far below, and she knew. Soon it would be her turn.

TWENTY-THREE

Their footsteps rang out over yet another cobbled walk. This late, the block was fairly deserted. The trees lining the footpath cast suspicious shadows as they walked. "You're certain it was Paris?" Jonah growled.

"I'm certain," Darby snapped.

He increased his pace. The wind whistled through the branches overhead.

"Would you mind slowing down?"

He merely grunted, his feet biting hard into the ground. He'd been like this ever since they'd arrived in the city. A machine driven to find Sorcha. He knew he was behaving less than logically, but he'd been the one to send Sorcha away—directly into danger. It ate at him, clouded his thinking. She hadn't wanted to go, but he'd forced her to. Shut her out of his life even though she'd wanted to stay. He'd failed her again. Just like before. Only if something happened to her this time, he would not be able to go on.

The irony, of course, was that he'd never *wanted* her to leave. He'd denied himself Sorcha by thinking that he was helping her. Doing the right thing. If he found her again—*when* he found her again—he would not let her go. She was his. Forever.

He nodded to himself, glancing around. "Does any of this look familiar?" Scanning the area, he motioned to the patisserie. The wood door was faded, more pink than red, but maybe . . . He could no longer recount how many patisseries they had visited since arriving three days ago, searching for one with a red door.

Even this late at night, the delicious aroma of baked bread encircled him. "Let's go over it one more time."

"Maybe, no . . . I don't think so. Jonah, they're all starting to look alike now." She flung her hands up in the air in frustration.

"It is or it isn't, Darby," he growled.

Darby's shoulders slumped and she moaned, "Jonah, I'm tired. It's late. Let's go back to the hotel." She strode ahead, her steps fierce slaps on the sidewalk.

He followed, not even close to quitting. Quitting meant quitting on Sorcha. Jonah seized Darby's arm the exact moment she jerked, coming to a halt. She pulled her head back, almost as if she were looking up at something, seeing something in all the winter-gnarled branches of the tree stretching over them.

He stepped around her cautiously, uttering her name quietly. "Darby?"

She stared upward without blinking. As if she hadn't heard him. As if she didn't know he was beside her at all.

He didn't speak again, merely waited, watching her as the moments crawled past. It could only have been a minute, but the time stretched agonizingly slowly as he waited for her return.

Finally, she sucked in a deep breath, as if emerging from a great pool of water. Blinking, she looked around, her eyes losing their glassy quality. "This is it, where they took her. She's here. Close."

Elation swelled inside his chest.

She turned, staring into the distance, into the memory of her vision. "The demon witch . . . she's powerful. Too powerful for Sorcha. For any of us. Sorcha can't beat her."

He'd given very little thought to the demon witch. He'd been more worried about the lycans who'd taken Sorcha. He'd fought hard not to think about them . . . with her all this time . . . the horror she could now be enduring at their hands. He knew what they could do to her. Moonrise was tomorrow. Whatever anguish she endured with them now would magnify then.

Darby closed her eyes for a long moment, as if still seeing it all in her mind. Her breath released in a slow shudder. She reopened her eyes and turned her head to look slowly around, as if finally returning to herself and the present.

"They took her that way." He stared where she pointed, at the dark alleyway the patisserie shared with an antiques shop. "There's a service entrance on the side of the antiques shop. They went through that door, to an elevator belowground." She focused her gaze on Jonah again. "But you can't go, Jonah. You'll never come out. You can't beat these monsters."

And there was more. He could read it in her eyes. He didn't have to think hard to come up with what it was. "You still see it?" His voice fell flat. "She kills me?"

She gave a jerky nod, her eyes dark in the shadows, full and gleaming. "I'm sorry, Jonah, but it's still the same as before. We've done nothing to change the future course of events."

So Sorcha would kill him? As Darby had first predicted.

He supposed there were worse ways to go. He lifted his face and exhaled, watching the white cloud of his steaming breath for a moment before nodding, a calming peace settling over him. As long as Sorcha lived, he would be at peace. "It's fine, Darby."

She grabbed hold of his arm. "She's already lost, Jonah. Don't you get that? And so are you if you press on." She bit her lip, her shoulders sagging. "It's all so hopeless. Maybe I should never have called you."

"I'm glad you did. I can't walk away and leave her to whatever fate—"

"Yes. I know," she choked, her voice a rough scrape on the air. Her eyes gleamed wetly up at him. "You love her and you'll go after her. And you'll die. And she'll still be in their prison. No one wins, Jonah."

"Wouldn't you want someone to come after you?"

A flicker of something passed over her face before she answered him. "Not if there was no hope. Not if it would put him at risk, destroy him. We need you, Jonah . . . I . . . do." She shook her head. "I might be lost, witout hope, but you can still help the covens. Isn't that more reasonable than following a useless cause?"

He'd let logic and reason get in the way before. That's what had led Sorcha into danger in the first place. Logic could go to hell for all he cared.

He touched Darby's face then, brushed his thumb against her cheek. "You've taken me this far. Thank you, Darby."

"Sure. Thank me for getting you killed."

"You've always been a friend to me, Darby, even when I wasn't much fun to be around. You got me to Sorcha. Whatever happens, I owe you for that. Go home . . . or wherever it is you need to be. And try to stay out of trouble."

She smiled weakly. "I can't ever seem to do that." Her smile slipped then. "I'm a witch. Trouble always finds me."

He dropped his hand from her face. "If I survive this, you know I'll always be there for you. If you ever need—"

"I know, I know." She nodded brusquely, her smile resurfacing as she burrowed her hands in her pockets and tossed her fiery hair. "I'll be okay. I'm tough, like you. I'll figure it all out. I hear they make excellent coffee in Greenland. Best in the world."

With a grim smile, he nodded, hoping she was right, hoping she would be okay.

Turning, he hurried away, redirecting his thoughts to Sorcha and how he was going to save her.

TWENTY-FOUR

When the elevator doors slid open, Jonah had no idea what to expect, but it wasn't a smiling *human* receptionist sitting behind a mahogany desk. Smooth music piped in from overhead. He stepped warily out into the heated room.

"Hello. May I help you?" She looked up from her computer screen, a glossy red smile on her lips, as if she worked in a plastic surgeon's office and not some antechamber of hell.

Without altering her gaze, her arm shifted, dipped low beneath her desk. An imperceptible move. Instantly he knew she touched some kind of hidden alert button—or was about to.

His gaze narrowed on the single door behind her desk.

"Do you have an appointment?" she asked.

"I want to speak with whoever's in charge."

She scanned him, up and down. "I think that can be arranged. One moment." She made several taps on her keyboard, then paused, reading something on her screen. Her gaze snapped to him. If possible, her smile beamed several shades brighter. Falsely bright. "Excellent." She stood from her chair in one graceful move and waved him toward the door. "You can go through this door. Someone will meet you to show the way."

Right. He could just imagine who that someone might be. The demon witch responsible for abducting Sorcha? Lycans?

He rounded the desk, the bump of his sword at his side, beneath his coat, the only reassurance necessary.

He'd defeated lycans and demon witches before. He'd do it again tonight. He'd fight harder than he ever had because his motivation was stronger. He had to win. He must. Sorcha's life depended on his beating whatever waited for him. He had to get her out of here.

Before she kills you? He shoved the nagging voice aside, unwilling to dwell on Darby's predictions. It wouldn't stop him, and it didn't make sense anyway. Why would Sorcha want to kill him? Even if they'd parted on a less than warm note, she'd never wish him dead.

Passing through the door, he found no one there to meet him. He didn't see anyone or anything as he advanced, just a yawning stretch of hall. Concrete floor and bare walls closed in around him.

With careful steps and one hand tucked inside his coat, he advanced, muscles tight and screaming with awareness. Only one thought pounded through his head. Sorcha was here. *Near.* He could feel her, almost taste her on his lips. It was enough. All he needed to keep going.

He passed door after door, all closed. Not a sound scratched the air other than the hum of the ventilation system. Cameras were stationed in every high corner, following his progress. He was walking into the jaws of the beast, descending into the abyss. It wasn't even a trap. It couldn't be a trap if he was aware that something nefarious and dangerous awaited him. If he embraced it voluntarily.

"Jonah." The voice boomed from above.

He whirled around, searching for the source, the nape of his neck prickling at the familiar voice. The long chuckle that followed only confirmed the suspicion.

"Old friend, good to see you again. This is quite the week for reunions."

He should have felt surprise at the sound of Ivo's disembodied voice, but given that he'd discovered Sorcha survived the blast in Istanbul, he was beyond assuming anything anymore.

"Ivo," he called out, spotting the speaker vents in the ceiling. "Where is she?"

"Ah, looking for my little girl, are you? She did grow into a stunning creature. Too bad these aren't the old days or I would gladly give her to you. Alas, my goals have changed . . .".

Suddenly a door opened, as if by magic, swinging quickly near his right side. He jerked, flattening his back to the wall, braced for anything that might emerge from the shadowy space.

"You don't hold quite the same appeal. I don't need you in the same way. Funny how time alters one's perception."

"What happened to building your army of lycans? Ruling the world and subduing man?"

"There are different kinds of power, I've learned."

Jonah's gaze drifted back toward the yawning door. He knew it hadn't opened randomly or accidentally. "Where is she?"

"Go ahead"—Ivo's voice floated over him—"if you want to find her, she's down there."

Not for one moment did Jonah trust him, but he didn't have much choice except to play this out.

"Bet you wish you'd taken her when I first offered her to you on a platter."

"I think she was twelve the first time you tried to get me to take her to mate," he growled.

"Yes, and something tells me she's not such an easy conquest now. Tell me, have you bred with her already? From the possessive way you're be-having, I suspect you have." Ivo chuckled and the sound curled menacingly on the air.

Jonah stiffened, sick at the thought of Sorcha back in the hands of her father.

Ivo chuckled. "Apparently I'm right. So much for your grand morals that prevented you from fucking her before."

Black rage swept through Jonah. "You should have burned in that fire. I'll see you burn yet . . ."

"Promises, promises. What are you waiting for? Sorcha's just below. Get going, hero."

Jonah moved through the door and descended steps onto another floor . . . even as he knew something was wrong. Ivo wouldn't hand Sorcha over to him so easily.

The air grew dimmer, smelled dank and rot-ting. The doors he passed now were heavy slabs of metal. His skin felt chill to think that Sorcha was behind one of them. Knowing now that Ivo ran this little operation, he hoped he hadn't sicced his lycans on her—she was his daughter, after all.

A sudden loud click reverberated in the air. Jonah stopped, staring straight ahead at the door at the end of the corridor. Larger than the rest, it drew his eye. It was bolted from the outside. He watched as that bolt lifted, the screws creaking noisily, oil-starved.

Warmth began to build at his center, spreading out through his pulling limbs. His teeth grew, thickening in his mouth as he transitioned.

The metal door slid open slowly. Jonah stopped, stared hard at the swelling darkness that dwelled inside the room. His heart hammered. Without a thought for the cameras following his every move, he pulled out his sword.

Instinct blared as loud as a horn in his head, telling him to hold the sword ready, that Sorcha wasn't inside this room. Something dark and hungry, ready to pounce, watched him from the confines.

Gradually a sound penetrated as he stared into the swirling black of that room. His ears pricked, adjusted for the slightest sound, undetectable to human ears. But he heard it. Steady and heavy as the rhythm of a metronome.

The fall of breath.

Demon breath, gurgling deep and rancid. Even where he stood, it reached his nose, made his limbs pull harder, deeper, and snap into their final position.

An actual demon watched him in corporeal form, staring out from that lightless room. He flexed his hands around his sword.

He'd only come across a demon in the flesh once. He'd barely survived the encounter, but the experience had taught him what to look for. Had taught him to expect that he might not survive.

The moment it charged into the light, he caught only a flash of the large animal shape. The two-headed creature shot toxic spit from its mouth. Jonah swerved to avoid the hissing liquid. It landed on a metal door with an incinerating sizzle.

Jonah lunged forward in a blur, stabbing into the demon's thick, meaty chest. He grunted as he pulled his sword back out, the blade glinting with blood as black as tar. The demon bellowed, in either pain or rage. Maybe both. Jonah knew only that his efforts didn't stop it, didn't slow it down.

Jonah crouched and swung around, surveying the demon's body as quickly as possible, his gaze moving in a feverish sweep as he searched for the mark that would glow, a red handprint—the mark of the fall, God's handprint casting the demon into hell. Every demon bore it, though never in the same spot.

One of its dragonlike heads spit again, and Jonah moved too late. The acid grazed his shoulder in a poisonous burn, devouring his flesh, tissue, muscle. The demon saliva reached his bone and began eating through it. He couldn't stop the scream from escaping his throat, shuddering through the corridor and lifting up in the air.

With a bellowed rage, he swung and decapitated one of the heads. It fell and rolled along the floor. Still the demon kept coming at him, its remaining jaw snapping, toxic spit hissing through the air.

Jonah dropped and rolled, planning to take a leg out from under it—and that's when he saw it. Buried beneath the belly, almost completely hidden, tucked inside the joint of the front right leg, glowed the mark of the fall.

Grasping his sword in both hands, he plunged it up into the glowing red handprint.

The beast howled, fell to its massive side with a loud crash. Its four legs flailed for a moment. Smoke swelled up around it. Jonah staggered back, remembering what had happened the last time. Holding a hand against his eyes, he squinted as it burst into fire and ash. Flames raged over the demon, devouring it and sending it back to hell. From a safe distance, he watched, feeling only grim satisfaction when the demon was almost instantly reduced to a pile of charred rubble.

The tinny sound of clapping rang out over the speaker system. "Impressive, Jonah. Your knowledge of demons is . . . unexpected. I've underestimated you."

Panting, he glared up at the ceiling as if he could

see Ivo. "Yeah, well, I've changed over the years." His voice fell thickly from his mouth. "Where's Sorcha?" he demanded.

"Did you think you could just waltz in here and leave with her?" Ivo laughed. "Nothing is that simple. You killed my demon. I must confess some shock over that . . . and disappointment. You'll have to pay for that"

"Enough with these games!" Jonah roared.

Ivo's demented laugh rumbled through the air again. "Games . . . funny you should say that. I happen to like games very much. Very much indeed. You should remember that about me."

That Ivo was a sick bastard who liked to torment those around him? Yeah. He remembered.

Steps sounded behind Jonah. He swung around, his bloodstained sword at the ready. The mark on his neck tingled and burned . . . as it had for some time now. From the moment he'd stared into the darkened maw of the room and felt the demon's eyes on him. He'd barely noticed, too worked up fighting for his life and struggling with the realization that Ivo was alive.

A nonthreatening-looking woman descended the steps. She was very earth mother in her brown wool dress and orange knit cap tightly fitted to her head. Her frizzy gray-streaked hair escaped the sides like straw bursting from a scarecrow's hat.

She reminded him of a vagrant he'd given change to outside his favorite restaurant in Seattle.

"Ah," she clucked, appraising him. "A dovenatu. Imagine that. Two in the same week. How lucky are we?"

"Ingrid." Ivo's voice rolled over the air with a touch of impatience. Clearly he had tired of playing with Jonah. He had always been like that, given to wild swings in mood. "You know what to do."

"Yes, of course." She gave a very businesslike nod.

Jonah poised the sword above his head, ready to defend himself and attack . . . not about to let the fact that she looked like someone's grandmother deter him from shielding himself. Dying now was letting Sorcha down, and he'd vowed not to do that. Not ever again.

Then something changed. He felt the shift on the air current, a sharp thinness.

His muscles constricted. His skull pounded, a twisting pain squeezing at the temples. A buzzing filled his ears, gradually turning into a soundless voice. *Drop the sword. Drop the sword. Drop the sword.* Pain thudded at his skull, tiny hammers seeking a way inside.

He resisted, his arms trembling from the force it took to hold on to the sword. "What are you?"

he ground out even as he already knew. His sixth sense around witches was clamoring loud and clear. This was the witch from Darby's vision. The powerful one, the one who'd overtaken Sorcha. The one, Darby had predicted, who would overtake him. The one he couldn't beat.

She frowned. "You're strong," she muttered, narrowing her eyes and working her fingers in the air as if she were performing a magic trick on him.

The voice in his head intensified, a whispering mantra. *Drop the sword. Drop the sword.*

His fingers unfolded. A violent bellow ripped from his lips as his sword clattered to the floor. She pointed at the demon's cell, directing him.

Without a word, he felt himself turning, twisting around. His feet moved, each one in a leaden step, one after the other. The dark cell loomed closer and closer. He couldn't resist, couldn't fight the witch mind-fucking him into doing her bidding. No wonder Ivo was able to control lycans, demons, Sorcha . . . *him.*

Maybe Darby was right. Maybe he would die at Sorcha's hand. Maybe this witch would have her kill him.

The door clanged shut behind him. With a curse, he rotated in the room that stank like the demon who'd occupied it before him. He muttered, "Nice shithole."

As he was coming to expect, Ivo's voice rolled out over the air. "There are better accommodations to be had. Please me, and who knows, maybe you'll get an upgrade. Or maybe not. Maybe I'll put an end to your life tonight."

Jonah squinted, adjusting his eyes to the swelling darkness. "Just tell me what you're going to do with me."

This time there was no answer.

SORCHA FELL BACK ON her cot, the scream she'd heard moments before ringing in her ears. It had sounded unearthly and full of pain but oddly familiar, too. Almost as if the cry had been her own. The sound still echoed in her head, made her heart pound faster.

Rolling to her side, she curled her legs and tucked herself into as small a ball as possible. "Jonah," she whispered, and the sound of his name made her feel better, closer to him even though he was a world away from her. Where she wanted him to be. Where she needed him to be. Safe.

She felt warm inside, light and free, knowing he was safe and far from this.

"Jonah." Closing her eyes, she let his face fill her head, remembering the times she'd studied him asleep in bed beside her. She would always have that. Every time she closed her eyes, she would have him. It was all she could hope for. Right now it was everything.

The manner in which life ends means nothing, she decided. It's meaningless. She almost laughed when she realized she was contemplating the end, her death. For so long she'd thought that was virtually unattainable for her.

Now that it was real, looming close and a very likely possibility, she felt human. For the first time since she was a girl. Then, she did laugh. The sound spilled out, rusty and broken. Innately human. Human was something she had hoped to be on more than one occasion.

It's the living that counts, and the time she had lived with Jonah was what she would hold close, tucked to her heart forever.

TWENTY-FIVE

Ingrid came for her the following morning, grunting in satisfaction to see that she was dressed and her tray was empty of food. Did she think Sorcha wouldn't eat? Sorcha snorted. She wasn't about to go without nourishment. She needed her strength for whatever her father planned for her.

She walked with firm steps, in steady silence, her jaw aching from the tension knotting it as she followed Ingrid through the myriad corridors, deep into the unknown.

They finally arrived at a large, airy room she'd passed through once before. Lonely manacles dangled from the walls and floors. It had been empty then. Now the hard eyes of four others followed her. Apparently none of them required restraints. She eyed them openly in return, combatants, she guessed from their attire . . . attire so like her own.

"Here you are. Pick a seat."

Sorcha sank down beside one of the players.

She didn't even hide making a study of them. If

she was to fight alongside them—*against* them— she wanted to know as much about them as possible.

For a brief moment, she wondered when she had become this. So mercenary, so intent on her survival that she measured everyone for their weaknesses. And then she didn't think about it again. She wouldn't. Not if she wanted to live through this. To see Jonah again—

To see Jonah again? Is that what mattered to her most right now?

She blinked once, hard, letting herself absorb this realization, take it deep inside her and then tuck it away. For later dissection. Now, she could only think about life. About winning her life.

As far as she could tell, none of her companions was lycan. They wouldn't be sitting before her with all the appearance of humans if they were. She could tell it was moonrise. Even buried beneath the earth, she felt the pull of the moon deep in her bones. Her skin tingled and her core smoldered with heat. She could turn in an instant if she willed it. And in the ring, she very well might. Anything to survive.

But then, that's what her father was counting on. He wanted a show. She frowned darkly. Like it or not, she would give him what he wanted. As much as she loathed the idea of playing in his death games, she was not ready to die in some form of indignant protest. If she needed to turn to live, she would.

She eyed the others again, hardly registering Ingrid leaving her with them alone. So if they weren't lycans, what were they? Mere humans wouldn't satisfy her father's sense of drama. Not if he'd wanted Tresa to compete among them. They had to be serious threats.

Her companions in the holding room seemed equally fascinated with the mystery of her.

"Hey, newb. What's your story?" the lone female asked. She was the epitome of female warrior. Her long blond hair was pulled back in a tight ponytail. Armor covered all her vital parts, but the rest of her was tantalizingly bare.

"Isn't it clear?" a guy asked. He was big, brawny, with arms like tree trunks. "She's like me."

Sorcha inhaled, her nostrils flaring wide. He was right. He was a dovenatu like her. Her pores snapped open, recognizing her own species.

Leaning forward, he propped his elbows on his knees. Every inch of his bulging muscles looked greased. Better for the fight, she supposed. "Not too many of us around, huh? Name's Sheppard."

"Is that your first name or last?"

"Both." He smiled, a blinding flash of teeth, and sent her a wink.

"Just great." This came from a scrawny boy who looked barely out of his teens. "Just what we need . . . you two bonding." He rose and paced a few feet with angry strides. "I can't keep doing this every week. None of you likes me," he accused.

"No arguing with that," the blonde woman muttered.

"See!" he continued. "I'm not going to make it—"

"Shut the fuck up, Phillip. None of us is going to last very long down here. That's the whole point," the female bit out. "So why don't you stop acting so helpless? We've all seen what you can do."

The third guy held silent, his ink-dark eyes slowly assessing Sorcha, as well as the others. He somehow managed to hold himself apart from them, and it wasn't just because he was silent. With his head dropped back against the wall, he looked removed, untouched by it all. Almost as if he were bored.

Waving his reed-thin arms, Phillip shouted at the brooding man, "Would you stop looking at me that way?"

What way? Sorcha wanted to ask. It seemed as if he were looking through the teenager rather than at him. It seemed as if he were looking through all of them. Clearing her throat, she asked, "So are we supposed to fight each other or what? What's going on?"

The four exchanged looks of mild surprise.

"You don't know anything, do you?" The female sounded annoyed.

"None of us is here to fight one another," Sheppard volunteered.

"Tell her nothing!" Phillip hissed. "Let her figure it out for herself. She doesn't need an advantage over us."

"God, Phillip, chill out." The blonde wrapped her fingers around her ponytail and smoothed her hand down the waist-length rope of hair. "As I recall, we told you how the cow ate the cabbage when you first got here."

Phillip's face reddened, the blemishes standing out more brightly, now angry purple splotches on his pale skin.

"You should be glad the gamekeeper gave us someone to replenish the ranks."

"We began with thirty fighters! She'll hardly improve our odds."

"Can someone tell me what's going on?" Sorcha persisted.

"We're supposed to fight the defender," Sheppard answered, moving to sit beside her. His thigh aligned with hers and she scooted over an inch. He was good-looking and he was a dovenatu. Two qualifications that should have sparked her interest. Two qualifications that would have delighted her a month ago. But not now. Now he failed to affect her at all. He simply wasn't Jonah.

"Who's the defender?" she asked.

"He's the reigning champion . . . and has been for the last year. Everyone expects him to wipe the floor with us." The blonde leaned back against the wall. "Like he always does. Once blood is drawn, once someone is killed, we're herded back and given another week of life." She shrugged. "I'm Mila, by the way."

A chill chased down Sorcha's spine at how matter-of-factly Mila related the depravity of her father's kill games.

"I'm Sorcha," she replied numbly, still running over all the blonde had just said. "A fight to the death," she murmured, sickened to know that Ivo's blood ran through her veins. That this was her father's doing.

"A fight to the death," Phillip echoed angrily. "For one of us at least."

"It's simple really," Sheppard said beside her. "We fight the defender together. They'll release us into the ring and we'll try to kill him before he kills one of us . . ." He paused to grimace. "So far, though, he always kills one of us."

"Don't tell her anything," Phillip cried. "Someone has to die. Let it be her. Give us another week!"

"If I'm prepared," Sorcha snapped, at the end of her rope with the kid, "I can better help *all* of us. What is this defender, anyway? A lycan? It's moonrise, he'll be stronger—"

"You'll wish it was a lycan." The dark-eyed quiet man finally spoke up, his black eyes drilling deeply into Sorcha.

"Ah, he speaks," Mila cheered in mocking tones. "Gonna bother telling us your name yet, stud?"

Apparently he hadn't been with them long either. He swung his dark eyes on Mila, but offered nothing else.

"No? Shame." Looking back to Sorcha, Mila answered the earlier question. "The defender is a demon. Nasty and big and invincible as far as we can tell."

A demon? In corporeal form? How had her father captured a demon? No doubt Ingrid had a hand in keeping it captive. Her mind raced, thinking over all Jonah had told her about demons. Somewhere on the demon's body was the mark of the fall. She just had to find it. "We can kill it," she announced, her voice ringing with conviction.

"You don't get it. There's no salvation here for

any of us," Mila interjected. "The gamekeeper won't halt the game until one of us dies."

"So what happens if one of us kills the defender?"

"Then one of us gets to be the new defender." Phillip waved his hands in the air. "Fun. Who wants that job? I'll just work on not getting killed."

The air came alive with cheering shouts. Sorcha looked in the direction of the door. "That's the arena?" she guessed. "What's going on out there now?"

"Pregame show." Sheppard shrugged his massive shoulders. "Every moonrise they fill the ring with a dozen or so lycans and an equal number of hunters. It's one big free-for-all. The hunters love it." He swung his gaze on the dark-eyed brooder. "Isn't that right?"

Sorcha stared back and forth between the two men, not missing the steady flow of animosity between them, the crackle of hate in the air. Then it clicked. "You're a hunter?" she demanded.

Dark eyes shifted to her, obsidian black. His lips barely moved as he spoke. "I used to be."

"Makes you feel warm and fuzzy to know he's fighting beside you, doesn't it?" Mila's lip curled up. "A year ago he was hunting your kind down like dogs. Now his buddies are out there cheering for his blood."

Something flickered in his gaze. Just for a fraction of a second, but Sorcha hadn't imagined it. The mention of his friends turning on him had stung deeply. "I never hunted dovenatus," he murmured. "Even though the Federation ordered me to."

"Is that how you got thrown down here? Because you're . . ." Sorcha searched for the right word. "Uncooperative?"

"Rogue hunters aren't much better than lycans to EFLA." His lip curled as he looked at her. "Just like dovenatus, we're deemed expendable. They thought this might be a more entertaining way to end my life."

Sorcha shook her head, marveling that some of the spectators were his former friends and comrades.

A door clanged loudly. Ingrid appeared, breathless, as though she'd just jogged a mile. "It's a madhouse tonight. The crowd is wired," she exclaimed as if the news might please them.

Sheppard stood and clapped the hunter on the back as if they were old friends. The animosity flowing between them told otherwise. If they weren't about to fight a demon for their lives, they would gladly be fighting each other. "C'mon, let's go see all your old friends."

The hunter flung Sheppard's arm away with a growl.

"Oh, leave each other alone already and let's get this over with." Mila stalked forward. Instead of using her hand, she nodded once and the doors were flung wide open. Without a blink, she strode ahead to lead the way.

"A witch," Sorcha noted beneath her breath, but she'd already suspected as much. Only Mila wasn't like Ingrid. No demon possessed her. She was a white witch. The tough-as-nails blonde answered to no one, that much was clear, and Sorcha could understand how she'd survived this long in the arena when others had not.

The boy lingered, clearly reluctant to enter the arena. She stared hard at him, trying to figure out how he had stayed alive this long. What was his *talent*? "And why are you here?" She knew her father well enough to know that the boy couldn't be helpless. For all his complaints, Phillip had to possess an advantage. If he survived where so many others had not, he was no weakling.

"Nothing . . . I'm . . . just a mage. A mage in training. I was an apprentice when they took me and my master almost a year ago. He owned a magic shop in Dublin . . . mostly sold books, novelty items."

A mage? As in a wizard? She'd never even known they existed. Sorcha shook her head, feeling her world shift again beneath her feet.

Although if witches were out there, why not mages?

He strode past her, his voice high in defense. "I didn't even get but a few months of training before we were captured. Trust me, I'm nothing . . ."

"And yet you're still alive." Striding ahead of the boy through the doors, she hardened her heart, not fooled for a moment by his helpless act.

Entering the narrow tunnel that led into the arena, she emptied her head of all thoughts, of Jonah, of everything but what waited ahead of her. She didn't need any distractions if she was going to make it through this.

The other three walked steadily in front of her, their movements indicating a certain jaded familiarity that only heightened her sense of inadequacy. Not a good feeling. She pulled back her shoulders. *Game on, Sorcha. You can do this. Until you figure out a way to escape or talk Ivo out of this insanity, you must.*

Music played in the distance. The pounding bass, guitar and drums blaring louder as the light at the mouth of the tunnel grew and grew. Her pulse increased, hammering in her throat as she quickened her pace to match the others speeding into the arena.

When she cleared the mouth of the tunnel and stepped into the arena alongside the others, the crowd went wild, shouting, clapping, feet stomping. She marveled that hunters cheered at the sight of her when they lived by a creed that demanded the extermination of her kind. How ass backward was that?

Lycan agents had definitely lost perspective in the last few years if they condoned these blood games, even sponsored them. Were they any different from the soulless, flesh-hungry lycans they hunted? As a girl, she had almost romanticized them—thought them heroes killing that part of herself she hated . . . the part of herself she wished dead, too. The part of herself that her father saw only as an asset, her greatest strength.

As it turned out, they were as bad as the prey they hunted. Even worse. They were as bad as her father.

The double doors slammed shut behind her. Ingrid was gone. It was just the five of them.

A loud horn cut the air, broke through the din of hunters crowded around. Close enough to observe the spectacle but a safe enough distance away that the spectators weren't in danger. Heavy wire mesh surrounded the arena in a great drape. Even if she could scale the twenty-foot wall to the first row—and she probably could—she would have a hard time breaking through the wire mesh. Knowing her father, it was made of some super-resistant material the government didn't even know existed.

She surveyed the cheering hunters, hundreds of blurred faces. They looked more beast than man, hungry for blood, their eyes wild and wide, mouths gaping. Her gaze drifted to the rogue hunter in her midst. Sure enough, he was staring at the crowd, too, his dark eyes intense and glittering as they fixed on his former comrades.

Her gaze narrowed, following the direction of his stare, to a single individual. A hunter sat there among the screaming crowd, the only one not cheering. Still and silent, his gaze locked on the rogue. Apparently the rogue still had one friend amongst the jeering hunters. Or at least a sympathizer.

"Look alive!" Sheppard shouted, urging them on as a team.

Her gaze snapped to him, grateful. With a nod, she turned her attention to the arena. Empty so far. Just the five of them.

A cold breeze puckered her flesh. Various weapons dotted the dirt-packed floor. Various guns. Little good they would do in fighting a demon. A crossbow. A sword. An ax. A few hand knives. A whip. She eyed the shield. No telling what power the demon would have at its disposal, but she wanted the shield.

Mila beat her to it. Her hand shot out, and the shield flew across twenty feet, into her grasp. Into her other hand flew the ax.

With a shake of her head, Sorcha muttered, "Not too hard to figure out why she's still alive."

"Right," Phillip grumbled, a good distance behind her. Behind all of them. How he'd survived remained a mystery.

The crowd suddenly stilled, waving fists stuffed with money for bets as her father's voice rang out over the speakers, filling the shifting fog. "Welcome, welcome! Tonight we have something special planned for all our brave hunters!"

Sorcha tried not to choke on this—her father kissing the asses he'd once fought.

No one breathed. Time was suspended.

The wild, hungry eyes of the crowd seemed black as a starless night as they gazed down into the arena.

"Tonight we declare a new defender!"

"What the fuck?" Sheppard flung out beside her. He'd moved close to her. She reminded herself not to trust too much in his nearness . . . not to think he'd allied himself with her and relax her guard. For all she knew, he was plotting to throw her to the demon beast . . . or whatever *thing* they had to fight. No one was going to look out for her but herself.

The crowd broke out in agitated murmurs. Some shouted at her father where he stood on his balcony, a dictator overlooking his kingdom.

A man, an agent of EFLA, she presumed, sat beside Ivo, looking none too happy. The prospect that they had missed a possible fight where the demon defender was defeated did not sit well with the crowd.

Ivo waved his hands as if calming a group of small children. "Recently we were infiltrated by an unforeseen assailant who thought he could put an end to our beloved games!"

The arena filled with loud boos. The tiny hairs at the back of Sorcha's neck prickled.

"This trespasser slayed our demon defender—"

"Shit." Sheppard shot her a glance. "Looks like a new game tonight. Who knows what we're up against."

Her stomach churned.

Her father shouted into the microphone, "And you know the rules!"

"Kill the defender, become the defender!" the crowd shouted back with fanatic zeal.

Her father brought up both arms, swinging them violently in the air. "Let the killing begin!"

A large gate cranked open on the opposite side of the arena. The noise scratched her nerves, heightening the drama . . . the horrible anticipation. As the gate lifted, a rolling fog of smoke flowed into the arena.

Her eyes ached as she stared unblinkingly at the opening. She waited, breath trapped in her constricting lungs at the sight of all that billowing fog, slowly filling, filling . . . obscuring her view.

"Breathe," Sheppard advised from beside her in a humorous voice. "It's kind of important."

"How can you joke at—"

She didn't finish. She caught a movement. A flash of dark in all that fog.

"It's coming!" Mila shouted, bracing her shield before her.

The crowd took up a chant, *Kill, kill, kill* . . .

The boy at her back took up another chant, the low muttering indecipherable. His words ran together in a rhythmic mantra, and she realized it was no language she knew, but some kind of foreign incantation. Glancing over her shoulder, she caught only a glimpse of Phillip muttering to some kind of talisman he wore about his neck before he vanished, disappeared in a blinding flash, a zip of light.

She gasped.

"That's *his* trick," Sheppard snapped, grabbing her hand and moving her toward one of the weapons lying on the ground, indicating that she should pick it up. "He makes himself invisible," he spit out as he snatched up a sword for himself. "Convenient, I know. You won't see him again until this is all over."

"Nice," she muttered, thinking of all his complaining and woeful eyes as she snatched up a knife and tested it in her grip. An ammonia odor reached her nose. Her nostrils twitched at the sharp, familiar smell. She lifted the blade close to her nose and sniffed—silver nitrate. Poison to lycan and dovenatu. Sheppard tossed her another knife and she tucked it into her belt.

Phillip probably had the best defense out of all of them. And she'd actually felt sorry for the little shit.

"He's coming!" the hunter-turned-prey shouted, swinging his crossbow left and right.

"Where?" Mila shouted, looking around wildly.

A stillness came over Sorcha then, the loud shouts of spectators dulling to a low drone in her head. She hardly noted her companions. Her gaze penetrated the opaque air, detecting the shadow emerging through the mist. Her skin rippled, snapped, burning from the inside out as the familiar pull of her bones began, her instincts reacting as she braced herself for the battle ahead.

TWENTY-SIX

Jonah stared through the open door into the shifting fog. There was nowhere to go but forward.

The demon witch's voice broke out behind him. "Go on. Don't keep the audience waiting."

The cries of the crowd filled his head, a deafening din.

She prodded his back. "Go on. Your fans await."

"What's all this?" he growled.

"You have one simple task. Kill or be killed."

Suddenly, he was moving, one foot dropping down in front of the other, the pain in his head crushing as she forced him forward. He was helpless to resist. The door clanged shut behind him.

The roar of the crowd was deafening now. Smoke swelled up around him as if the earth itself breathed fire.

He sucked in a deep breath. He really couldn't afford to die. Besides wanting to live for himself, there was Sorcha to consider. How was he going to get her out of here if he got himself killed? How was he going to see her again? Smell her hair? Taste the honey of her skin? Feel the warm heat of her body?

Quite simply, he needed to do all that. He needed her. Craved her as deeply as he craved his freedom from this stinking cesspit. Once he found her, he vowed to keep her. Hold her so close he could never lose her again. If that meant killing the faceless opponents awaiting him, then so be it.

The gate clanged shut behind him, the harsh sound reverberating in the mist-filled air, and he was moving, slinking into the fog, looking for his first victim.

THE WAITING HEIGHTENED HER anxiety, and made her pulse jump wildly in her neck. She whipped around at every imagined sound or movement, hoping she wouldn't cleave apart one of her comrades in her movements. Her fingers flexed on her weapon, mouth watering and drying interchangeably. The rasp of her breath filled her ears.

Then she saw it.

Mila shouted out a warning.

Sorcha didn't have time to process a face or even much of a form. The shadow broke through the fog with deathly speed, a dark blur that marked its inhuman origins.

"What the hell! Look out!" This came from the disembodied voice of Phillip somewhere close.

Sorcha whipped her head left and right. The shadow continued to zip among them, taking recon, assessing for weakness.

Sorcha felt the panic rise within the group of them at the new threat, one none of them had studied and faced before. *An entity strong enough to kill a demon.*

Mila shrieked and charged, diving deep into the mist to meet the shadow.

Sheppard shook his head. "She's got balls."

The ax whistled through the air as she swung. The shadow moved, skipped around the witch with dizzying speed . . . and something about that movement struck Sorcha as familiar. She squinted and crept closer through the swirling mist, the racing of her heart taking on a new speed . . . a speed born of true fright. Panic.

"What are you doing? Get back," hissed Sheppard.

She ignored him, inching forward, muscles braced, knife at the ready. The mist cleared then and she had a perfect view of the witch, pinned beneath the new defender, his sword at her throat.

Mila's face was flushed red, her nostrils flaring with loud, gusty pants.

The defender inched the sword closer to her throat, but the effort had him panting, hand shaking from the strain. Clearly the witch was using her special talent to keep the blade from cutting down and into her throat.

Even before Sorcha registered all this, she recognized *him*—knew him with every fiber of her body before she ever saw his face.

"Jonah," she whispered, then again louder, screaming, "Jonah!"

His head whipped in her direction. Shock rippled across his fully turned features. She felt her own flesh contract, react to him on a primal level.

The witch acted then. With his guard down, Mila flung him from her. Jonah launched through the air, landing near Sorcha's feet.

She rushed toward him with fear in her heart. Not for herself, but for him. He was the target, after all. Any moment, they would be on him.

Crouching beside him, she growled in a fiery rush, "What are you doing here?"

"I'm here for you." Springing to his feet, he circled her wrist with the hard band of his fingers, as if she might disappear in a puff of smoke. "What are *you* doing in here?" He motioned around him with a wave of his hand.

"Father stuck me in here. I pissed him off with my less than thrilled reaction at seeing him."

Jonah shook his head with a growl. "You never could put up a front . . . even if it was to save yourself."

The horrible reality of their situation washed over her then, bitter and acrid. *Jonah had to kill one of them . . . or die himself.*

The crowd shouted down at them.

"C'mon," Jonah said, grabbing her hand. The warm clasp of those fingers around hers felt so achingly good as they cut through the hazy air. *Right. Natural.* Even with all that was wrong, she felt a surge of relief. That somehow everything would be right for her. For both of them. "We're getting out of here!"

It was on her tongue to ask how precisely they were going to manage to escape the arena and a hundred-plus bloodthirsty hunters when Jonah jerked and stiffened, his hand crushing hers in a death grip. His face turned upward, as if seeing something floating above them in the melting fog.

"Jonah!" she demanded over the ear-bleeding din, bewildered. His glassy-eyed stare frightened her, filled her mouth with a bitter tang.

A horrible sputter sounded from his lips.

"Jonah! What's wrong?" Her gaze scanned him, stopping, locking in horror at the tip of a sword in his chest, buried deep. She sniffed. Beneath the coppery scent of his blood another odor tickled her nose.

No! No, no, no, no, no . . .

Silver nitrate. Poison to their kind.

She slapped a hand over her mouth to stifle her scream.

Her only thought for Jonah, she dropped her hand and inhaled shallowly, peering around him to where the sword penetrated his back. There was no sign of his killer. She winced, her mind shying from the word. He was not dead. Not *killed*.

Silver nitrate might be poison to them, but they weren't lycans. It didn't have to be lethal. He could recover. It was possible. He could regenerate. He would—if she had to breathe life back into him herself.

At first she thought whoever had stabbed him had turned and fled . . . but then she saw the sword's leather grip turn, twisting as it drove deeper, harder into Jonah, pushing, pushing . . .

Jonah cried out, his throat arching. She choked on a sob at the low, pained sound.

Fury fired through her . . . and awareness.

She lifted her blade and let it fly, stabbed it through the air. She heard the thud, felt her knife make contact. For a moment, her weapon appeared to have suspended itself in midair, in nothing but space.

Jonah dropped to his knees. She tried to catch him, to hold him up, as though that might keep him well and with her, keep him from being seriously hurt.

At the sound of a wet gurgle, she looked up, flicked a glance toward her suspended knife, to the boy who was there but invisible to the eye.

Gradually the fog receded in the arena, melting like fast-fading smoke. As it did, Phillip appeared. Dead, impaled with her knife.

Sorcha pointed a shaking finger at Phillip. "Tonight's kill," she called out, her warning clear. She hovered over Jonah, clutched him close, not about to let anyone pry him from her arms and live.

"You're protecting him?" Sheppard cocked his head at a dangerous angle, glaring at her.

Her fingers flexed around Jonah, running through his hair. She'd missed him too much. She wasn't going to lose him.

"Well, that's pretty evident." Mila kicked Phillip's lifeless body. "She killed for him."

"Are you fucking him or something?" the rogue hunter asked, but in a way that made her think he didn't really care. It was just an idle question.

He looked from her to the jeering crowd, his dark eyes shifty, nervous in a way.

Jonah growled. A quick glance down revealed a feverish light burning in his eyes. "Jonah," she whispered.

"Sorcha, don't risk yourself. Move away from me—"

"Shut up," she said, her voice cracking.

"Ah, so touching," Mila mocked with a roll of her eyes. "Spare me."

Over Jonah's protests, Sorcha blocked him from the others. He was too weak to stop her. She did it unthinkingly, with no hesitation, her heart full and deep with love, desperate for him to live, to avoid another attack . . . even if it meant losing her own life. And that was the humanity she craved, the soul, she realized in a flash. It was love. It lived in her for Jonah. And maybe it always had. *Maybe?* Who was she kidding—it always had.

A loud horn blew. The crowd stilled, their shouts dying as all eyes swung toward the balcony.

She held her breath, meeting her father's gaze across the distance. He looked down at her, his eyes, for all their glitter, dead and uncaring. He looked right through her with that stare.

"Finish it." His voice jumped through the air. "Fight to the death!"

She flinched, her fingers tightening on Jonah's arm. Her gaze flicked wildly to the others, frozen still, all of them a horrified tableau. No one knew what to do. She read it in their eyes. Felt the same way. Everything slowed. A roaring sound filled her head. This was it. Any moment death would congest the air.

"Shit," Sheppard muttered, and her stomach twisted sickly as she noticed his fingers tighten around the grip of his sword. His foot scuffed the ground, inching closer to her.

"Sorcha!" Jonah bit out. "Get up! Defend yourself."

She snatched up a discarded blade from the ground and held it before her. She'd defend herself. She'd go out defending them both.

The quiet hunter still seemed oddly focused on the crowd. Especially odd considering that they were supposed to start killing one another. He might want to be looking at any one of his potential opponents.

With the roaring swelling inside her head now, she followed his gaze, saw him staring, eyes locked on the good-looking blond guy again.

"What are you waiting for?" her father shouted, his face growing red from where he looked down at them.

"Crazy bastard," she muttered, every line of her body taut and singing with readiness, waiting for the first assault.

Still, the three of them didn't move. Mila looked the rogue hunter over, clearly marking him for the first attack.

Then he nodded, moving his dark head in a sharp, decisive jerk. Deliberate. And she knew then. He was signaling the guy in the crowd. A split second after she reached this realization, heat and fire blasted the air. She was lifted, flung far.

Someone screamed. Shrill and piercing. The sound endless. The pain consuming.

She could see nothing beyond fire and rolling black clouds of smoke. Every nerve screamed in agony. She tried to move, into what she didn't know. The world seemed turned inside out, upside down. She couldn't move, couldn't budge. Intense pressure held her down, pinned her like a bug.

And then she realized that the screaming—the shrill incessant screech in her ears—was her own.

JONAH DRAGGED HIMSELF ALONG the ground, hauling his body over burning debris that scorched through his clothes and devoured his flesh. Bodies and human remains spotted the arena—or what used to be the arena.

He squinted through the billowing black, the gnawing wound in his back nothing compared to the pain in his heart, the squeezing fist inside his chest.

He followed the sound of Sorcha's scream. The smoke cleared and he spotted her at last, her body buried beneath a slab of ceiling. Her face peeked out from twisted steel and concrete, streaked in blood and soot.

Pandemonium shrieked around them. Chunks of ceiling continued to fall, caving in, shaking the air and vibrating the earth.

The moans of dying hunters filled the air. Shadowy figures staggered around, trying to find a way out of the nightmare—hell's tomb. At least Ivo was buried somewhere in the mounting inferno.

Jonah dropped next to Sorcha and curled his hands around the wedge of slab. His body screamed in agony as he tried to lift the chunk of ceiling off her. He grunted, blood vessels popping from the effort.

His grunt strangled in his throat, twisting into a scream of agony as he realized he couldn't. He couldn't move it. Couldn't save her. It weighed too much. Even considering what he was, what she was, he was too weak, his body still battling the poison coursing through him.

Damn, damn, damn. Hot tears that had nothing to do with the burning smoke or hungry flames licking toward them pricked his eyes.

Sorcha whispered his name beneath the mangled concrete and metal, her eyes glassy with pain.

He laced his fingers with hers. "I'm here, baby. I'm here." The smoke thickened. The smell of burning flesh stung his nostrils, and he wasn't sure it wasn't his own. The heat encroached, gaining on them like an advancing beast, edging closer and devouring all in its path. "I'm not going anywhere."

For several moments, he lay there, an odd contentment sweeping him. If he had to die here, now, at least he would be with her. Dying together, with someone, with *her,* he realized, beat what he'd had before. A nonlife where he'd turned his back on all, on everything.

He laughed hoarsely. It had taken him long enough to reach that conclusion, but now that he had, he felt as if he'd come home at last. If ever, by some miracle, he survived this, he knew his life would be with Sorcha. It would be hunting demons, protecting witches . . . living out the fate God had somehow chosen for him.

"Jonah." Her voice sounded stronger, driven and more aware of her surroundings. Her eyes glinted up at him—the Sorcha he knew and craved. "You have to go."

He shook his head, refusing to hear the words, to absorb them. He would stay. He would stay if this—mere moments—was all that was left for them.

His gaze crawled over her face, memorizing her every feature, soot-covered, blood-smeared, bruised and torn . . . taking peace from the sight of her. "I have to stay," he said simply, quietly, as if chaos and madness didn't rage around them.

"Damn you, no," she choked out, tears running down her smoking cheeks. Smoke rose off both their bodies now. He didn't feel any of it. Not anymore. He didn't feel the heat. He felt only this moment with her. "You have to save yourself," she hissed.

"I'm already saved. You saved me."

Her face crumpled then. She sobbed, tears trailing shiny tracks on her face. He inched as close as he could, holding her arm, his fingers tightening around her fingers, wishing he could feel all of her pressed against him.

"Hey!" The voice jarred him, so close. He looked up at the other dovenatu who had been in the arena with Sorcha. "Move it!" the guy shouted, leaning down and grasping a jagged edge of concrete in his hands. The female was there, too, the blonde whose throat he had tried to cut. The mark at the nape of his neck throbbed in recognition. A witch.

As the dovenatu worked to lift the slab off Sorcha, the witch stood close, holding up her arms, working whatever skill she possessed, her face screwed up tightly, as if she were in pain from the effort.

As he squinted through the curling black, it seemed that the tips of her fingers glowed.

Finally it rose, tiny inch by slow, unbearable inch.

With a grunt, Jonah grasped Sorcha's arm and dragged her clear of the wreckage, ignoring her cries.

"You're free!" he cried, feeling as if he'd saved himself. Because if she lived, he knew a part of him always would.

The dovenatu didn't hesitate. He bent and scooped her up. Jonah suppressed his rage, the hot flash of possession, at seeing Sorcha clasped in another's arms. But he would bear it. He didn't care how she got out of here, as long as she did. *As long as she lived.*

She looked back for him, twisting her head desperately, her dark hair whipping into her face as the dovenatu bore her away from him. He tried to rise, tried to move after her, follow, but his body didn't feel a part of him anymore. He couldn't command it, couldn't force the dead weight to action. He felt as if he were being pulled, squeezed through a too small hole, wrung out and twisted dry, empty.

Staggering, he dropped, unable to keep up. A warped steel beam fell beside him, shuddering the ground. He heard Sorcha scream his name as she vanished into the black smoke.

TWENTY-SEVEN

Stop! Put me down!" Sorcha writhed, cursing, feeling as helpless as a child in Sheppard's arms. She tried not to worry about the fact that she couldn't feel her legs, or that her ribs ached as if a herd of horses had stomped all over her body.

Her broken body would heal and repair itself in time. Time she didn't have. Time she needed to see to Jonah, to purge the silver nitrate from his body in the hope that he would survive.

She blinked tear-filled eyes. Now wasn't the time to break down. Jonah was still back there. He needed her.

She struggled harder. "Put me down!" She would crawl back to him with her bare hands if necessary.

"Would you stop?" Sheppard shouted, navigating his way though the burning, smoking wreckage. "The elevators are up ahead." He glanced back over his shoulder. A foul expletive fell from his lips. "Where the hell's Mila?"

"You left her, too," Sorcha accused.

"Honey, in case you didn't realize it, this is war—be grateful I grabbed you!"

"We have to go back for Jonah!" She beat a knotted fist against his shoulder, hating that she was too weak to stop him from carrying her away.

Sheppard shook his head fiercely, lips pressed into a grim line. "I can't carry both of you. Sorry." Except he didn't sound sorry.

"Then go back for him," she choked out. "Leave me."

He laughed, then coughed against the suffocating smoke. "Love really does render people stupid." She caught the motion of his shaking head. "Trust me, if I'm not going back for Mila, I'm not going back for him."

He reached the elevator and kicked the up button with his booted foot, muttering, "Let's hope it works."

And Sorcha hoped it didn't. Because she couldn't imagine going on without Jonah. Not now. Not ever again.

Over the roar of fire, the din of crumbling earth and debris, the elevator binged open in front of them. Sheppard dove inside.

Only they weren't alone for long. Two others jumped in beside them before the doors had a chance to slide shut. The rogue hunter and his blond friend, the guy in the crowd he'd signaled to the split second before the explosion. Somehow he'd done this. They both had. They had destroyed her father's little kingdom, killed hundreds. *And why not?* she asked herself dully. She couldn't blame them. Her father had only ordered them to kill one another. At least with the explosion there was a hope for survival . . . escape. It was that hope the two men had seized.

She stared hard at them, resenting that it worked out so well for them. They were getting out alive. Jonah, Mila . . . they weren't.

As the elevator began its glide upward the two hunters sagged against the back of it, shoulders touching. In the flickering, dying light of the elevator, she watched them. The fair-haired hunter's hand brushed over the other hunter's hand, closed around the fingers in a tight grip. *Intimate.* As if he was afraid his friend would be ripped from him again at any moment.

Not friends, she realized flatly, her heart a squeezing fist in her chest, each pounding beat for Jonah, lost in burning chaos even as it dawned on her that these two men were much more than friends. They were lovers.

The sight of the two hunters only made her want to weep for Jonah, at what she was losing . . . what she would never have again.

"Please," she whispered, but she wasn't sure who she was asking for help. Sheppard? Or God himself. And why should he help her, a creature not of his making, an abomination. Why would he hear her call?

Her last sight before she closed her eyes and buried her face in Sheppard's chest was the elevator doors rolling open, delivering them from the fire and smoke and returning them to civilization.

SHEPPARD CARRIED HER A safe distance into the gathered crowd of onlookers. Behind them the building was gone. In its place, a pile of smoldering rubble and broken, fiery walls cast a deep red glow on the evening. A great serpent of black smoke, several shades darker than the pulsing night, rose into the Paris sky.

A song of sirens wailed, growing closer. She caught a glimpse of the two hunters before they disappeared into the crowd, swallowed up in the press of crawling bodies.

"Clear the fuck out of the way!" Sheppard shouted. Aside from a few glares, no one even seemed aware of them, too fixated on the mesmerizing fire.

"Move!" he snapped, clearly desperate to get away before the authorities arrived. Not an easy feat when the crowd surged and pushed back at them, more people arriving every second to gawk at the burning hole in the earth. She stared bleakly at the disaster, certain no one was alive in there anymore. She turned away, hiding her face in Sheppard's chest, unable to bear the sight of it . . . the thought that Jonah was forever buried in the burning ruins.

Then something pulled at her, urging her to lift her head. Heat built at her core and her scalp tightened, tingling. Her heart fluttered wildly beneath her breastbone. She craned her neck for another look at the building she had just decided never to look upon again.

And she saw him.

Materializing out of the billowing black, he staggered beside Mila, one arm draped over her shoulder for support.

"Jonah," she breathed.

"I'll be damned," Sheppard muttered, turning to face Jonah and Mila as they approached.

"You brought him?" Sheppard asked as they came together in the throng.

Mila shrugged.

Jonah broke free from her and grabbed hold of Sorcha, pulling her from Sheppard. Even though she doubted he could support her—he could hardly stand by himself—she didn't protest. To have him again, with her, alive, his arms surrounding her even if they fell to the ground . . . It was heaven.

But they didn't fall. He staggered for a moment, balancing himself with a hiss of warm breath in her ear. Her name sounded like a prayer on his lips. "Sorcha. Sorcha . . . *mine.*"

"Jonah." She closed her eyes, squeezed her lids tight, as though she could trap the moment, lock and freeze it inside her. "Let's go home."

Where home was failed to matter. Home was the two of them. Together.

EPILOGUE

The Seattle lights winked through the mist-shrouded city. Sorcha and Jonah barely moved where they lay, wrapped around each other like two contented cats.

Jonah kissed Sorcha's neck, urging her awake. "C'mon, time to head out."

She blinked unfocused eyes, pulling herself from her sex-sated doze. "How am I supposed to move now?"

He glanced at the clock. "It's the best time to hunt," he reminded her.

She dragged her pillow over her head and moaned. They'd been back in Seattle for over a month now. It had taken Jonah a while to recover from his wounds, to completely exorcize the poison from his system. Now that he was fully recovered, she could hardly keep up with him when they scoured the city hunting demons.

"You can sleep," he offered. "I'll be back in a few hours."

"Uh-uh. Not a chance. You're not going without me." She tossed the pillow aside and sat up, teasing. "You're not changing your mind on me and leaving me behind while you have all the fun."

"I haven't changed my mind. We're in this together. This is what you want to do . . . and what I *have* to do." His eyes looked far away for a moment before fixing back on her. "I'm not running from anything ever again. Not this . . ." He rubbed the back of his neck where he was marked, touched by God to hunt demons, to protect white witches from possession. "Not my heart—*you*. I was stupid to let you go." He winced, and brushed a hand against her cheek, his thumb lingering on the soft skin. "And it nearly killed us."

She traced his bare chest, scraping him lightly with her nail. "Let's not go over that again. No one made you come after me, but you did. And now we're here, together and happy, and that's not going to change."

He stared down at her, his eyes stark and fathomless, a sea of blue that she could happily drown in. "There was never any doubt. I'll always come for you. Without you, I cease to exist."

Her chest heaved with a sharp breath. "Careful, I could get used to you saying things like that."

Jonah lowered his head, his mouth savoring

hers as he spoke. "Then brace yourself, because you're going to hear it. A lot."

"I thought we were heading out," she murmured between deep, drugging kisses, curling her fingers into his muscled shoulders and giving as good as she got.

"We will. We will. But first things first." Jonah's hand delved between their bodies, finding her pulsing warmth, feeling the beat of her heart, a matching rhythm to his own. "This is important, too."

She gave a tiny gasp as he invaded her with a touch, a penetrating stroke. "Oh, very important. Life-and-death important."

She smoothed her palm against the side of his face, relishing the scratchy bristle. "I could get used to this, too."

He arched a brow. "Yeah?"

She smiled. "Yes. I'm afraid you're stuck with me."

He released a deep, exaggerated sigh. "Then I might as well marry you."

She stilled, the blood rushing from her face. "Don't tease, Jonah—"

"I'm not. Trust me. A man doesn't joke about marriage. Especially not me. For us, 'until death do us part' is a really long time. Marrying me is forever, Sorcha."

She dropped back on the pillow, shaking her head, her hair tumbling around her, rippling against her shoulders. "Why do you want to marry me? You don't need to. I'm not going anywhere—"

"Sorcha." A touch of exasperation laced his voice. He feathered her bangs back from her forehead as he leaned over her. "It's what people do when they love each other."

"Love each other," she echoed, her belly fluttering as those words wove through her.

"Yes, of course. What else are we doing here?" He stared at her expectantly, as if waiting for her to get it, to understand . . . to accept.

He was right, of course. Why else had she come back with him to Seattle? Why else had she forgotten about her life in New York—discarded even her determination to kill Tresa? For now, at least. If she ever decided to resume her hunt, she was content with the knowledge that Jonah would be with her, at her side.

Without uttering a word, they had both understood as soon as they left Paris that neither one of them would leave the other's side again. She found more than love in his arms. She'd found her soul.

She nodded, felt a silly, happy grin breaking out on her face. "We're loving each other," she breathed. *Loving*.

"Exactly." He pulled her flush against him, smiling, sighing his pleasure, clearly savoring the press of her body against his. "I've waited my whole life for you . . . and I'll spend the rest of it with you. Never apart."

Never apart.

His voice rolled through her, husky and warm. *Never apart.* Never alone again. No matter what happened, no matter where fate led either of them, they would be in it together.

The darkness hungers...

Bestselling Paranormal Romance from Pocket Books!

KRESLEY COLE
PLEASURE
OF A DARK PRINCE

An *Immortals After Dark* Novel

Her only weakness...is his pleasure.

ALEXIS MORGAN
Defeat the Darkness

A *Paladin* Novel

Can one woman's love bring a warrior's spirit back to life?

And don't miss these sizzling novels
by *New York Times* bestselling author
Jayne Ann Krentz writing as

JAYNE CASTLE
Amaryllis Zinnia
Orchid

Sometimes love needs a little help from beyond...

Bestselling Paranormal Romance from Pocket Books!

JILL MYLES
SUCCUBI LIKE IT HOT
The Succubus Diaries

Why choose between the bad boy and the nice guy... when you can have them both?

CARA LOCKWOOD
Can't Teach an Old Demon New Tricks

She's just doing what comes supernaturally....

GWYN CREADY
FLIRTING *with* FOREVER

She tumbled through time...and into his arms.

MELISSA MAYHUE
A Highlander's Homecoming

Faerie Magic took him to the future, but true love awaits in his Highland past.
